THE CIDER SHOP RULES

A CIDER SHOP MYSTERY

THE CIDER SHOP RULES

JULIE ANNE LINDSEY

WHEELER PUBLISHING
A part of Gale, a Cengage Company

LIBRARY OF CONGRESS CIP DATA ON FILE.
CATALOGUING IN PUBLICATION FOR THIS BOOK
IS AVAILABLE FROM THE LIBRARY OF CONGRESS.

ISBN-13: 978-1-4328-9541-9 (softcover alk. paper)

Published in 2022 by arrangement with Kensington Books, an imprint of Kensington Publishing Corp.

Printed in the United States of America
1 2 3 4 5   26 25 24 23 22

To my daddy

CHAPTER ONE

"What on earth is going on here?" I asked, wheeling my grampy's old farm truck into the field just outside Potter's Pumpkin Patch. I puzzled at the gorgeous, though insanely crowded, view through my windshield. The Blue Ridge Mountains in northern West Virginia were breathtaking in November, but that didn't explain the hundred or so people milling in the distance. "What's everyone doing at the pumpkin patch? Halloween was two weeks ago."

Families typically flocked from far and wide to spend the day at Potter's Pumpkin Patch during September and October, but I'd never seen the place so busy mid-November.

My best friend, Dot, a ranger at the national park and lifelong animal activist, strained against her seat belt on the passenger's side, craning her neck at the crowd. "No way." She slapped the dashboard and unbuckled with a soft squeal. "Winnie. Look!"

"What?" I cut the engine, then followed her gaze through the glass, trying and failing to see whatever had gotten her so excited.

She tugged the handle on the creaky passenger-side door and jumped out. "Crusher is here today," she said, shooting me a wild-eyed expression, then shutting the door behind her.

I pocketed my keys and met her in the overgrown grass, enjoying the warm autumn sun on my cheeks. It wasn't uncommon to receive a few extra weeks of nice weather this late in the year, but 72 degrees and sunny was more than I could've asked for. Especially since the Fall Harvest Festival was in full swing at my family's orchard. Hopefully the beautiful weather would keep the guests coming through our gates all day as well.

"I used to beg my folks to bring me up here to see Crusher," Dot said, gathering her thick auburn hair over one shoulder. "I can still remember how mesmerized I'd been by the original one, and it was just a green backhoe with red eyes painted on the bucket."

The new Crusher was worlds cooler. I'd

never been a fan of the old one, mostly because I liked pumpkins, and the original Crusher destroyed them. The latest version was a rental from the monster truck show. The massive silver vehicle breathed fire from its grill and drove over pre-destroyed cars. Pumpkins were rarely damaged in the process.

Dot slowed as we crossed from the field to the jam-packed gravel parking lot. A giant hand-painted sign featured the words FALL FAMILY FUN DAYS and a schedule of key events. Dot's jubilant mood flattened as she traced her pointer finger over Crusher's schedule. The next performance was several hours away. "Rats."

"Well, at least we know why the pumpkin patch is so packed," I said. "The Potters have enough things going on here today to keep folks busy until dark. Plus, Crusher is always a hit. Maybe Granny and I should get a fire-breathing, car-crushing monster truck for the orchard." I nudged her with an elbow, and she perked up.

"That would be amazing."

We moved through the gates, admiring the controlled chaos. Potter's Pumpkin Patch was an annual tradition for most locals, and it drew crowds from three counties. There were hayrides, cornhole tournaments, piglet races, pumpkin picking, and a corn maze few could navigate. Plus, on occasion, an appearance from Crusher. Children loved climbing and sliding on the stacked hay bales and playing in sandboxes filled with dried corn. Parents enjoyed the concessions stand and picnic pavilion, where they could rest while keeping their busy children within view.

I couldn't help wondering what my options were for increasing traffic at the orchard. Granny and I had delicious produce, baked goods and cider, plus hayrides, cornhole games, and a local jug band every Friday. Was that enough? Did we need more entertainment? A pair of orange tabby cats and a fainting goat lived on the property, but Kenny Rogers and Dolly wouldn't do anything on command, and we had to keep Boo away from the commotion or he'd collapse.

Dot raised a finger to a wooden arrow directing visitors to the petting zoo. Her brows lifted in question.

"Let's go," I said with a grin. "I have to find Mr. Potter to pick up Granny's order. Maybe he's with the animals."

Dot's blue eyes twinkled, and she picked up her pace. "Thank you!"

Our orchard held an annual Fall Harvest

Festival from Halloween until Thanksgiving. Traditionally, our special events picked up where the pumpkin patch's left off. Until last year, our fall festival had been the final blowout before the season's end. Afterward, the orchard would close until the next summer, but that all changed when I opened a cider shop inside the historic Mail Pouch barn on our property. Now our open season lasted through Christmas, and we could sell our products all year long.

The cider shop had been a bang-up addition so far, and we needed more props and décor for the additional space. Normally, Mr. Potter's leftover hay bales, cornstalks, pumpkins, and gourds found a good home at Smythe Orchard, but with the crowd around us, it was hard to think of any of those things as "leftover." In fact, everything seemed to be in use.

Dot buzzed with excitement when the petting zoo came into view. I smelled it before I saw it, then laughed as Dot climbed onto the bottom rung of the wooden fence like one of the children. She leaned her torso on the rough-hewn wood and stretched one arm into the pen, beckoning the mini-flock of sheep and pair of alpacas. "Come here, sweet babies."

I tucked a quarter into the feed machine

beside her and gave the knob a twist. A pile of dusty brown food pellets dropped into the retrieval section, and I pushed them into a disposable cup for Dot to distribute. Dot loved animals like I loved old-fashioned caramel apples, deeply and without bias. Unlike my passion, hers kept her active, fit, and strong, while mine made my pants tight. "Here you go," I said, offering her the small cup of animal food.

She beamed up at me, quickly accepting the cup. "Aren't they perfect? Don't you just wish you could take them all home?"

I gave the pack of spoiled livestock a sideways glance. They were all pretty cute, but I had my hands full helping Granny as needed, running the cider shop, and taking night classes at the local community college. Plus, Dot had already talked us into three animals in the past year. As a ranger in our national park and budding wildlife rehabilitation guru, Dot had a perpetual Noah's ark worth of animals in need of forever homes, and I'd reached my limit.

"I'm going to look for Mr. Potter," I told her, scanning the crowds in search of his familiar face and deciding which direction to go. "I won't be long."

The world was aglow around me. A vibrant fireworks display of autumn color

12

stretched across endless fields and over mountains to a cloudless blue sky. The bold green grass beneath my feet bled seamlessly into the rich oranges and browns of a pumpkin field, the brilliant amber and scarlet of leaves on reaching limbs, and the distant walls of a massive corn maze. Blossom Valley was always beautiful, but dressed in her fall finest, she was truly a sight to behold.

I slowed at the sound of a grouchy male voice seeping beneath the door of a large red barn, then changed trajectory. I was nearly positive the angry voice belonged to Mr. Potter, though I'd never heard him angry. A moment later, one door swung open, and he stalked into view, rubbing the back of his neck and grimacing blindly into the crowd.

I waved a hand overhead and smiled brightly as I wound my way to him, dodging wayward toddlers and moms blindly pushing double strollers.

Mr. Potter's expression cleared a bit as I drew near. He cast a backward glance in the direction he'd come. The door had closed, successfully sealing whatever had upset him inside.

"Morning, Mr. Potter," I called, shading my eyes from the brilliant sun.

"Hey there, Winona Mae," he said cheerfully, despite the obvious frustration in his eyes. "I thought that was your grampy's Ford over there."

I gazed across a sea of pickup models from this century, my eyes latching easily onto the bulbous red work truck Grampy had painstakingly restored. Some people thought it was a shame to use it for hauling and towing, but Grampy had insisted that was what the truck had been built for, so I kept up the tradition. The nice thing about old trucks was that I could usually fix them when they broke, thanks to years under their hoods at Grampy's side. "It's me," I said. "You've got quite a crowd today. This is wonderful."

He bobbed his head in distracted agreement. "I've got your Granny's order on a trailer behind my four-wheeler. I'll take it over and load it up while you see the missus about getting your receipt."

"Okay," I said, hesitantly. Normally, I would've insisted on helping him load the truck, but he looked like he could use a minute alone. "Mrs. Potter is inside?"

"Yep." He pulled a worn white handkerchief from his pocket and drove it across his forehead and upper lip.

"I'll meet you over there in a minute," I

said. "Just pull the tarp back, and I'll tie it all down when we finish."

"No problem," he said, already moving away. "Take your time. Enjoy the festival." He raised a hand overhead, waving his good-byes.

I went inside the small market space to pay for Granny's order, a load of hay, corn, pumpkins, and gourds. The line was long, and the people impatient, but it gave me time to shop the racks of goodies. I added a pair of candied apples to my bill, paid, then went to collect Dot.

"Thanks!" she said, eagerly taking the second caramel-covered apple.

We moved in companionable silence for several minutes, concentrating on the crisp snap of green apple beneath the thick, sugary caramel coating. I moaned and let my eyes flutter with each delectable bite.

"This was fun," Dot said when we reached the field beyond the gravel parking lot. "Did you get everything you came for?"

"I think so," I said. "Mr. Potter is loading it up."

A few steps farther and his four-wheeler came into view, then parked among the pumpkins not far from my truck. The trailer was empty, and the tarp had been secured over my order, leaving only the tips of

15

cornstalks and rounded sides of several large pumpkins partially in view.

Dot plucked the bungee cords that were stretched over the tarp on her way to the passenger door. "You know what would go great with this delicious apple?"

I scanned the area for signs of Mr. Potter, wishing I'd been at least a little helpful as he'd loaded up my order. There were people everywhere, but none looked like him from where I stood. I supposed he was in high demand on a day like today, and I'd thank him the next time I saw him.

"Ice cream," Dot continued, as I climbed onto the faded bench seat beside her and slid the truck key into the ignition. "This apple needs a French vanilla milk shake chaser."

"What doesn't?" I asked, impressed and excited by her suggestion.

We made our way back to town slowly, enjoying the view and finishing our apples.

"You should send Harper to the Potters' place," Dot suggested between bites. "Maybe she'd come back with new ideas for your Fall Harvest Festival."

I'd been thinking the same thing.

Harper Mason was Granny's new orchard manager, a first for us. Once we'd realized there was no way we could run a busy orchard and a newly opened cider shop on our own, we started looking for help. I found Harper at school. She'd been taking business classes like me and also helped with an FFA group. Harper was self-motivated, hardworking, and happy, the perfect trifecta for an orchard manager. As an added bonus, she was local. No need to renovate an outbuilding for her housing, or cause Granny to share her home, not that Granny ever minded sharing anything. Harper had been on-site daily for most of the summer and into early fall, organizing and overseeing the harvest crews. She'd kept them on task and on schedule, protecting the fruit and saving us a ton of money in the process. These days, she stopped by a few times a week to check in and meet our off-season needs. She was basically an answer to prayer.

"I'll mention it when I see her," I said. "She and her FFA group have been making scarecrows for local farmers all week. She's hung a few at the orchard for show, and they're pretty good. They've added a little extra fun to the harvest festival. People stop and take pictures with them."

Dot shivered. "Not me. I've never liked scarecrows. I appreciate their work, but they creep me out."

I rolled my eyes. Dot was a horror movie–watching chicken. She'd probably seen some B-rated film where a scarecrow *had* come to life, and it'd stuck with her. I, on the other hand, loved scarecrows with their baggy borrowed clothes and hay-stuffed heads. They were the protectors of produce, the jesters of the land.

Dot groaned as we floated over the final hill into town and stopped at the light behind four other cars. "Traffic."

It took a moment for my brain to put it all together. A crowd at the pumpkin patch in November, five cars at one stoplight, tourists flocking down Main Street . . . "I'll bet everyone's here for the John Brown reenactment."

"That's in October," Dot said, looking perplexed. "Isn't it?"

"Normally, yes." The light changed, and I eased through the intersection behind the row of cars. "It had to be rescheduled this year. The guy playing John Brown has a kid who plays travel ball, and the team went to state."

Dot nodded. "That makes sense. I know I've been busy, but it's not like me to miss a bunch of men in uniform rolling through town."

The reenactment of the raid at John

18

Brown's fort was a long-standing tradition in Blossom Valley. John Brown was a famous abolitionist who led militia in a radical movement against slavery, inciting slave rebellions and supporting their freedom by any and all means. The site of his eventual overthrow in a raid by US Marines still stood on a bluff overlooking the Shenandoah River. Civil War reenactors celebrated John's memory, his work, and the enduring brick building where he took his last stand against Colonel Robert E. Lee every fall.

A smile spread over my face before I could stop it. Not to sound like an ogling woman, but Dot was right. I didn't hate the uniforms. There was something about a man who'd give up his life for a stranger that got me right in the heart every time. Soldiers, firemen, lawmen. I shook the last thought from my mind. It was no secret I'd been idiotically developing a crush on our new sheriff for a year. Unfortunately, he'd sooner put me in lockup than a lip-lock.

I angled into the last available parking space in front of the ice cream shop and shifted into PARK. The line snaked around the building. "Wow."

Dot met me on the sidewalk. "At least we can chat while we wait. Did I tell you I love this outfit, by the way? You look super cute.

Very country chic."

I stared down at the faded jeans I'd owned at least a decade. The holes at the knees were earned, not purchased. My black fitted Patsy Cline T-shirt was a Christmas gift from Granny, and the sneakers on my sockless feet were probably from high school. Given I was twenty-nine years old, they really shouldn't have impressed. "Thanks," I said, taking up the end of the line.

"Did you cut your hair?" she asked, now scrutinizing me.

I squirmed under her keen and knowing eye. "No." I tugged the length of my mousy brown locks over one shoulder and averted my eyes. "I used my blow-dryer."

"And you're wearing makeup."

I made a sour face. "It's ChapStick and some mascara."

"Makeup." Dot beamed.

"Stop it."

Her smile widened, and I squirmed. Dot thought I'd begun paying more attention to my appearance since my aforementioned crush had begun.

I tried not to think about the crush at all.

A broad shadow fell over us as we shuffled forward with the ice cream line. "Excuse me." A handsome stranger rubbed one hand through his tousled sandy hair and smiled.

"I don't mean to interrupt, but I think I'm lost." He chuckled. "No. That's not true. I'm definitely lost." His brilliant blue eyes twinkled as he moved the hand from his hair to his neatly trimmed beard, managing to look slightly bashful and instantly more endearing.

"Well, where are you headed?" I asked.

The man's brows crowded together. He pulled a folded sheet of paper from his back pocket and gave it a glance. "The Murphy Farm."

Dot rocked back on her heels. "Are you one of the Civil War reenactors?"

"Kind of," he said. "A friend's dad asked me to fill in for him. He said something about this usually happening last month, and I guess he couldn't do it this month, so I came in his place. My family's here too. We're making a whole vacation of it." He lifted and dropped his hands in a show of defeat. "Lemonade from lemons, right?"

My traitorous gaze dropped to his left hand. No wedding ring. "Your family will have a great time. There are always plenty of activities for children."

He puckered his brow. "I don't have any children." A moment later, his eyes widened. "No. Not *that* kind of family. I meant my parents. We're meeting my brother here, but

21

he's also not a child. My sister has kids, but she's not coming. Not her cup of tea."

I smiled back at him, thankful I'd worn the ChapStick and mascara. "The fort is about five miles north. You can take the county road out of town," I said, pointing to signs on the next block. "Make a right at that stop sign, then follow the markers. You can't miss it once you get on the right road."

"Okay," he said, nodding, but making no move to leave. "Thanks."

Dot looked from his face to mine. "Tell you what," she said, pulling a pen and receipt from her purse and scribbling on it. "Call this number if you need anything else while you're in town this week. Winnie is an expert on Blossom Valley and everything in it."

He smiled. "Is that so?"

I laughed, simultaneously wanting to hug and smack Dot. "That's me. A regular BV Wikipedia."

The line moved again, and he took a step back. "Great. I'll leave you to your ice cream. Thanks for the directions." He lifted the receipt before tucking it into his back pocket with the refolded flyer. "And for the number."

I inched forward with the line, refusing to watch him go. My phone rang before we reached the ice cream shop's door, and I answered eagerly, hoping it might be Granny. She'd gone to the Roadkill Cookoff in Marlinton with two girlfriends and a new turkey chili recipe, and she hadn't bothered to call or check in all weekend. "Hello?"

"Winnie?" a man's voice asked.

"Yes?"

"Just checking to see if your friend gave me a bogus number," he said. The jovial tone immediately put the handsome stranger's face in my mind. "Thanks again," he said.

I made a weird, strangling sound, but he'd already hung up.

"Oh my goodness. Was that him?" Dot asked, grabbing my arm and wiggling it. "What did he say?"

"He wanted to see if you gave him a real number."

Dot did a quiet squeal and marched in place. "He was so cute!"

He really was, but my mood drooped slightly as I stared at the darkened phone screen. "I didn't get his name."

Dot took my cell and tapped on the screen, then returned it to me. "There. All fixed."

She'd added his number to my contacts list and assigned him a name. " 'Tall, Dark, and Yummy?' " I asked before expelling a bark of laughter.

"Wasn't he?" she challenged.

Thankfully, it was my turn at the counter, so I ignored her.

I placed an order for a massive chocolate malt, then stepped aside so she could order.

I couldn't put my finger on a specific reason, but something about the man had felt strangely comfortable to me, like I'd known him long before we'd met. I smiled. *Write a romance novel, why don't you?* I told myself. *Tighten up, Montgomery.*

A few sips of chocolate malt cleared my head as Dot and I walked back into the sun. "What's going on over there?" she asked, pumping the straw in and out of her thick vanilla milk shake.

"I don't know."

A clutch of people had gathered behind my truck to stare at the ground. My stomach pinched as I realized I might've somehow hit a squirrel or chipmunk and not even known.

"Hey," I said, moving around to join the group. "What's going on?"

I followed their gazes to a dark puddle forming beneath my tailgate.

"Deer season hasn't started yet," an older man said. "If you've got a buck back there,

24

he'd better have been hit with a bow. Not a gun."

"It's not a buck," I said, offended by the accusation and concerned by the growing puddle. "I don't hunt."

"What is it, then?" he asked.

I gave the drips another look, and my stomach churned with awful memories.

The man was right. Gun season for deer didn't begin for another few days, but the fact was irrelevant. All I'd done today was make a pickup at the pumpkin patch. Pumpkins, gourds, and hay, nothing that would spill or bleed.

Dot moved in close, uncertainty rolling off her in waves. "Did you order anything from Potter's place that would leak like that?" she whispered, probably already knowing the answer.

"No."

I reached for the tarp's edge, breath held, back rigid, then peeled the protective covering away.

Dot screamed, and I jumped back, stumbling over my feet and nearly toppling onto the pavement.

Mr. Potter lay lifeless among the pumpkins and fall décor in my truck's bed. A deep and clearly fatal head-wound scored the back of his skull.

CHAPTER TWO

Sheriff Colton Wise and his deputies arrived within minutes. An ambulance, crime scene team, and coroner's van weren't far behind. Emergency vehicles clogged the street between wooden roadblocks that had seemed to manifest from nowhere.

Dot and I sat uselessly on the curb near my front bumper, horror-struck and in stunned silence. Neither of us was able to comprehend the unfathomable discovery or resulting scene unfolding before us.

Why would anyone hurt Mr. Potter? He was beloved. A local icon who spread joy with his pumpkins, corn maze, and wholesome family activities.

My gut demanded that whatever had happened to him was some sort of accident. It didn't make sense that it could be anything else, despite the gash on his head. Except he couldn't have covered himself with my tarp and secured the bungee cords. Only the person responsible for Potter's death would have done that. Anyone else who might've happened upon him would've called for help.

I pressed a fist against the ache building in my chest.

Dot leaned her shoulder to mine for a long beat, offering a silent share of what remained of her strength and emotional stability.

Colton headed our way a moment later, a deep scowl on his handsome face.

"Dot," he said, bracing broad palms over narrow hips. "Winnie. Either of you have any idea how this happened?"

I shook my head.

"Is he dead?" Dot asked, the words catching and cracking in her throat.

I patted her knee. If by some freak chance, Mr. Potter's slack expression and lack of breath and heartbeat had meant nothing at all, surely the expanding puddle of blood beneath my truck confirmed his demise.

"Afraid so," Colton said, his tone flat, his features carefully fixed into the perfectly unreadable cop-mask I hated. "And you just found him like that? Riding under the tarp on your truck bed?"

I nodded.

"Did you see him in town before you got

ice cream?"

I froze, momentarily mistaking him for a mind reader. Then I recalled the ice cream shop behind us and forgotten drinks at our sides. "No."

"We'd just come from his place," Dot said. "Mr. Potter owns Potter's Pumpkin Patch. Do you know it?"

Colton widened his stance. "I do. That's where the rest of your load came from?"

"Right," Dot said. "We stopped there to pick up an order for the orchard's Fall Harvest Festival."

"Did you see Mr. Potter while you were there?" Colton asked, eyes narrowing as he mentally put the story together.

"No," Dot whispered, then turned to stare at me.

"I did," I said hoarsely. "He sent me inside to pay the bill while he went to load the truck. That was it."

"So, he was killed back at the pumpkin patch." Colton checked over his shoulder. The coroner and his men were moving Mr. Potter onto a gurney. "This isn't our murder site."

I shut my eyes to stop the tears from falling again. It had taken me several minutes to pull myself together the last time the tears had started. "Someone hit him with something."

Colton turned back to us. "Probably with a shovel. I'll know more in a day or two. Can either of you think of anything you saw or heard at the pumpkin patch that could be related to what happened to Mr. Potter? Anything that might've struck you as unusual? Even if you dismissed it at the time. It could matter now."

I racked my brain for some small detail that would send Mr. Potter's killer directly to jail, but found my thoughts too jumpy and scattered to recall anything other than his lifeless body under my tarp.

Colton's gaze swept continually over the crowd, assessing, evaluating, missing nothing. He'd arrived in his usual version of a uniform: blue jeans, a Jefferson County Sheriff's Department T-shirt, and a ball cap. Sometimes he wore the big brown hat or uniform button-down, but I couldn't recall the last time I'd seen him in all the proper pieces at once. Today, he'd removed the ball cap upon arrival, out of respect for Mr. Potter, which was nice, but the move hadn't made it any easier for me to read his expression.

"Why don't you give me a rundown on your time at the pumpkin patch?" he asked, turning sharp blue eyes on me. "Start with your arrival, then move through your steps until you discovered him in your truck."

I wet my lips, then did my best to comply, though the details were a little fuzzy. Overall it had been an absolutely ordinary day. Hadn't it? The crowd at the pumpkin patch was surprising, but only because I hadn't known about the Family Fun Day. And I'd forgotten the John Brown reenactment had been rescheduled, bringing our usual October tourists into town now. "Wait." A flash of Mr. Potter's uncharacteristically sour expression came to mind. "He looked upset when I saw him," I said. "I asked if everything was okay, and he said he was fine, but it didn't seem like that was true."

Colton scraped a hand through his hair. "All right. I need written statements from both of you, but I can swing by and pick them up later. You probably want to get home. I'll have a deputy take you."

"I'm fine to drive," I began, then realized a moment too late. "You're taking the truck."

"Crime scene," Colton said. "The bed needs to be processed before we can release the vehicle."

I slouched. "Right."

He fixed me with an exasperated look and

sighed. "You have some kind of luck, you know that? You've been present at almost every murder scene since I became sheriff, and probably at more crime scenes than most lawmen."

I lifted my finger at him, and my cell phone rang, successfully halting my rebuttal of his pointed and mildly accusatory statement. I dropped my gaze to the buzzing device beside my chocolate malt cup. I snatched the thing off the curb and rejected the call, turning the illuminated screen facedown on my lap.

Colton's gaze raised and locked with mine. "You sure you want to miss a call from Tall, Dark, and Yummy?"

The phone rang again, and Colton crossed his arms.

I held his stubborn gaze as I answered. "Hello. This isn't a great time," I said.

"I guess not." The voice on the other end was deeper than I remembered, more tense and hurried. "There are emergency crews all around the ice cream shop. What's going on? I was nearly to the fort when all these vehicles went racing past me. I followed them back."

"Why would you do that?" I asked, suddenly unconcerned with Colton's disapproval and extremely worried Dot had

31

given my name to a stalker or lunatic. Who chased emergency vehicles to crime scenes while on vacation? Or ever?

A car door slammed on his end of the line. "I'm here. What happened?"

"There was an issue with my truck," I said. "It's fine. I'm fine. You shouldn't be here."

Colton shot me an incredulous expression.

"Too late. I am here." This time, Tall, Dark, and Yummy's voice came in stereo, both through the phone and on the air.

Colton's head jerked up and turned in the newcomer's direction. Shock swept across his features at the sight of my new friend's approach.

The tall man smiled. "I thought that was you."

"It's me," I answered at the same time that Colton asked, "What are you doing here?"

Dot cocked an eyebrow. "You two know each other?"

Colton's frown returned. He trailed his gaze over my face, then stared at my phone.

I disconnected the call and tucked the device into my pocket as I stood.

"This is my baby brother," Colton said. "Blake. This is Winnie and Dot."

"We've met," Blake said, clapping his big

32

brother on the back and shooting me a smile.

"Your brother?" The realization was like a bucket of ice water to my head.

I'd looked Colton up online after we'd first met, and he'd accused me of murder. He didn't have a social media presence, but his mother did, and I'd gotten a fast rundown on all things Wise from there. "Blake," I said softly. "The Marion County sheriff." I nearly hung my head in defeat and humility. No wonder he'd looked familiar. He looked like his brother and the photos I'd seen of him last year.

Blake shot me a quizzical look and laughed. "How'd you know that?"

"Oooo," Dot said. "Another sheriff. More Wise men in uniform."

"Some are wiser than others," Blake said. "Do you guys need a ride home?"

Dot and I both said, "Yes."

Colton said, "A deputy can do it."

Dot cocked a hip and made a crazy face at him. "Which one? Because it looks to me like all your men have their hands full." She gestured toward the busy, crowded street.

Colton examined the scene while Blake grinned. "What about your granny?" Colton asked.

"She's in Marlinton for the Roadkill

Cookoff," I told him. "She's in a chili competition."

Dot frowned. "I didn't think she liked chili."

"Grampy didn't like chili," I corrected. "Apparently she does, and she's determined to win a ribbon for her family recipe."

"Sheriff!" A familiar, high-pitched voice screeched, turning us all in Birdie Wilks's direction.

Colton groaned as Birdie hurried our way, a line of women trailing like ducklings behind her.

"Sheriff! Is it true? Is that Jacob Potter they're hauling away?" She pointed wildly at the coroner's van easing past the wooden barricades. "Is he dead? Where was he found? How did it happen?" Thick rivers of tears rolled over her round, heavily rouged cheeks. "He's my best friend's husband. Has anyone called Hellen?"

Colton rubbed his chin.

I wrapped Birdie in a warm hug, and Dot offered her a tissue from her purse.

Birdie's ladies stood back, looking unsure if they should come any closer, given the generous amount of clearly visible crime scene tape several feet behind them.

"I have to call Hellen," Birdie cried.

"Now, Mrs. Wilks," Colton began.

Birdie pulled out of my embrace, the billowing sleeves of her emerald blouse lifting on the wind. "Don't you 'Mrs. Wilks' me, Sheriff Wise. If my best friend's husband is dead, she deserves to know." Birdie liberated her phone from a massive quilted handbag and dialed. She pressed the device to her ear with one dimpled hand and tapped her foot. A moment later, she let her shoulders droop and returned her phone to her bag. "No answer. We'll have to go and tell her ourselves," she told the women who'd crept back nearer the yellow tape. "Winnie," she said, spinning back to me. "You'll find out who did this, and you'll make it right. Won't you?" She pressed a soft palm to my cheek and implored me with her tear-filled eyes. "I need you to do that for me, okay?"

"Of course." I set my hand over hers on my cheek. "I'll do whatever I can."

"No," Colton blurted. "She will do no such thing, and I will inform Mrs. Potter of this situation myself. Meanwhile, you all need to take a big step back because you're presently skirting obstruction."

The other ladies ducked under the tape, putting themselves on the right side of the law.

Birdie glared up at him.

35

Dot and I exchanged a glance. What would happen next was anyone's guess. Birdie always got her way, but Colton had only been around a year. He probably didn't know that. Yet.

Blake coughed to cover a snort of laughter. He rubbed a big tan hand over twitching lips, failing to hide the grin that had bloomed there. "I love small towns. Don't you, brother?"

Colton stared at Blake, jaw locked and eyes hard.

Blake's twinkling blue gaze flicked to me. "You're going to look into the murder?"

"No," Colton said. "She definitely is not."

I bit my tongue.

"Of course, she is," Birdie insisted. "She always finds the killer."

"No," Colton repeated. "Winnie doesn't always find the killer. Winnie is usually abducted by the killer and nearly killed by the killer. Is that what you want, Mrs. Wilks? To put her in danger?"

Birdie's jaw dropped. "Of course not!"

"Hey." I bristled. "I've only looked for two killers," I said. "It's not as if I've been abducted dozens of times. And I'm getting better at it."

Colton rubbed his forehead.

Birdie patted my back. "He's right. I'm so

36

sorry. I shouldn't have put that burden on you. You should only look into this if you feel comfortable," she said. "Don't do anything to put yourself in danger."

Colton stepped in close and scowled down at Birdie and me. He curved his palms in front of him, as if he were grasping an invisible basketball. "Have you considered that announcing Winnie's plans to investigate a murder in front of a hundred onlookers might be a great way to put her in danger already? That maybe the killer is one of these eager-faced spectators, hanging on your every word? Because whoever did this won't want anyone looking into it. The sheriff or otherwise."

Birdie scanned the crowd. "I know most of these people. They aren't killers."

"Yet a man is dead," Colton said. "Someone is a killer, or do you presume it was a random crime? A tourist or stranger murdered the local pumpkin farmer for no solid reason? Happenchance?"

Birdie lifted her chin and squared her shoulders. "I'm going to see Hellen." She turned on her heels and led the other women back across the street.

Colton flashed hot, angry eyes at me. "I have to beat her to the pumpkin patch. Meanwhile you will not, under any circumstances, investigate this." He raised his eyes to Blake. "Take her home. Make sure she stays there."

Blake shrugged. "I can get her home safely, if that's what she wants." He turned a charming smile on Dot and me. "Offer stands, ladies. My truck's just over there."

"Thanks," Dot said, moving to his side.

Colton groaned. "I'll call you later, Winnie."

Blake tossed his keys in the air and caught them with a grin. "See you, bro."

CHAPTER THREE

The gravel lot outside our orchard gates was full, and my chest expanded with gratitude that the extra folks in town had found our place too.

Blake had dropped Dot at the local vet's office after she'd received a call about a goose that had been hit by a car. Dot was training with Doc Austin, learning veterinary triage firsthand so she could better stabilize injured animals found in the national park and elsewhere.

I directed Blake under the arching Smythe Orchard sign and along a winding dirt lane to the historic Mail Pouch barn. The barn was about a quarter mile from my home and Granny's, with rows of apple trees and all the Fall Harvest Festival fun in between.

Harper and some of Granny's needlepointing friends were running the show in her absence, and I'd called ahead to ask one of them to open the cider shop. It was afternoon when I finally stepped inside. Despite my solid, horrific reasoning for being late, I still felt awful. The business was my baby, my dream job and responsibility.

"Wow," Blake said, moving slowly into the barn behind me. "Impressive."

My spirits lifted by a fraction. "Thanks."

I'd poured my heart and soul into the interior design and recent renovation. I'd spent months plotting and planning, then pillaging local flea markets and estate sales for the perfect combination of items to tell the story of Blossom Valley's history. Now, the café space was strategically filled with memorabilia from the town's past. Mismatched dinette sets from former restaurants and homes polka-dotted the floor. Faded and framed black-and-white images hung with care on every wall, showcasing families, farmers, coal miners, and local sports teams. Even the former milkman who'd made deliveries from a flatbed pulled by his mule had a place on my wall. Each table's centerpiece was made of china or milk glass from generations before and filled with seasonal flowers from Granny's garden. Beyond that, I'd dressed the space in shades of crimson, eggplant, orange, and gold for fall.

I'd arranged hay bales with gourds and

pumpkins under windows and near the open doors. Festive signs marked the bathrooms, and I'd added apples everywhere I could. The barn made the perfect location for my shop. There weren't many barns like it still standing, and none were in as great of condition as mine. I could thank Grampy for that. He'd taken an active interest in the barn's preservation from the moment he and Granny had purchased the land. He'd done his personal share to see it maintained, plus he'd pursued all state-offered resources for the same purpose. The barn being historic and specifically significant to our region, there were grants available to keep it painted and structurally sound. Today, the building stood as majestic and steadfast as it had the day it was raised.

The renovations I'd had commissioned last winter did a great job upholding the integrity of the structure while shifting its purpose. Granny and I didn't need a massive two-story barn, but I'd needed a home for my cider shop. We'd removed the remaining stables and most of the second floor, save a small area at the back for potential expansion and a walkway around the perimeter, leaving a glorious view of the high, arching historic rafters. I'd added bathrooms and storage to the first floor, as

41

well as a full kitchen and service bar.

Granny's friend Sue Ellen stood behind the counter, wiping a wet rag in big circles over the heavily lacquered surface. Her eyes widened at the sight of me. She made a throaty, *poor you* sound and hurried in my direction. "Sweet baby girl." She wrapped me in strong arms and rocked me back and forth. Hanks of her sleek brown bob stuck to the corners of her glasses when she pulled away. "I'm so sorry for what you've been through today. Are you sure you want to be here? Maybe you should go home and rest, process what's happened. I can handle the shop."

As the pastor's wife in a small congregation, Sue Ellen was sugar to the core, never without her pearls and an arsenal of encouraging words. She was also a force of nature, and I had no doubt she'd run my shop successfully and for as long as I wanted. But this was my job, regardless of my mood or energy level. Plus, it was Mr. and Mrs. Potter who'd suffered today. I was shocked and sad, but I could work, and I'd been raised to do exactly that.

"Thank you," I said, squeezing her hands briefly, "but I'll be all right. I think the busyness will help take my mind off things."

Her thin brows knitted together. "*Off* of

things? Birdie told me you'd be looking into this for the Potters."

"Actually," I interrupted, rudely, but with an apologetic smile, "this is Blake. Sheriff Wise's brother." I pointed over my shoulder to the man standing a few feet behind me, still surveying the room. "Blake and his folks are in town for the reenactment."

Sue Ellen gave Blake a startled look, as if he'd just appeared. "Dear."

He strode forward, hand extended. "Nice to meet you. Sue Ellen, is it?"

"Yes." She took his fingers daintily in hers and tipped her head back to get a good look at him. "There certainly is a family resemblance now that you mention it."

"Don't tell Colton," Blake said. "Our younger siblings and I like to tell him he was the milkman's kid. We think it's funnier than he does. Actually, Dad doesn't love that joke either."

I smiled, enjoying the tenderness in his voice as he spoke of his family. I'd always dreamed of siblings, wondered what life would've been like with two parents who loved and wanted me, but that wasn't in the cards for my life. Instead, I'd been given two overattentive grandparents determined to do a better job with me than they had with my mother. Honestly, I think my

43

mother was just a bad apple, getting pregnant in high school, then marrying and running off with the guy when he joined the military, only to divorce him within a year and leave me behind. I couldn't imagine Granny and Grampy not being enough reason to live right. They'd been my everything.

Sue Ellen straightened her glasses. "Welcome to Blossom Valley," she said, hustling back behind the bar. "And to Winona Mae's new cider shop. What can I get you?"

"What do you recommend?" he asked.

"It's all amazing. You can't go wrong with Smythe Orchard apples and Winona Mae's recipes."

Blake took a seat at the bar, his gaze moving over the massive antique mirror on the wall opposite him. I'd doodled swirling leaves and piles of apples around the mirror's edges and in the corners with a dry-erase marker. Then I'd neatly scripted the menu in the center. Drinks in red. Snacks in orange. I'd learned in my marketing courses that theme and presentation were everything.

Ciders to Whet Your Whistle
Green Apple Cider
Caramel Apple Cider

Spicy Cinnamon Stick Cider
Fireside Cider with Toasted Marshmallows

Snacks to Quench Your Cravings
Cinnamon Apple Chips
Granny's Homemade Apple Pie
à la mode
Apple Pie Fries
Granny's Sweet Cream Pumpkin Roll
Fried Bologna

Blake smiled as he read a few of the items aloud. "Well, I wasn't hungry before I saw this. Now I guess I'm going to need to try that fireside cider and some apple pie fries."

"Good choices," Sue Ellen said, turning to get the order started.

"Fireside cider is something new I'm trying out," I said, leaning my elbows on the counter across from him. "I smoked the apples to give them a little kick, then I went heavy-handed on the brown sugar, but the marshmallows are what really makes it fun."

"Ta-da!" Sue Ellen set the steaming mug before him, piled high with mini marshmallows. She lit my newly purchased butane torch and browned the marshmallows into one big lump of melty goo.

"See?" I said, hoping he'd like the cider's taste as much as its presentation.

Blake laughed. "You're right. That was fun."

Sue Ellen disappeared, then returned a minute later with a basket of apple pie fries.

Granny had generously stuffed narrow logs of dough with apple pie filling, fried them, then rolled them in cinnamon sugar. The effect was something like ecstasy.

Blake's expression went from pure awe to reverence as he chewed and swallowed the first bite. "How is this place not packed 24/7?"

"Sometimes it is," I said. "Be sure to spread the word to all those reenactment soldiers, would ya?"

Blake nodded, his mouth full of apple fries.

Sue Ellen leaned a hip against the counter and stroked her pearls. "How is it that you hadn't heard about this place? Surely your brother has mentioned it." Her gaze shifted to me, and an infuriating blush burned my cheeks.

"No," Blake said, wiping the corners of his mouth with a napkin. "Colton's always been a tight-lipped, solitary guy." He squinted, as if searching for the right words, then nodded, apparently satisfied he'd already found them. "I bring him out of his shell as much as I can, but he'll probably die with state secrets."

The corners of my mouth tugged into a sad half-smile. That description sounded exactly like the Colton I was getting to know.

Sue Ellen patted my arm, then buzzed away to tend to guests.

"How are you really doing?" Blake asked, sipping the cider and sounding infinitely more serious. "There was a dead guy in your truck today. A guy you knew."

"Yeah." I swallowed a lump of emotion and told my stinging eyes to stow it. There would be plenty of time for a proper breakdown later. "It's hard to believe that it's true. Mr. Potter was a really nice guy. I've known him most of my life. Everyone liked him."

"Someone didn't like him," Blake said, returning to his fries.

"It just doesn't make any sense." I felt the weight and truth of the words in my core.

"So, you'll look into it?" He feigned nonchalance, but I could see the deep interest in his clear blue eyes.

I responded with a noncommittal smirk. I hoped the look said something like, *oh, please,* or *be serious.* If Colton hadn't told him about the cider shop, maybe he also hadn't mentioned its meddling owner.

He tipped his head and grinned. "I know you are going to. You don't have to say it. The ladies around here all seem to think you will. They know you better than me."

I pressed my lips together, refusing to bite. I hadn't decided whether or not I'd get involved in what had happened to Mr. Potter. Much as I'd like to help him get justice and please Birdie in the process, I hated to peeve off Colton again. He seemed stressed enough for ten men when I'd seen him.

Blake narrowed his eyes, and they crinkled with humor at the sides. "So, you're definitely not getting involved?" he asked, shoving the next fry into his mouth. "You're not going to ask any questions about why a man whom you say was beloved by the community, a man you've known for years and who is apparently your friend Birdie's best friend's husband, was murdered and hidden in your pickup?"

My jaw sank open. He clearly hadn't missed a thing while listening to Colton and me outside the ice cream parlor. I chastised myself for letting Blake's guy-next-door appearance trick me into forgetting he was one hundred percent a sheriff, just like his brother. Blake might seem perpetually ready to play ball or grab a drink, but that made him even more dangerous to me than Colton. Blake made me let my guard down. "You're good," I said, returning his intent stare. "I'll bet you always play the good cop in a good-cop, bad-cop scenario."

His smile widened. "You still haven't answered my question."

I crossed my arms. "I will likely visit Mrs. Potter tonight with a casserole or pie, as custom dictates. It's appropriate to pay my respects at a time like this and let her know I'm available for whatever she needs."

He chewed smugly, eyes twinkling, lips curled slightly at the edges.

"Don't get cocky," I told him. "It's basic Southern manners and Blossom Valley protocol. What kind of neighbor would I be if I didn't?"

"I haven't said anything," Blake said, lifting his mug for another slug of cider.

I bristled. It suddenly felt as if we were playing a game, and I was losing.

He wiped bits of marshmallow from his neatly trimmed mustache and leveled me with a suddenly serious stare. "So, what's up with you and my brother?"

I blinked. "What? Nothing. What do you mean?" I crossed my arms, then uncrossed them when his gaze lowered to take note of the action. I recrossed them a moment later to stop him from thinking he'd been the reason I'd uncrossed them to begin with. "Colton and I are friends, I think." I shifted. *What do I normally do with my arms?* Did they just hang there? Like fallen limbs? "We're friendly," I amended, unsure *friends* was the right choice of word. "It's complicated. We've got this pattern where I make him crazy, then he saves my life. Is that friendship?"

"That sounds unhealthy."

My hands landed on my hips. "Well, it's our thing."

He dusted cinnamon sugar from his fingertips, still evaluating me. "Are you sure the two of you aren't dating?"

"I would know if I was dating someone," I said. "Now you're just miffing me off."

He smiled. "Want to have coffee later?"

I gaped, and it took extreme mental effort to force my mouth shut.

"Winona," Sue Ellen whispered sharply and cleared her throat loudly, as if she'd swallowed a frog.

I started. When had she returned from waiting tables?

The white noise of my busy shop hummed back to my ears.

Sue Ellen tipped her head over one shoulder and flicked her gaze toward the open barn doors, where Colton's silhouette was backed by the blinding sun.

Blake turned to look too. "Brother," he said, rising to greet him.

"I thought I'd find you here." Colton dragged his attention from Blake to me, then back. "Mom's looking for you. Dad's at the fort, talking to the militia, and she wants to go to dinner. I said you'd take her."

Blake smiled. "I guess that's what favorite sons are for." He clapped Colton on the back, then extended a hand to me across the bar.

I accepted the offering, and he held on.

"What do I owe you?" he asked, still holding my hand in his broad, warm fingers.

"Nothing," I said. "It's on the house. You brought me home when I needed a ride, and I served you a snack. I think that makes us about even."

"About," he said, focusing on the single unnecessary word. "Coffee should settle things between us, then. I'll give you a call to set it up." He released my fingers and was gone.

Colton followed his brother out, promising to be in touch with me later for my written statement.

I blinked in their absence, then hurried to collect my marbles.

CHAPTER FOUR

I threw myself into being the best cider shop owner on earth until the crowd waned and the sun set. Then I locked up and headed home to make a casserole.

Two orange tabbies found me on the long dirt road home and weaved their way around my feet, arching and rubbing against my calves as I moved. It'd only been about a year since Dot had rescued them from the national forest and delivered them into my heart. Back then, they were frail, orphaned, and weak. They'd both fit into one inside pocket of Dot's park ranger coat. Now the little fuzz balls were about eight pounds each and as healthy as a couple of very small horses.

Dot had lovingly named them both Kenny Rogers, the name she gave all her rescues. She claimed it was easier to remember one name than forty, faster to call the herd for mealtime, and she flat-out loved the actual human Kenny Rogers, so it worked. I'd kept the name for my tomcat and chosen the name Dolly for his sister.

They mewed up at me, begging for snuggles and their dinner. "Almost there," I told them, picking up my pace. Much as I wanted to stop and play, I was in a hurry.

The long shadows of a fall evening crept across the ground around me. They reached toward my feet from rows of looming trees and a scattering of outbuildings across the orchard's landscape.

The shadows had only recently started to bother me. Until a few months ago, I'd embraced the nights as lovingly as the days. Then I'd learned that a hired gun and current fugitive named Samuel Keller might have been stalking me. Keller blamed Colton for the life sentence he'd swiftly avoided by killing his transport guards, and he wanted to punish Colton for the inconvenience. Since I'd been spending a lot of time with Colton while investigating a summer murder, he suggested it was possible that Keller had mistaken our relationship for something more. And he might want to terrorize me as a means of hurting Colton. Fortunately, that hadn't come to pass, but the possibility was never far from my mind.

Members of Colton's former police team

and a handful of FBI agents had chased and tracked Keller into Kentucky months ago. In theory, I had nothing to worry about anymore. But given the man had eluded authorities once, my confidence that he'd never return was low. In fact, in my experience, people with an ax to grind usually found a stone. So until Keller was captured and tucked safely behind bars, I'd always wonder if he was out here again, watching from the trees.

Something moved in the shadow at the edge of a building, and the cats hissed.

I gasped, and the sudden, unbidden sound gonged in the darkness.

A pale white goat bobbled stiff-legged into view before toppling completely over.

"Oh, Boo!" I whispered, rushing to his side. "I'm so sorry. You scared us. What are you doing out here? You know you're supposed to stay in your pen after dark." I stroked his side until he rolled onto his feet again, then I patted his head and curled my fingers under his collar.

We made a detour to Granny's backyard. "Let's get you home."

Boo was another one of Dot's rescues. He'd stolen Granny's heart when he came with some of Dot's other, non-fainting goats to help mow the lawn. Apparently, the other goats picked on him, and Granny couldn't take it, so he lived in her yard now.

"In you go," I told him, opening the small wooden gate outside my spruced-up childhood playhouse. The pastel pink clapboard and white trim had been refinished for him in a more masculine palette of grays and blacks. The letters of his name were stenciled in thick square-edged marks above the door. "You did a nice job on the grass today," I told him, closing the gate carefully when he was safely inside.

Harper had since hired an affordable and effective lawn crew to manage our grass, but Granny didn't think we should point that out to Boo. She believed he needed to have purpose and praise to feel good and be healthy. So, she walked him while the lawn crew tended her backyard, and we complimented his work ethic and craft when he returned. Silly, maybe, but who was I to mess with a goat's self-esteem?

I left Boo to his hay bed and headed across the empty field between Granny's historic farmhouse and my renovated-outbuilding home.

My phone buzzed with a text message from Blake as I unlocked my front door. He'd sent a photo of himself beside a food truck outside the John Brown fort selling

"West Virginia's Best Apple Fritters." His right eyebrow cocked in disbelief, and his thumb was distinctly pointed down.

I laughed, then tucked the phone away and headed for the kitchen. A whole lot of people buying those fritters were going to be disappointed. Especially if they'd ever tasted one of Granny's. Blake hadn't had one of her fritters, but he'd made short work of her apple pie fries, and I supposed they were a solid frame of reference.

I sprayed a 9x13 baking dish with cooking spray, then set my oven to preheat. I carried my recipe box to the couch and got down to business. It wouldn't matter to Mrs. Potter what sort of casserole I baked, but I wanted to pick the right one anyway. She'd likely be too grief-stricken to eat and too inundated with other food deliveries to get to mine for a month, but I couldn't go empty-handed, and on the off chance she decided to set tonight's offerings out as a buffet for her visitors, I wanted mine to be the best.

My phone rang, and I found Dot's face on the screen. "Hello?"

"Are you going to the Potters' place tonight?" she asked. Something honked in the background, and she shushed it.

"Was that a goose?"

Dot sighed. "Yeah. It's the one from Doc Austin's office. He saved it, but he doesn't think it'll ever fly again. The wing will heal, but the damage is irreversible." The sorrow in her voice was enough to break my heart. "I made a place for him to stay at my house while I take a pie to Mrs. Potter," she said. "Do you want to ride together?"

"Absolutely. Give me an hour to get something in and out of the oven, then I'll pick you up." I loved to drive, and this was the sort of thing I'd normally take Granny to, but she was still at the Roadkill Cookoff.

Sixty-seven minutes later, I rushed out the door in jeans and a black sweater. I'd wrangled my hair into a headband and skipped the mascara. I put a ChapStick in my pocket just in case.

The world was impossibly dark as I beat a path through the nipping wind to my grampy's cavernous pole barn, where he used to store his classic cars. He and I had spent hours there working on his cars and talking about our days. It was where he'd taught me the hard truths in life, about being a woman in a farmers' world. About sometimes having to work harder than the guys to get the same acknowledgment. About how it was unfair, but persistence could change anything, even stubborn people's minds. He'd taught me everything he knew, patiently and without boundaries, because there was nothing I couldn't do. It'd been four years since he'd gone to heaven, and I missed him every day. Sometimes so much I couldn't catch my breath.

I opened the barn doors wide, inhaling the familiar scents of earth and oil.

My eyes jumped instantly to Sally, my nineteen-sixty-eight-and-a-half 428 Cobra Jet Mustang in Wimbledon White. I'd sold her sisters to Doc Austin for money to renovate the barn and open my cider shop, but I could never willingly let go of Sally. Sally sang to me.

I climbed in and let my palms glide over the curve of her steering wheel before giving her engine a start. Together we rolled into the night.

A shiver rocked down my spine as I reached the driveway's end. The familiar sensation of being watched crept along the base of my neck and curled icy fingers into my hair.

I checked my door locks, then gave Sally's pedal a little press and launched us onto the silent country road. She charged easily ahead, floating silently around the winding ribbon of road between the mountains and leaving my fears far behind.

Dot's front door sucked open as I pulled into the drive. She nearly leapt into Sally's passenger seat with a foil-covered pie on a dish towel inside an upturned cardboard box lid. The lid and towel worked as a platter and insulator to keep the piping hot pie from burning her legs. She flipped the towel's edges up and over the foil on top of her pie, then reached for her seat belt to buckle up. "Get moving before my pie goes cold."

I shifted into gear and pressed the gas.

I had an insulated carrier for my casseroles, complete with extra padding on the bottom and Velcro handles on top, but I'd yet to find one for pies.

"What kind of casserole did you decide to make?" she asked as I eased back onto the road and pointed us in the direction of Potter's Pumpkin Patch.

"Tater tot," I said, pulling my lips to the side and partially regretting my decision. "It's not fancy or special, but everyone likes it. I figured it'd be easy to give away if her freezer's full when we get there."

"Smart," Dot said. "I hate that so many people use times of tragedy like this to show off in the kitchen. As if that's what matters instead of the fact our community is grieving a loss and consoling a widow. I mean, come on, people, save your made-from-scratch pasta and canned-by-hand sauces for a party. Right? I made a pecan pie."

"I love pecan pie."

"Good, because ever since those trees I planted a few years ago matured, I've got pecans coming out of my ears. I might have to start selling them by the roadside before I'm buried alive in them."

I gaped. "I could never be buried in pecans. I'd eat them. If you need help, I'm your girl."

She smiled. "You're going to regret saying that, but no take-backs. Now, we have about ten minutes before we get to the Potters' place, and you have to fill me in on what happened with Sheriff Wise's brother after you dropped me off."

I puffed out a breath. "I don't know what to say."

"I'll get you started," she said pertly, then paused to clear her throat. "Holy crow! Can you believe you gave your number to a total stranger? And he turned out to be Sheriff Wise's brother? What are the odds? Then the sheriff saw that you'd nicknamed his brother 'Tall, Dark, and Yummy!' Could that have been any more awkward?"

I cast a deep frown in her direction. "*You* gave him that nickname — and my number," I reminded her. "And yes, I'm horrified, so I'm trying not to think about it."

"Sound strategy," she said. "So, what's he like? Is he always as charming as he was on the street? Did he stay awhile when he brought you home? Did he know who you were once he saw you with his brother?"

"He stayed for cider and apple fries," I said, "but he didn't know who I was. Apparently Colton isn't much of a sharer. Blake had never heard of me or that my cider shop existed. He said his brother's a private person."

Dot balked. "I guess so. You're the only person in town I've ever seen the sheriff spend any time with. If he didn't tell his family about you, he must not tell them anything. Was it weird flirting with his brother? Do you think Blake thought it was weird that you knew his brother? What did the sheriff think about you calling his brother 'Yummy?' "

"I didn't call him that. You did," I repeated. Though she was right, Colton couldn't know that.

"Are you going to see Blake again?"

I made the final turn onto the Potters' street, biting my lip against a nonsensical rush of nerves. "He invited me out for coffee."

61

"No!" She gasped, swiveling to face me on the narrow seat. "Are you going to tell Colton? Will Blake?"

"Colton heard him ask me," I said, my voice dropping to a guilty whisper. "He showed up unexpectedly at the cider shop and overheard the whole thing. Then he sent Blake to have dinner with their mom, and he left too."

Dot shook her head slowly, eyes wide with disbelief. "I don't even have words for that."

"It's not like Colton and I are dating," I said, sliding Sally in line behind what seemed like a million other vehicles on the road along the Potter property. The gate to the pumpkin patch entrance was shut. A set of heavy chains and an impressive padlock hung from the center, forcing everyone to walk around to the home's front door.

Dot climbed out, careful not to dump her pie. She peered at me over Sally's roof, a strange, pensive look in her eye. "It's not as if you *aren't* dating either."

"I don't even know what that means," I said, shoving my seat forward to collect my casserole from the backseat floorboard. "It's all just very weird and complicated." I straightened and shut my door. "I'd rather spend my time figuring out what happened to Mr. Potter than thinking about the Wise brothers."

Dot met me at Sally's side and joined me on the slow processional to the Potters' front door. "Fine, but keep me posted. You're quick to complain Sheriff Wise doesn't tell you things, but pulling information out of you isn't so easy either."

The door opened as we reached the porch, and a couple I recognized from town passed us on their way out. Birdie held the door and ushered us inside.

The house was full and warm. Dozens of locals, families, couples, and kids crowded into the small rooms. Every flat surface overflowed with food, drinks, and desserts. Dot and I delivered our offerings to the first available table, moving the other dishes as needed to create more space.

Birdie helped. "I'm so glad you're here," she said when our hands were empty. She squeezed us in a group hug, then stepped back to lock her gaze on mine. "Have you heard anything?" Her raised brows and wide eyes made the meaning of her words crystal clear. *Had I heard anything about who had killed Mr. Potter?*

"Nothing at the cider shop," I said. "What about you?" I dragged my gaze pointedly around the crowded room. "Seen or heard anything that didn't add up or sit right?"

"No," Birdie said. "The crime scene folks poked around outside until just a bit ago, but they didn't come in to talk to us. The sheriff and his deputies are still here, combing through the barns and grounds. The sheriff asked a bunch of nosy questions earlier, before folks started bringing food."

"What kind of questions?" I asked, lowering my voice to a whisper.

She pursed her lips and sighed. "Had Hellen and Jacob been fighting? Had he been behaving strangely lately? Did he have any enemies? That sort of thing." She rolled her eyes. "Hasn't anyone ever told our sheriff it's bad luck to speak ill of the dead?"

I offered a sad smile. I knew what she meant, but I also knew Colton had to ask those questions. He had to find a thread to pull. Something to set off the investigation. "Do you mind if I slip out for a minute and take a look around?"

Birdie's face lit up. She motioned me through the home toward the back. "The sheriff already cleared the barns and fields nearest the parking lot. If you start there, you shouldn't run into him."

Dot stopped at my side. "Keep your phone in your hand in case you need it."

I brought her number onto my cell phone screen. "Okay. If you get a call from me, it's because I'm in trouble, so come immediately."

She nodded.

Dot opened the back door, checking over her shoulder for lookie-loos. No one paid any attention to us.

I slid out and stood under the cone of motion lights on the rear porch, unsure where to begin, then I saw the red barn and a memory surfaced. Mr. Potter had come from that direction today, and he'd been obviously irritated by something. Or someone.

I headed for the barn, listening carefully for signs of Colton or his deputies nearby. Their flashlight beams bobbed and flashed in the distance, closer to the corn maze than the petting zoo, and both were too far for me to still be visible in the night.

A pair of four-wheeler tracks caught my eye in the moonlight, and another memory flashed into my mind. Mr. Potter had left his four-wheeler and trailer in the pumpkin patch near my truck after hauling my order to the field where I'd parked. I used the tracks to guide my path to the barn, then slowed at the flicker of light peeking around red gingham curtains on the front window and beneath the partially open doors.

"Hello?" I called, rapping a knuckle on

the wooden frame, and hoping a cold-blooded killer wasn't inside. "It's Winona Mae Montgomery," I said, toeing the door open a bit further. "Anyone here?"

A young man strode toward me in visible pain. I didn't see any blood, or anyone else, so I assumed his pain was emotional rather than physical. "Can I help you?" he asked, throwing the door wide with a forced smile. "I think most folks are inside the Potter home. You can try the back door. Someone will let you in, I'm sure."

"I was just there," I said. "Why are you out here all alone?"

He shrugged. His ruddy cheeks and puffy eyes suggested he'd probably come to cry and be alone. "Why are you?"

I looked around the barn. No smoking guns in sight. "I came out to get some air and saw the light. Are you hungry? There's plenty of food and no way Mrs. Potter can eat half of it on her own. There's a buffet set up in the dining room."

He rubbed a handkerchief under his nose. "I don't really know those folks. I mean, I recognize them from a lifetime in this town, but I wouldn't feel right going in. And I'm not hungry."

"I get it," I said. "It's fine. Most of the folks inside are older than me, and you're

66

still young. It's not exactly a youthful crowd." I eyeballed him, taking a closer look, absorbing the details. He was in jeans and a white T-shirt. His hair was combed, but longer than the fashion. The soles on his boots were thin. His hands were clean, but his nails dirty. "How did you know Mr. Potter?" I asked, already formulating a few guesses. He was probably a farmhand. Young, strong, tireless. Someone who wouldn't mind the hard work and low pay.

"I work for him," he said. "Worked." He ran a palm across his lips. "He gave me a job when no one else would. I've been here two years now. Potter was a good man. This shouldn't have happened."

"I agree," I said, stepping closer. "I'm Winnie, by the way. I run the cider shop at Smythe Orchard."

"Wes," he said, offering me his hand.

"Why wouldn't anyone else hire you?" I asked, my thoughts circling back to the strange comment. Wes seemed nice enough. He looked presentable, was articulate, and must've been a hard worker or he wouldn't have lasted at the pumpkin patch for two years.

He wrung his hands and averted his eyes. "My mom's sick," he said. "I quit high school to care for her when she couldn't work anymore, but we needed money. I tried to get a job, but I didn't realize how tough that would be for a dropout. All companies see is a young, uneducated quitter. Mr. Potter was the only one willing to give me a chance. He told me I was a hard worker, and he wanted me to take the night courses offered at the high school and get my GED. No one ever believed in me like that before, you know?"

"Yeah," I said. "I do." I wasn't sure what else to say, but I liked the idea of having a friend at the pumpkin patch. "I'd like to come back in the daylight and look around after the sheriff and his men are finished. Would that be okay with you?"

"Sure," Wes said, "but the sheriff wants us closed tomorrow."

I mulled that over, unsure if that would be a better or worse time to peruse the grounds. On the one hand, no one would be around to mess up any missed evidence. On the other hand, it would be easier for Colton to spot me if he dropped by.

The low drone of male voices drew my attention, and I froze. The voices might belong to friends of Mr. Potter's, dropping by to pay their condolences to his wife, or the voices could belong to the sheriff and his deputies coming to speak with Wes.

"One more question," I said quickly. "Can you tell me anything about today that might explain what happened to Mr. Potter? Did you see him arguing with anyone? Was someone angry about something?"

Wes's nose wrinkled. "No. Why?"

"Well, someone did this to him," I said. "I don't know who or why, but it must've been someone who was here today before I left." I shoved the tip of my thumb into my mouth and chewed the nail. "There were so many people here. I wouldn't know where to start."

I listened for the men's voices again, but they were gone. Probably friends of Mr. Potter's.

Hopefully friends of Mr. Potter's.

"I guess I should get back inside," I said, suddenly afraid I would be busted by Colton himself. Caught red-handed asking the help about the victim. "I made a tater tot casserole if you're interested."

"I'm fine," he said, forcing a smile. "I think I need a few more minutes."

"I can bring a plate out to you," I offered.

"It's all right," he said. "You don't have to worry about me."

I slumped. For all the height and muscles, Wes looked like a lost kid.

"Okay," I said, resolving to leave him. I'd

69

be back another day to prod a little more. For now, this was enough. "I'll see you later," I said, and slipped back into the night.

My phone lit and buzzed in my palm, creating a spotlight in the darkness. A new text from Dot.

Alert! Alert! Sheriff! Sheriff!

I made a run for the back porch.

Dot wrenched open the door and pulled me inside just as Colton rounded the corner from the living room.

He stared at us as we pressed our backs to the closed door.

I raised a palm hip high and waved.

He sauntered closer, eyes tight. "What are the two of you doing?"

We shook our heads in unison. "Nothing," I said. "You?"

"I just finished walking the grounds," he said. "I stopped in to let Mrs. Potter know we've finished up for the night."

Birdie swooped into view behind him, waving her arms overhead to catch my attention.

"Excuse me," I said, slipping away from Dot and moving past Colton. I hurried into Birdie's personal space, then tugged her several more feet away from the sheriff before stopping.

70

She cupped a hand around her mouth and leaned her lips close to my ear. "I just spoke with Hellen, and she says the neighbor has been complaining for two months about the noise whenever they have special events and local bands here. I think you'd better talk to him and his wife."

"Okay," I said. That seemed like a good lead, but I wanted more, and I wasn't getting anywhere on my own. "Can I talk to Hellen privately for a minute?" I asked, catching the widow in my line of sight. "Maybe we can step into her bedroom or somewhere else with a door and no prying ears. Actually —" I paused. Mrs. Potter looked a little wild and unsteady as she straightened the buffet. "Is she okay?"

Birdie gave her friend a quick look. "She's fine. Probably had an extra nip or two of brandy to settle her nerves," she said. "Why don't you speak with her another time, and visit the Brumbles as soon as possible? I told the sheriff about the neighbors when he came inside, but I don't think he took me seriously."

"I think he takes everything seriously," I said, casting a look toward the kitchen, where I'd left Colton alone with Dot. "Did the Brumbles come over tonight?"

Birdie tented her brows. "Nope." She let

71

the *p* pop on her lips.

"Wow." Not showing up when your neighbor was murdered was definitely suspicious. "Okay," I promised. "I'll stop by their place tomorrow."

"Excellent. I'll let Hellen know." Birdie craned her neck, scanning the crowd, presumably in search of her friend. "I'd better go and check on her." She patted my shoulder on her way past.

Dot hurried toward me, looking thoroughly amped up. She hooked her arm with mine as she motored past, turning and pulling me along with her. "I don't want to rush you, but I'm worried about Kenny Rogers," she said. "His wing needs to stay in the splint, and he won't stop fussing at it."

I allowed Dot to pull me onto the porch before I dug my heels in. "What are you doing?"

"Escaping," Dot said. "I couldn't stand another minute of that tension. Sheriff Wise knows we were up to something. He just kept looking at me with this flat expression, like he could read my mind."

"I call that his cop face," I said, moving with her again. "You were smart to run before he started asking questions. He always gets me with the questions." Plus, it'd been a rough day, and I wanted to go to

72

bed. Not that I'd be able to sleep, but I'd trade my best sneakers for a hot shower and some comfy pajamas.

We moved swiftly past a dozen parked cars. I peeked over my shoulder a few times as the icky sensation of being watched returned. Normally that feeling was specific to my property, where I suspected Samuel Keller had stalked me before.

I picked up the pace until Dot and I were both in a sprint.

We stopped short at the sight of broken pumpkin shells littering the ground near Sally's tires and stringy orange pumpkin guts smeared over her pretty white hood and formerly spotless windshield.

"Oh no!" Dot gasped. She inched closer, while I stood frozen and dumbstruck several feet away.

"I can't believe it," she said. "Who would vandalize your beautiful car like this?"

I dialed Colton and pressed the phone to my ear. "It's not vandalism," I said. "It's a message."

Whoever did this wasn't crazy. More likely, he or she was a killer.

CHAPTER FIVE

The tow truck arrived quickly and loaded Sally onto its bed. Colton considered her a crime scene now, so I was out two cars in one day. A personal record I wasn't proud of. His deputies scanned the ground for footprints or evidence to point a finger at the pumpkin smasher, but in truth, there were a ton of people visiting Mrs. Potter tonight, and they all had easy access to my car and the property, which was a pumpkin patch.

Eventually, a now-familiar black truck crawled to a stop beside the tow truck. Blake hung his arm through the open window and shook his head at Colton. "You must run a tight ship out here," he said. "Two crimes in ten hours."

Dot moved immediately toward the truck.

Colton's frown deepened. "What are you doing here?"

Blake hooked a thumb in my direction,

and Colton blanched.

"You called him?" Colton asked, looking as if the idea was absurd.

"Well, yeah," I said, a little confused myself. I'd assumed Colton would be happy with the choice. Who could be more trustworthy than his brother? "You're working. Granny's in Marlinton, and I drove Dot here. It was him or Hank."

"Who's Hank?" Blake asked.

"No one," I answered as Colton said, "Her ex."

I shot him an annoyed look as I moved toward the open passenger door. Dot had let herself into the backseat portion of his extended cab and left the door agape.

We drove away with Colton staring in our wake.

My stomach pinched with misplaced guilt and rightly placed terror. Someone had attacked Sally outside a recent widow's home where I'd been snooping, which could only mean one thing. I'd ticked off another killer. I didn't have time to worry about how Colton felt about who drove me home.

"Hey," Blake said, catching my eye. A shrinking reflection of Colton in the rearview mirror between us. "Don't worry about him. You did the right thing. I'll get you both home safely, and he knows it. Sometimes it just takes him a while to figure things out." The words sounded sincere, but Blake's smile seemed to say otherwise, and I couldn't make sense of the two together.

"You don't have to look so pleased that I irritate him," I said.

He lifted a palm in mock innocence before hitting his turn signal at the end of the road. "I just like to get his goat. It's what little brothers do."

I considered his words. "How much older is Colton?" The pair looked to be the same age. Though, personality wise, Blake was more like a frat boy and Colton an aging professor.

"Sixteen months," Blake said, still smiling. "Mom treated us like we were twins for the first ten years or so. Even dressed us the same. Drove Colton crazy. I never minded. He was my big brother. I wanted to be like him."

"Jeez," Dot said, piping up from the back seat. "Sixteen months? No wonder your mom dressed you alike for a decade. She was probably too tired to remember both your names until then."

Blake laughed, bobbing his head and drumming his thumbs against the steering wheel to an old Tim McGraw song. He found Dot's house without asking for directions despite the fact he'd dropped her at the local vet's office earlier, and not her home. He waited for her to go inside and close the door before pointing us in the direction of my place. She didn't seem to notice, and I didn't mention it, but I added the fact to a growing list of details I'd been mentally collecting about the newest Wise man in my world.

I scanned the roomy, painfully clean truck cab. No mud on the floor mats. No crumbs or change in the cup holders. It could have been a rental if it wasn't for the silhouette of a bucking bronco clinging to the rear window and the dummy emergency flasher on the dashboard. I couldn't help wondering if he ever used the flasher and where he'd bought it. Could I get one for Sally?

Blake shifted into PARK outside my house several minutes later. "I don't suppose you have another vehicle around here somewhere?"

"No, but Granny does, and she'll be home tomorrow. I'm sure she won't mind sharing her truck if the need arises. Plus, Sally wasn't damaged, so I'm not sure how much evidence Colton expects to get from pumpkin guts. I figure I'll have her back soon."

" 'Sally?' " A fresh smile spread. "Like Mustang Sally."

I blushed, feeling slightly childish for naming my car, or rather for calling her the name Grampy had given her the day he'd had her battered body towed home to restore. "My grampy named her. It stuck."

"I'm pretty sure Wilson Pickett named her, but I can appreciate your grampy carrying on an excellent tradition. Maybe I should name my truck."

I rolled my eyes dramatically for effect. "You think on that," I said. "Don't ask Dot for help. She'll name it Kenny Rogers."

I opened the door and slid out. "Thanks for being my white knight again."

He shrugged. "I look tough and rescue pretty ladies. It's what I do."

I did another eye roll and closed the passenger door.

Blake powered down the window between us. "Give me a call if you need another ride. I've got nothing going on besides marching and being shot up at the fort. Consider me at your beck and call."

I stared back, dumbfounded.

He winked. "I'll wait for you to get inside and lock up before I leave."

I turned silently and marched up my front steps. I'd never had a man at my beck and call before, certainly not a strapping, handsome one, and I didn't hate the thought.

Surely he was joking.

He'd probably only said it to get a crazy response from me.

I slipped inside and locked the door, then waved through the front window before kicking off my shoes and collapsing onto my couch. Blake gave a little honk as he pulled away.

I tipped over onto the cushions and curled my legs up beside me. Kenny Rogers and Dolly came to sit on my head.

The phone rang.

I groaned and dug it from my pocket, pushing cats aside and hoping it wasn't Colton calling to complain. I didn't want any more drama tonight. I had plenty of my own to deal with. I smiled when I saw Granny's face. "Hello?"

"What on earth is going on over there today?" she said, sounding thoroughly and appropriately exasperated. "I just got in from the cookoff and checked my messages. I've got about a dozen from my needle pointers saying you found another dead body. In your truck! And Sue Ellen says there was a man flirting with you at the cider shop, and Sheriff Wise didn't look very happy about it, and now someone saw Sally covered in pumpkin guts going into town on a flatbed. What? Is? Happening?" she

79

asked, breaking the last question into pieces.

I wasn't sure where to begin. She'd been filled in rather well, evidence the town rumor mill was going strong. I'd had it in my mind to call her tonight, after a hot shower, from the comfort of my bed. I'd planned to relay the details to her, then go directly to sleep. "It was Mr. Potter," I said finally, realizing that was the only thing she hadn't stated specifically. "I just got home. Dot and I took Mrs. Potter a pie and a casserole."

"Apple pie?"

"Pecan. Dot baked it. I made a tater tot casserole," I said.

Granny sighed. "I'll fix her some chicken and corn bread tomorrow."

I waited through a long beat of silence. "I'm sorry, Granny. I know you've known the Potters a long while."

"Everyone loved him," she said, her voice cracking a little at the end. "It doesn't make any sense."

"I know."

She sniffled, and I imagined her working a tissue under her nose and wiping tears from her cheeks with careful fingers. "I'm heading home after breakfast tomorrow, so try not to do anything rash or dangerous until I get there."

I sat up and frowned at the empty room. "Why would I do anything rash or dangerous?"

Granny gave a low, humorless chuckle. "Just stay put until I get there, okay? Then we'll sort things out."

I wrinkled my nose. "I'm not sure what there is to sort out. There's no need to hurry home. Your friends and I have this place covered."

"Well, I'm ready to come home. It sounds like my grandbaby and my community are in crisis. Plus, my chili didn't even place. Those darn Stitch Witches rigged the judging."

"The Stitch Witches?" I repeated, trying to force sense from her words. "Your needle-pointing nemeses? What do they have to do with the cookoff?"

"Apparently they're from this town," she said, sounding exhausted. "They knew I was coming. Saw my name on the roster and stacked the judges against me. I spent all that time perfecting a recipe that never had a chance."

I rubbed my forehead. The Stitch Witches seemed to be everywhere these days, and they were mean to Granny and her needle pointers just for the sake of being mean. Granny didn't know what to do with that.

Honestly, neither did I. So far, she and her ladies had tried killing them with kindness, ignoring them, and swapping ideas for vengeance that they would never perform, but which had proven therapeutic over coffee.

We disconnected several minutes later, then I went to take a highly anticipated shower.

As predicted, twenty minutes under a steady stream of steamy water followed by a pair of flannel jammies and fuzzy socks did wonders to raise my mood and lower my tension. I padded to the kitchen and put a kettle on for tea, then grabbed my laptop. I tried searching for information on Blake while I waited, but like Colton, he didn't keep any social media accounts. Aside from a few accolades for bravery and honor in his local paper and his mother's Facebook updates, there was nothing to be learned about him.

I'd discovered most of what I knew about Colton from his mother's Facebook page, because Blake was right. Colton was a closed book. His mother and sister, on the other hand, kept active and busy pages. In a matter of minutes, I'd learned Colton Wise was thirty-three, thirty-four now, a full five years older than me. He had a big family, retired parents, a schoolteacher and a coal miner, and three siblings. One sister and two brothers, all grown. They attended church, participated in fund-raisers, and seemed to adore Colton, though it was rare to find him in any of their photos. The same was true for Blake.

I switched gears and looked up Mr. Potter. He didn't have a personal page, but he had a business page for his pumpkin patch. I scanned the photos for familiar and unfamiliar faces, then took a look at the reviews in case someone had been hurt on the property and blamed him.

Most of the comments and reviews were from people who'd treasured their experiences at Potter's Pumpkin Patch, but there were a series of one-star rants from a user named Nathan Brumble. I clicked on Mr. Brumble's name and found myself staring at a vaguely familiar face, only I knew him as Nate the Butcher. I cringed. Not the sort of professional I'd want to make an enemy.

A creepy sensation raised the hair across the nape of my neck, and I turned to stare out the window above my sink. I focused hard on the shadows of trees and bushes, fences and scarecrows. Maybe I didn't like the latter as well as I'd thought.

My kettle sang, and I slapped a hand to

my chest hard enough to leave a mark. I moved the wailing pot, then went to peek into the decorative mirror in my living room. As suspected, my skin, already pink from the heat of my shower, was red where my palm had collided with my collarbone. "Yikes." I plucked the fabric a few times, hoping to cool my stinging skin. When it made no difference, I went back to the kitchen for my tea.

A shadow moved across the porch, and someone pounded on my door before I reached the kettle. I forced my shaking limbs to redirect, first grabbing my baseball bat, Louisa, from her spot in the corner, then to take a closer look through my window.

"Winnie?" Colton's voice warbled through the glass. "It's just me. I probably should've called first."

I set Louisa down, rubbed sweaty palms over my pajama bottoms, then opened the door. I tried to look as grown-up as I could in wet hair and pants with little frogs on them. "Come on in," I said, stepping out of his way, then locking up behind him. "Everything okay, or did something else completely horrendous happen?"

"I'm just checking on you," he said, his gaze darting around the room. "You must be shaken up after a day like this."

"I am," I said. "I made tea. Would you like some?" I set out a second mug just in case.

"Sure." Colton removed his hat and turned it over in his hands. "You want to talk about it?"

I shrugged and filled the mugs, then dropped a bag of apple cinnamon tea in each. "I've had better days. My emotions are all mixed up, and my brain is scrambled, but I suppose that's to be expected. I just can't understand why anyone would hurt Mr. Potter, or Sally for that matter."

Colton took the offered mug and spoon. He paddled the little tea bag through the water, dunking and prodding it. "I'll get to the bottom of those mysteries," he said. "Right now, I'm concerned about you. You've been through a lot of tough things in the past year, so it would be completely normal if you were feeling exceptionally uneasy, irrationally heartbroken, or plain old terrified. Sometimes the compilation of bad experiences like the ones you've had can lead to a tipping point."

I pulled my tea bag out and blew over the steaming liquid in my cup. "I'm okay."

"It's fine if you aren't," he said, following suit with the tea bag, then motioning me

85

into my adjoining living room. "The human psyche can only take so much."

I sat on one end of the couch and wrapped my fingers around the warm cup. "Nothing bad happened to me today. The Potters, yes — but not me. I can hardly be upset about my car in comparison to what Mrs. Potter has experienced." *Or Mr. Potter,* I thought morbidly.

"You can absolutely be upset about your car," Colton said, setting his teacup on the coffee table. "You can be upset about Sally, and about your truck, and about the raw deal you keep getting by finding these bodies. Heck, I'm mad for you. Surely someone else in this town can find the next one."

I grimaced. "Does there have to be a next one?"

He raised and dropped a hand. "You know what I mean, and sadly yes. People die every day, and other people find them. It doesn't always have to be you. Or murder," he added belatedly.

"Maybe it hasn't hit me yet," I said. "This day seems more like a bad dream than reality. None of it makes any sense."

"Agreed." He stretched back on the couch, straightening long legs out in front of him. "If you need to talk, you know I'll listen."

"Back at you," I said pointedly.

Colton cocked a questioning brow, and I took that as a request to elaborate.

"Why didn't you tell me your family was coming to visit?" I asked. Didn't they get along? Was he ashamed of my town? Of his new position here? Of me?

"I only found out a couple of nights ago," he said. "The trip was planned on the fly when Blake agreed to fill in for someone in the reenactment. Then my folks decided to tag along because that's what they do since they retired. They go. Anywhere. Anytime. Because they can. They don't want to sit around and gather moss. Their words. Not mine." He sighed. "I never expected you to run into Mr. 'Tall, Dark, and Yummy' before I did. They weren't even supposed to get here until dinnertime."

"Dot named him that," I said, feeling the senseless need to point it out again. "Not me."

Colton pursed his lips, but he didn't comment. "I'm glad he was around to bring you home tonight. With everything that's been going on, I wouldn't have trusted anyone else."

Exactly what I thought. "If we're being

87

candid," I said softly, testing the water and eagerly changing the subject, even though I'd brought his family up. "I will admit I've felt a little extra paranoid since finding Mr. Potter today. So, maybe I'm not dealing with it as well as I could be."

"Paranoid in what way?" he asked, sitting taller, on alert.

"Well." I wet my lips. "Sometimes I feel as if I'm being watched again. I'm usually here when it happens, maybe because so much of the awful stuff I've been through has happened on the property, but I also felt that way outside the Potters' home tonight when Dot and I were running to my car, before I saw what had happened to her."

Colton's body tensed. He lurched onto his feet. "You've been feeling watched? Here? When?" He moved to the window and stared out.

"Earlier. Walking home from the cider shop," I said, thinking back to the other times I'd felt the chilling sensation crawl up my spine. "Then in the car, as I was leaving to pick up Dot, and again right before you got here."

He turned to look at me, a strange mix of emotion on his face. Was it fear? Anger? Something else? "Have you seen anything or anyone on the property who put you on edge? Anything that set your intuition on alert? There are a lot of new faces in town for the reenactment. Could one of them have rubbed you the wrong way or reminded you of a past trauma?"

I shoved onto my feet and went to meet him at the window. "I don't think so. Why?" I watched his face fall back into the blank cop stare I hated, and I realized I wasn't the only one acting squirrely. "Do you think there's a chance someone was really watching me today?"

His skin went pale, though his expression remained carefully unchanged.

My gut twisted. "You told me Samuel Keller was in Kentucky. Your former team members and some FBI guys chased him there. So, who's following me now?"

Colton scratched his head. "Keller's trail went cold around Lexington."

"What!" My heart leapt, and my stomach revolted. "When?"

"About ten days ago. His case was transferred to the US Marshals, but every lead ran cold and they returned home to regroup the night I got the call from Blake saying he and our folks were coming into town."

A lump of fear lodged in my throat, bitter and hard with betrayal. "Were you going to tell me?" I croaked. "What if I'd been in danger and didn't even know? What if I'd felt the urge to run, but told myself not to be silly and walked right into his hands?"

Colton turned to me, his eyes dark and burning with regret. "I'm sorry."

I cupped my hands to my mouth and flopped back onto the couch when I feared my knees would buckle. "What were you thinking?"

"At first, I was thinking they'd pick up the trail again. When they came home empty-handed, I was hoping Keller had boarded a boat for Alaska. I knew that was wishful thinking, so I traded sleep to follow online leads and gather details from my old team. I made sweeps of half the county yesterday, checking every hotel, motel, and dive bar with his photo and a list of every alias he's been known to use. No one saw him. Then you know how today's gone."

My temper cooled a bit. "You should have told me."

Colton dipped his chin once. "I'm going to take a walk around, then head home. Call if you need anything." He paused, one hand on the doorknob. "I mean it, Winnie. Even if you're sure it's nothing, just call. I'd rather respond to a thousand false alarms than not show up the one time you needed me."

"Okay," I whispered.
He bobbed his head and was gone.

CHAPTER SIX

I tossed and turned until dawn, then gave up the effort and opened my laptop. Relieved of the pressure to sleep when I couldn't, I went back to something I could do with some success. I snooped virtually.

I opened Facebook and searched the page I'd been reading before Colton had arrived and rocked my already shaky world with news of Keller's possible return. I followed the one-star pumpkin patch reviews back to Nathan Brumble, then I clicked onto his personal page. Nothing. No photos. No updates. No favorite movies or family members listed. It was as if he'd created the account just to leave the nasty reviews on the pumpkin patch. I navigated back to his reviews and read them again. Nate's complaints ranged from excessive noise at late hours to trash in his yard, which he believed came from careless pumpkin patch guests. He claimed to have lost large amounts of sleep and clearly all of his patience. I'd definitely pay a visit to Nate's home as soon as possible, preferably while he was at work.

I typed *Brumble* into the website's search bar and looked for his wife's profile.

I found a familiar face and clicked the link, surprised to see a woman I'd met multiple times when I'd worked at the diner. Funny I'd never put the two of them together. Polly had breakfast at the Sip N Sup with friends at least twice a month. She always ordered a yogurt parfait with granola and coffee.

I scrolled through her feed, making plans to bring her some fresh cider and apple strudel as soon as possible. Her page was a gold mine of information on Nate's beef with the Potters. Between cheery photos of her with her husband, their home, gardens, and activities were a series of short videos taken by Nate. All were of Potter's Pumpkin Patch and the loud partying across the field. Cheers from crowds as local bands wrapped up and screams for more when the Crusher rolled loudly over previously destroyed cars. Worse was Nate's low, muttering promise in the background about making Mr. Potter pay.

I closed the page and took a deep breath, then scratched Kenny Rogers behind his ears. "Things aren't always as they appear," I told him. "Nate was mad and made a threat, but it doesn't mean anything." I'd vowed to kill my ex, Hank, at least a dozen times this month, yet he was still alive and kicking.

I opened a new page and searched for Hellen Potter. I couldn't help wondering if she, like Polly, had kept robust social media accounts while her husband had none.

Hellen's page was bright and welcoming with fall recipes and photos from the pumpkin patch, but no pictures of her husband as far as I could see. I scrolled back for what seemed an eternity in search of him, but it was months before he appeared. I slowed at a set of selfies taken last spring. She and Mr. Potter looked happy, yet he vanished from her page after that. Had they simply been too busy preparing for fall business to take more photos together, or had something happened between them?

Maybe Polly Brumble wouldn't be the only wife I'd visit after breakfast.

I hurried to get ready, choosing comfort over fashion in my clothes and shoes, then pulling my wild hair into a manageable ponytail.

My phone buzzed with a text from Blake as I scrubbed my teeth. He wanted to buy me breakfast, and seeing as I had no car or desire to cook, I accepted. Plus, Blake was good company and fun to look at. Breakfast with him was a no-brainer.

When we arrived at the Sip N Sup before they ran out of Freddie's homemade biscuits and gravy, I knew it was going to be a great day. The familiar hustle and bustle of the busy diner made my feet itch to jump up and help out. I missed the clattering plates and rich greasy scents of salt, butter, and coffee that had long ago permeated the walls and faux-leather booths. Sometimes I even missed the soft swish of material as the ice-blue vintage waitressing uniform brushed my thighs. I took a minute to enjoy the large black-and-white-checkered floor and wide wall of windows facing Main Street before suggesting a booth near the entrance.

Blake clasped his hands on the table after Reese, the young blond waitress, took our orders and went to fetch drinks. "I love this place," he said. "I stopped by yesterday for coffee, and I wound up with a quarter-pound mushroom cheeseburger that tasted like my best dreams come true."

I smiled. "My granny says her mama told her that the way to a man's heart is through his stomach. I guess some things never change."

He rubbed his ridiculously flat stomach through his T-shirt. "Your great-grandmama was a smart woman. I might order one of those cheeseburgers to take with me. For lunch."

I laughed. "You can always come back, but trust me. If you manage to finish your biscuits and gravy, you'll be too full to think about eating again for a while."

He looked skeptical. I didn't blame him. The Sip N Sup made a great burger.

"Did you know I worked here for ten years?" I asked, feeling wildly nostalgic for something I'd only given up eleven months ago. "I started on weekends in high school, then I stayed on full-time after graduation. I waitressed to pay for college as I went so I wouldn't graduate with any student loan debt." Also, probably to defer the inevitable. I'd wanted to open a cider shop, but until the orchard had been in danger, I'd lacked the confidence and motivation to make it happen.

Blake looked impressed. "Not many people get out of college debt-free these days. That was quite a goal. And I've been to your cider shop, so that's two gold stars for you. How long ago did you graduate?"

I felt the heat of pride on my cheeks, then the sting of awkward misunderstanding on the back of my neck. "I'm still in college," I admitted. "A senior this year." Possibly the only twenty-nine-year-old in any of my classes. "We're on fall break now, but we go back after Thanksgiving. I'll graduate next May."

"Nice," he said. "Be sure to send me an invitation to your party."

Reese arrived with a carafe of coffee and a pair of mugs. She set them all before us with a smile. "I'll be right back with your breakfasts."

"Thanks," I told her as she spun gracefully away, her corkscrew ponytail bobbing behind her. Reese made waitressing look like fun. She was never short on smiles or pep, and just being near her was somehow energizing. I wished she worked with me at the cider shop, but I could never offer her enough hours or guarantee the kind of tips she earned here.

She returned a moment later as promised. "Here you go." She arranged the plates, then added two sets of silverware neatly rolled in napkins. "Winnie," she began, tentatively, casting a cautious look at Blake.

"He's fine," I told her. "Go on."

She pursed her lips a moment, then leaned

in conspiratorially. "I heard about what happened yesterday, with Mr. Potter in your truck, then the other thing, with your car. I'm real sorry about all of that. You have the absolute worst luck."

I sighed inwardly. Of course she'd heard. The Sip N Sup was often gossip central, and there had been hordes of witnesses for both discoveries.

"Birdie Wilks was in here last night and told me all about it. She said she'd been with Mrs. Potter all day and didn't have time to make dinner for Mr. Wilks, so she stopped by to pick up a potpie and some mashed potatoes. We got to talking while she waited."

"Did she say anything else?" I asked, hoping Reese was about to unload an incredibly useful clue.

"Just that you're looking into it for Mrs. Potter. As a favor to Birdie. I want you to know I'll keep my ears open and let you know if I hear anything hinky." Reese peeked over her shoulder to where a couple waited at the counter, bill in hand. "I've got to get the register," she said. "Holler if you need anything else."

Blake forked a hunk of gravy-soaked biscuit. He popped it into his mouth and groaned. "This is fantastic."

"It's Freddie's personal recipe," I said. "We're lucky to get any because it's normally gone by now. He must've planned ahead for all the visitors this week." I worked the pepper shaker over my meal before digging in.

Blake was quiet for several minutes, until his plate was nearly empty. "Maybe we should talk about the dead guy. Seems like every lady in town is rooting for you to solve his murder. You want to tell me what you know about him? Maybe I can help. It's what I do, you know?"

I considered his offer, sure it was probably a trap, then marched in anyway. "His name is Mr. Potter," I said. "Was," I corrected, cringing at the necessity of past tense, though even that was better than hearing him called "the dead guy."

Then I spilled every detail I had.

"So, you're going to talk to Potter's neighbor today?" he asked. "The butcher with an ax to grind?"

"I plan to visit his wife," I corrected. "I want to know if Nate only complained online or if he and Mr. Potter had ever argued in person about it. Something like that could easily have escalated yesterday. There were a ton of people there at the time he was killed, lots of noise, and Crusher was scheduled to perform later. Maybe Nate had had enough."

Blake wiped his mouth and dropped the napkin beside his plate. "You want some company?" he asked. "I don't have anywhere I need to be right away. There's an informational meeting at the fort in an hour, but it's optional. The real training and details will come in a day or two. Today is mostly for mingling and trading stories. I don't usually pretend to be a militiaman from two hundred years ago, so I don't have anything good to share."

"Yet," I said, lifting a finger to make the point.

"Yet," he agreed. "So, what do you say? Need a ride to question a suspect's wife?"

I debated. "I hate for you to miss your militia's mixer, and I'm not sure we'd make it to the Brumbles' place and back to the fort in an hour."

"I don't mind," he said, deep sincerity in his tone.

"Make it where and back in an hour?" Hank asked, manifesting at the side of our table with a smile.

"Nosy," I said, fixing him with my best warning face. "What are you doing here?"

"Looking for you, obviously." He motioned for me to scoot over, and I obliged on instinct.

"Why are you looking for me?" I asked, staring as he took a seat at my side.

Hank's attention flicked to Blake. "Oh, hey, man," Hank said. "I don't think we've met. I'm Hank Donovan, Winnie's former fiancé."

"Blake Wise," Blake said, extending a hand across the table.

"We were never engaged," I said flatly. "Stop telling people that."

I'd anticipated Hank's proposal two Christmases ago, after five long years of dating. It had been well past time to do it, but he hadn't. Instead, he'd announced plans to move to Ohio and work for a big oil company over his mama's Thanksgiving turkey. Then he'd said I could come with him if I wanted and sat there waiting for me to leap with joy. I'd dumped him after dinner and stewed over it for a year. "We grew up in Blossom Valley together," I explained to Blake. "We dated awhile, but that was over two years ago. More recently, he was a suspect in one of your brother's murder cases."

Hank frowned.

Blake nodded, recognition lighting his eyes. "I remember you. Colton told me all about that. What a crazy mess, right?"

"Colton told you about *him*?" I parroted, feeling utterly gobsmacked. He'd told Blake about Hank, but not about me? I ignored the punch of disappointment in my chest. That was fine. I didn't care at all. I shook it off and turned a pleasant expression on Hank. "I was just saying to Blake that I'd like to talk to Mr. Potter's neighbors today. Maybe they saw or heard something that can be used to find his killer. I brought strudel and cider for Mrs. Brumble." I patted the bag on the bench at my side.

"I offered to go with her," Blake said. "Questioning suspects doesn't seem like the sort of thing a civilian should do on her own. She was in the middle of turning me down politely when you showed up."

Hank shifted to face me. "I'll take you."

Blake shrugged. "I suppose that's better than nothing. Winnie?"

"Fine," I said. "I don't want you to miss your thing at the fort, and Hank's already here."

Blake slid out of the booth and offered Hank his hand again. "It was nice to meet you." He ended the shake and smiled my way. "I've got breakfast. Call me if you need anything."

"Thanks," I said, shooing Hank out of my way. I left Reese a huge tip, then followed him to the door.

I'd hoped to visit the Brumbles with Blake, a lawman trained to protect me if I knocked on a killer's door and ticked him off, but I'd somehow wound up with Hank instead.

I supposed the key to survival, if things went south, was just to outrun Hank.

CHAPTER SEVEN

"So that's Sheriff Wise's brother?" Hank asked, unlocking the doors of his pickup.

"Yep."

We climbed aboard, and Hank gunned his engine to life before easing us out of the parking space. "Interesting."

I powered down my window, refusing to bite, choosing instead to enjoy the warm fall air. It was cooler today than yesterday, but just as beautiful. I opened and closed my fist outside the truck, allowing wind to beat against my palm and tickle the skin between my fingers.

"Don't pretend you're mad I crashed your breakfast," he said. "I know you well enough to know you'd have told me to kick stones if you didn't want a way out of that date." He took the corner out of town looking smug and overconfident.

I narrowed my eyes at him. "Clearly you don't know me at all, Hank Donovan." A fact he'd plainly proven yet again. "I was having a perfectly nice time at breakfast, and it wasn't a date."

He shook his head contrarily but said nothing.

I ran my gaze around the truck's new and spotless interior. "Ever miss the fancy little sedan you used to drive?"

"Sometimes," he said, promptly smacking into a pothole. "But not at the moment. My BMW wouldn't have survived this road."

"That's the truth," I said. "I'd be house-bound all winter if it wasn't for Grampy's truck. Sally's awful on slush and snow." I needed the pickup for inclement weather and anytime I wanted to haul more than a load of groceries. If I didn't think it'd hurt Sally's feelings, I'd buy a more practical car, a small SUV or a gently used pickup, something more sensible for country living, and I'd save Sally for warm Sunday drives. Unfortunately, I suspected Sally would think I was a traitor.

"So, what was going on with you and Colton's brother?" Hank asked. "If it wasn't a date, then did Colton ask him to keep an eye on you?"

I puffed my cheeks in an exaggerated sigh. "According to Blake, Colton's never even mentioned me or my cider shop. Dot and I met Blake by chance when we were going for ice cream yesterday. It was weird. I don't want to talk about this," I said, frustrated. "How are things with you and the bridesmaid?" I asked, referring to the last girl I knew he'd been seeing.

"Didn't work out," he said. "What kind of ice cream did you and Dot get?"

"I got a chocolate malt. Dot got a vanilla shake."

"I want a root beer float. We should get ice cream on our way back."

"Might as well enjoy them while we can," I said. "Winter's coming for us eventually. Mother Nature can only put it off for so long."

"Excellent. Hey, how'd your granny do at the chili cookoff?"

I cringed. "Turns out the Stitch Witches live in Marlinton."

Hank grimaced. "No."

"Yep."

"Bummer." Hank slowed as he cruised past the Potter's Pumpkin Patch. "Talk about dumb luck."

"Yeah, but she'll be home by lunchtime today, so that's good." I sat up straighter, evaluating the eerily desolate property.

The place was closed. Gate shut. Lot empty. Fields, hay bales, and pavilion silent.

A complete contrast to the scene from yesterday, or even last night with all the well-meaning guests delivering food and the deputies combing the land.

My heart went out to Mrs. Potter. Granny and I had had one another when we lost Grampy, so neither of us had to get through it alone, but Mrs. Potter had no one. I supposed Birdie Wilks would do all she could to comfort her friend, but I wished there was more I could do too. "Let's stop and see Mrs. Potter first," I said. "I hate that she's all alone."

"Now?" Hank asked. "Or after we see Nate's wife?" He slowed to a crawl between the two properties, waiting for instructions.

I chewed my lip, unsure. "Now, I think."

"As you wish." He pulled his truck into the driveway outside Mrs. Potter's home and snuffed the engine.

A shotgun blast echoed in the distance as I opened my door.

Hank swung his hands overhead briefly, then let them drop. "I don't understand why people have to do that," he said. "There's always a few who just can't wait another few days for gun season. They have to jump the shark every year. Get a few deer before the season opens. Once they do, they probably don't even bother paying for a proper hunting license."

I gave him a sideways look. "What?"

"Did you know the money from hunting licenses supports our state Division of Natural Resources? Those funds support our wildlife, forests, and lakes."

I turned to frown at him for the little rant. First of all, I didn't know Hank cared so deeply about any of that, and secondly, there had to be a personal reason for it. Most of the things Hank cared about had a common denominator: They each directly impacted *him*. "People shoot all the time around here," I said, feeling a bit silly for stating the obvious. "Whoever pulled that trigger might've been killing a copperhead or a bobcat, protecting their livestock, or just doing some good old-fashioned target practice. Why assume they're shooting deer right before gun season?"

Hank fixed me with a droll expression. "What kind of target practice only takes one shot?"

"Maybe the shooter is really good," I said. "Maybe she hit the bull's-eye first try, and now she's done for the day. Why do you care, anyway?"

He climbed down from his truck, and I followed suit. We met at the front bumper.

Hank stuffed his hands into the front

pockets of his neatly pressed blue jeans and squinted against the midmorning sun. "I saw a few clearings in the forests around the county that had strategically planted patches of corn near the tree lines. At least two of those had tree stands visible within thirty yards," he said. "For poachers' purposes, obviously," he added, in case I couldn't have figured that out for myself.

Poachers were the worst. It wasn't as if the deer stood a chance against a hunter with a gun to start with, but poachers took it a step further. What ever happened to the thrill of the hunt? The challenge? Skills like tracking? I put a pin in my mental tirade as something else came to mind. "How'd you see the corn and tree stands? Were you out hiking?" I asked, trying to imagine Hank in the woods by choice.

"Satellites," he said. "Everything's visible with satellite imagery."

"Why are you looking at satellite images of our town? And while I agree poaching is wrong, I'm going to repeat my previous question. Why do you care?"

Hank didn't hunt. He never had. Hunting was primal and dirty. It was hours in the woods, sweating in camouflage, waiting for the perfect shot and often not getting it, then repeating the process the next day, and the next, until hopefully the stars aligned. Hunting was eating beef jerky from baggies tucked in vest pockets and drinking luke-warm water or coffee from a canteen or thermos all day. Worse, if a hunter had a shot, took it, and hit, hunting meant drag-ging a two-hundred-pound deer off a moun-tain, its body still warm with the life you'd taken. Not just anyone could do all that. Never mind the field dressing that came next.

"I just do," he said, tipping his head toward the Potters' front door. "Now, come on. Someone saw us from the window. We'd better knock and stop lurking in the drive."

The front door swung open as Hank and I reached the porch. Mrs. Potter's gaze trav-eled from his face to mine, then down my arm to the bag in my hands. "More food?"

"Strudel and cider from Smythe Orchard," I said, wishing I'd brought enough for two stops. I'd only planned to visit the Brumbles. "I hope you don't mind me com-ing back so soon. Hank didn't get a chance to pay his condolences last night, so I thought we could come together. We won't stay long or be in your way."

Mrs. Potter swung the door wide. "I never say no to anything from Smythe Orchard. Come on in," she said, sounding as exhausted as she looked.

We followed her through the über tidy living room to a small kitchen, where casseroles and pies were stacked on one another.

"Fridge and freezer are full," she said with a wave toward the piled-up food. "I tried to send things home with folks, but no one wanted to take anything. I can't seem to eat, so I suppose this will all go to waste soon."

I cast a look at Hank, hoping he'd take a casserole off her hands.

He helped himself to a seat at the table. "I'm very sorry about what happened," he said. "If there's anything I can do to help, please let me know. I'm not much of a cook, but I can help with the property or anything else less . . . domestic that comes up."

I handed her my offerings, then glared at Hank's dumb head. "Less domestic?" Like, he won't cook or clean, but he can what? Chop wood and change her oil?

Mrs. Potter poured three glasses of cider. "Thanks," she said. "I don't need anything right now. Honestly, I just want to be left alone. Unfortunately, the moment I am alone, I wish I wasn't."

"I understand," I said. I'd felt the same way after losing Grampy. The orchard had been overrun with people paying condolences and wanting to help. I'd wanted to scream for silence, but then, in the silence, I'd longed for company. Nothing about loss was easy, but having Granny nearby had helped. Sometimes all a person really needed was someone to be still with. "Is there anything we can do to help while we're here?" I asked. "Believe it or not, Hank and I are a pretty handy duo."

Mrs. Potter sipped and savored her cider. "Not today, but I'll need help cleaning up outside after all those busy festival days. I don't think anyone's allowed out there right now. The sheriff's got the whole place closed down while he and his crew tear it apart in search of clues." She leaned against the kitchen table and glared at the closed curtains on her back window. "That nasty Nate ought to be happy now. No more noise to upset him. No more sounds of joy and laughter or music and dancing. Ever." Tears welled in her eyes on the final word.

"I'm going to talk to Nate's wife," I said. "I'll bring her some cider and see if she has anything useful to say. Maybe she saw something from her home that will be helpful," I suggested. "The Brumbles aren't that far away."

Mrs. Potter dabbed the corners of her eyes

with a napkin and nodded. "I have to cancel the pumpkin cannon tonight," she said, her voice quaking. "And I guess I can tell the Crusher crew to pack it up and take it home. We won't be needing it again this year."

"I'm so sorry," I said softly, feeling my throat tighten with empathy and deep understanding.

Hank moved to her side, drawing her attention from the closed curtains. "I can make those calls for you, if you'd like."

Mrs. Potter released a small sob. She nodded and pointed to the refrigerator, where a pumpkin-shaped magnet held a list of contact names and phone numbers.

Hank pulled his phone from one pocket and took a picture of the list. "No problem. I'll get it done before lunch."

"Thank you," she answered softly.

"Mrs. Potter," I said, "can I ask you about Nate? I know he complained about the noise, but did that just begin, or has it been going on awhile? And if the change is recent, can you remember when the complaints started?" I hoped to match his complaints with the timeline on Mrs. Potter's Facebook account. Something had changed for the Potters in August, and I wanted to know what that was. I doubted Mrs. Potter would admit anything if I asked outright.

"Nate started complaining last year," she said. "He changed the hours on his butcher shop to open earlier and close later, which meant he was home less and needed more sleep. So, he thought we should have to follow suit with our business hours to accommodate the changes he'd made with his. Suddenly our festival was inconvenient to him, and we were supposed to fix it. He's so selfish and close-minded he can't even see how obnoxiously self-important his stance is. I mean, what kind of a person thinks their needs are more important than everyone else's?"

I offered a sad smile. "I'll talk to Nate's wife and see what she knows."

Mrs. Potter nodded, turning her attention back to the closed curtains.

I stepped forward, focusing on the figures beyond the glass. Colton's deputies were visible through the small space between the curtain panels, picking over the land and setting down little numbered evidence teepees. "How long have they been out there?"

Mrs. Potter tightened her arms around her middle. "All morning. Half the night."

I hadn't noticed them when Hank and I pulled up. They'd probably been going through the barns and buildings. I couldn't help wondering if the farmhand I'd spoken to last night was still in the red barn, watching as deputies searched for clues. I also couldn't help hoping he wouldn't mention running into me if he spoke with the sheriff.

Colton suddenly turned the corner, flashing into view, as if my thinking of him had caused him to appear. He marched up the cobblestone walkway in our direction, heading for the back door in long, steady strides.

I leaped for Hank, looping my arm in his. "Well, we'd better get going, Mrs. Potter," I said. "Looks like the sheriff is on his way to see you, and I want you to have enough privacy to talk."

Hank's eyes widened at the mention of Colton. "Goodbye, Mrs. Potter," he added quickly, presumably knowing the length of lecture I'd receive if Colton caught me there again. "I'll make those calls as soon as I drop Winnie back at home."

"Well, there's no need to rush off," she said, her words thinning behind us as we scurried away.

CHAPTER EIGHT

Granny's truck was in front of her house when we got home. I needed more cider and strudel to visit the Brumbles, plus I couldn't interview Nate's wife with Colton right next door. What if he stopped by to ask Mrs. Brumble about Mr. Potter and found me there?

I smiled at the small blue sedan parked with her truck. The owner's press badge dangled from the rearview. Not only had Granny beat me home, but apparently her high school sweetheart had already come to welcome her back.

"Looks like Owen Martin beat us to her," Hank said, shifting into PARK behind the sedan.

It wasn't much of a surprise, I supposed. Owen was so smitten, he might've been waiting on the porch when she got there.

"Five bucks says he brought flowers," Hank said, popping open his door.

"Obviously he brought flowers," I said. "And probably chocolates."

Hank and I climbed down from the cab and shut our doors in near unison. We took turns scratching Kenny Rogers and Dolly behind the ears as they yawned and stretched on Granny's porch steps.

I knocked as a warning, then let us in. "Welcome home!" I said, heading straight for Granny, seated at her kitchen table. I wrapped her in my arms and kissed the side of her head.

She squeezed me back. Her bobbed brown hair was tucked behind one ear, and she smelled of apples and spun sugar, as if she'd already been baking.

"I missed you," I whispered, not realizing until that moment how much it was true.

"Me too, sweetie," she said. "There really is no place like home."

Owen stood and extended his hand in greeting to Hank, then me, before retaking his seat across from Granny. "Penny was just telling me about the Roadkill Cookoff."

Hank took the seat beside Owen. "Folks say the entire event is fantastic. I want to hear everything." He tipped his head casually to the vase of white roses on the table and box of chocolates at its base, then flicked his smiling eyes to mine.

Owen was fighting an uphill battle to win Granny's affection. She wasn't ready to give her heart to another man. She might never be, but I had to give the guy credit. He was dedicated, and wholly devoted to his cause. He'd been Granny's high school crush, but life had come between them for about fifty years. Granny seemed to feel guilty for the time she spent with Owen, but I thought Grampy would approve, and four years was long enough to be alone. Especially when Owen thought Granny hung the moon.

She looked closer to my age than Owen's and had often been mistaken for my mother, which was closer to the truth than the guessers could have imagined. Granny was a dead ringer for Mary Steenburgen while Owen, on the other hand, had aged more . . . appropriately. I supposed he'd never been very tall, but now he also had a round bald head and glasses.

Granny tugged me into the seat beside hers. "What can I get you?"

I grinned. "Nothing yet." I'd spent countless hours of my life at Granny's kitchen table, eating meals or snacks, doing homework, and talking about my day. I'd peeled potatoes, sliced apples, shucked corn, and snapped string beans. I'd worked out my troubles and let Granny nurse my broken hearts.

The kitchen itself was great too. All original, save the occasionally updated electricity and appliance. Granny painted the walls and cabinetry from time to time for upkeep's sake, and she'd added dozens of framed photos to the walls, shelves, and counters. Mostly of me.

Granny hefted a bag from the floor near her feet. "As I was telling Owen, I missed you guys, but the cookoff was a hoot. I tried things I never thought I would. Like teriyaki marinated bear and turtle gumbo. Neither was for me, but I tried them! There were at least enough people to fill Disneyland. I've never seen the likes. Did you know the Travel Channel, the Discovery Channel, and the Food Network have all been there? That Roadkill Cookoff is a big deal. I felt like a celebrity just for being allowed to sell my chili. I told everyone who stopped to sample that I used locally raised turkey instead of wild, but it was still a hit."

Owen beamed. "I wish I could've been there to see you working your magic that first day. What a thrill that must've been."

"It was," she said, looking a little soft and wistful. "I felt forty-five all over again. Doing things I never thought I would. Travel-

119

ing. Trying new things. It's nice."

"I'm glad," I said, turning my attention to Owen. "You said you missed the first day. Does that mean you went to the festival?"

Granny's cheeks darkened, and I knew I was right. "Owen went to cover the event for his local paper. When he saw me there, he stayed through to the end."

Hank smiled. "Is that right?"

"Don't," Granny said, shutting him down with a shake of her index finger. "It's time to see your gifts." She dug into the bag and liberated a pile of keepsakes. "This is for you." She passed a commemorative T-shirt to Hank. White with black trim at the collar and cuffs. An official Roadkill Cookoff logo covered the front. "And this," she said, producing a ball cap with a matching decal. "For all your help getting me registered online. They sure don't make that easy."

Hank pulled the shirt on over his own, then worked the cap onto his head. "I love it."

"You look ridiculous," I said.

Granny handed me a pair of hairy brown slippers with stuffed black pointed toenails. "Bigfoot slippers," she said. "The American Sasquatch Society was there, and I know how you love your jammies. Now you have fun slippers too."

I put them on my hands and made them dance on the table. "Thanks."

"I've also got some jerky," she said, pulling small vacuum-sealed bags from her tote. "Bear, elk, vulture, snake."

"Snake?" I leaned away. "Got anything sweet in there?"

"I've got beaver pie," she said.

Hank barked a laugh.

I wrinkled my nose. "No, thank you."

"Try it," she said. "I think it's chocolate peanut butter."

I pressed my lips together, already turned off by the name. There wasn't any coming back from "beaver pie."

The oven dinged, and Granny scraped her chair backward, making room to get up from the table. "That's me," she said, humming as she went.

Owen folded his hands in front of him. "Penny promised me a hot apple turnover when we got back," he said, looking quite proud of himself.

My stomach growled at his words.

Granny pulled big mitts onto her hands like gloves. "Winnie? Hank?" she asked, looking over her shoulder as she lowered the oven door.

We accepted the offer with enthusiasm, and her smile grew.

121

Granny went to work drizzling icing over the warm pastries and plating them for us while I watched Owen watching her. He really liked her, and I couldn't blame him. In fact, his sheer, unabashed appreciation of her made me like him all the more.

He caught me looking and blushed.

"Did you enjoy the cookoff, Owen?" I asked. "Try anything new?"

"Well," he said, "I've been to the event before, so it was a bit of the same, though I thought Penny was robbed of her win. Her turkey chili was the best I've ever had."

Granny turned back to the table, ferrying turnovers to each of our seats. "Two of the Stitch Witches had husbands on the judging committee. I never stood a chance."

Owen shifted. "It was definitely an unfair decision," he said. "Your granny deserved that grand prize."

I had no doubt. "Are you staying in Blossom Valley to cover next week's reenactment?"

"I'd like to," he said. "Right now I'm on assignment to address rumors of a Blossom Valley specter, but the timing is excellent for covering both."

"A ghost?" I asked. "Hasn't Halloween passed?"

He nodded, using a fork to cut his turnover down the center and allow the pieces to cool. "Yes." He exchanged a speculative look with Granny.

"We're sure it's nothing," she said, focusing intensely on her turnover as she returned to her seat.

"Okay," I said, dragging the word out unnecessarily. Of course it was nothing to worry about. Ghosts weren't real. I frowned at Granny's strange reaction. I'd never taken her to be a believer, but as a whole, our town was superstitious to the extreme. Locals generally believed in any and all unexplained phenomena, including but not limited to "mountain magic," witchcraft, bad luck, bad omens, boogeymen, and just about anything they were told. Possibly even Bigfoot, considering my slippers had come from a chapter of the American Sasquatch Society. Even as a cynic, I played my cards carefully by never opening an umbrella indoors, stepping on graves, breaking mirrors, and a number of other little things that might sway the universe against me.

"Folks let their imaginations get carried away during all those late-night bonfires last month," Owen said. "That's all it is. Too many ghost stories. Too much spiked cider. Soon every shadow appears a little more ominous, and the gnarled tree limbs and barren branches begin to look like witches' hands." He bent his wrists and fingers until both hands seemed like misshapen hooks. "Add a little wind for motion and the things our imaginations can make of the shadows is limitless."

I swallowed a lump of instant fear as I pulled the phone from my purse and texted Colton a rundown on the ghost story. If there was any chance that Samuel Keller was behind those shadows, I'd sleep better if Colton stayed on top of it.

Granny gave me a quizzical look as I tapped my screen.

I offered a small smile. We'd have to talk later. I didn't want to give voice to the horrific speculations going around in my head until Colton could confirm them.

Granny seemed to understand my unspoken request for time. She dragged her attention away from me and smiled warmly at Hank instead. "What about you, Hank? What's new in your world?"

"Thank you for asking," he said slowly, shooting me a look. "No one else has."

I shoved a forkful of turnover between my lips to busy my tongue. I had bigger problems than upsetting Hank. I checked my phone for a response from Colton.

Nothing.

"Actually," Hank said, "I've been given a very important job at work."

I concentrated on chewing to avoid a groan. Hank was a public relations official for Extra Mobile, the big oil company in the next county. I wasn't a fan of any big oil company, so I made a practice of not asking about his work. Still, it seemed like I was going to hear about it anyway. I couldn't help wondering if he would be leveling yet another forest or buying more little old women out of their retirement homes in the name of fracking and commerce.

"I want to get folks excited about hunting again," Hank said. "Gun season starts this week for deer, and West Virginia as a whole is experiencing a downturn in registered hunters. That's a serious problem because wildlife and conservation organizations depend on sportsmanship fees and taxes to thrive."

"Interesting," Owen said, perking up. "I've heard about this."

Hank nodded, shoving another bite of turnover into his mouth. He chewed quickly and swallowed. "The state government plans to tax gas and oil companies to make up for the lost revenue."

I imagined bouncing a palm off my forehead. "So, that's why you're stalking deer stands from satellite imagery," I said. "You want more people registering to hunt because the income will benefit your company and you by default."

He widened his eyes. "Well, yeah. My company employs thousands of people, which means it directly impacts tens of thousands of lives."

I wanted to tell him he was being dramatic, but I knew what he'd said was true. The reduced number of hunting licenses had impacted Dot at the national park. Her boss had consistently reduced the number of free programs for the last three years in a row. I'd never considered whether or how the state might try to rediscover the lost revenue.

It was a little sad to know hunting was a dying sport. Hunting was a beloved tradition in Blossom Valley and an important part of our local identity and culture. Folks still hunted for bragging rights here, for the sense of community among sportsmen, and for the meat.

"Increasing taxes on oil companies isn't the answer," Hank said. "Increasing taxes means increasing a company's overhead and reducing profits. That will lead to job cutting, which will lead to higher unemployment rates and more families in need of cash and food."

Owen nodded, his bushy gray brows drawn together. "Interesting. A sure sign of the times. What do you think can be done about it?"

Hank smiled. "I plan to pass out flyers at the reenactment," he said. "Plus anywhere there are lots of men. No offense intended," he said, shooting a mischievous grin in my direction, "but statistically men make up the largest portion of registered hunters."

I ignored the statistically supported misogyny. "And what exactly will your flyers say? 'Please hunt because my mega-bucks company wants to keep its money'?"

"Funny," he said. He fished his phone from his pocket and tapped the screen a few times, then handed the device to me. "I'm thinking about printing this."

An image of a bearded man with a tight black T-shirt stretched over a clearly fit physique stared back at me. The man had a rifle on his back, a hunting license in his grip, and the words "Real men hunt" printed across his torso. An attractive blond woman in the background looked seriously impressed with him.

I handed the phone back to Hank. "Did you make this flyer?"

"Do you like it?" he asked.

"As an ad for a gym or beards? Yes." As an ad to promote hunting? No. "I'm not sure it portrays the sport accurately," I said.

"Ads aren't about accuracy," Hank said. "They're about creating an illusion and evoking an emotion."

"It evoked an emotion from me," I said, pushing to my feet.

I checked my phone once more. It was time to open the cider shop, and Colton hadn't responded to my text yet.

I couldn't be sure, but I had a bad feeling there was grounds to worry.

CHAPTER NINE

I lost myself in the beauty of the walk to the cider shop, putting thoughts of fugitives and specters behind me. I basked in the remarkable colors of the leaves. The beloved scents of fresh-cut grass and a distant bonfire on the breeze. I loved that specific scent, and it traveled for miles on the wind.

I unlocked the historic barn doors, then swung them wide on a deep inhalation of breath. I would never get tired of opening these doors and finding my cider shop inside. I flipped the lights on as I made my way to the counter and began my opening routine. I surveyed the menu, still scripted on the mirror hung behind the bar, then compared that to my inventory of ciders and sweets. Satisfied I had enough of everything to last the day, I moved the cash drawer from the safe to the register and counted it down. Next, I wiped tables and swept the floor, feeling grateful for my shop, the historic barn, Granny, and my home.

I returned to my place behind the counter as my first handful of customers arrived. "Come on in, y'all," I said, waving them forward. "What can I get ya?"

I poured ciders and served sweets with a smile, thankful for every order. At this time last year, my life had been on the cusp of an enormous change. Granny had just confided the extent of the orchard's financial problems to me, and I'd begun to concoct a plan. Our first annual Christmas at the Orchard. It was then that I'd first asked the bank for money to turn the barn into a cider shop. It was the beginning of extensive, life-altering changes, and a year later, it still felt surreal.

Customers served and satisfied, I turned to survey my cider supply. I wanted to create a specialty cider that would commemorate my shop's one-year anniversary, but what flavor should that be? So far, I had no idea. Or more accurately, no *good* ideas.

I pulled a test pint from the mini-fridge and gave it a good shake. I'd played with the idea of adding molasses and other spices to give Granny's standard cider a kick, and I was eager to taste-test the results.

The color was a little dark, and I didn't like the way it moved when I swirled the jug. Too thick and slow. I poured an ounce for sampling and gave it a sip in case my instincts were off. They weren't.

I upturned the pint into the sink and mentally scratched that recipe off my list of possibilities. I'd have to start over at home tonight. The cider shop was best equipped for making gourmet ciders in large batches, but home was where the recipes were formed. Each of my gourmet flavors began with one of the base options from Granny's orchard. Honeycrisp, Granny Smith, or Variety. Then I worked in other ingredients, mostly via trial and error, until the flavor was perfect and ready to share with others. When that happened, I made large batches at the cider shop and bottled it in half-gallon jugs for resale. Like most creative endeavors, my recipe trials ended in error more often than perfection, but I never minded. The process was half the fun.

"Good morning," I called as additional guests rolled in. I gathered napkins and followed one couple to a table. "What can I get you started with today?"

"Two mugs of your hot caramel cider," the woman answered eagerly. "We discovered this place yesterday and vowed we'd be back."

"I'm thankful to have you," I said. "Would

you like anything to go with your ciders?"

She glanced at her smiling companion, whose attention was glued to the menu board.

"Apple fries?" he asked her.

She raised two fingers in a peace sign. "Please."

"On it." I smiled as I headed back to the bar.

A man in jeans and a ball cap scanned the gallery wall near the window. His blue plaid flannel hung open over a white T-shirt, and his posture was painfully casual. *Tourist*, I thought. Obviously interested in the town's history. Probably in town for the reenactment.

"Welcome," I said on my way past.

He touched a finger to the brim of his hat without looking away from the framed newspaper clippings and town paraphernalia nailed to my walls.

I poured the hot caramel ciders and gave them each a cone of whipped cream on top, then popped some apple fries in the toaster oven to heat. I ran water in the sink to wash away the lingering scent of my failed cider while I waited. Hopefully I got better results tonight. There was no way I'd be sleeping, so I might as well make good use of the time.

The toaster oven dinged, and I plated the apple fries with the ciders and ferried the order to the couple at the table.

When I came back, the man in the flannel had made his way to the counter.

Behind him, a large group of women arrived, chatting animatedly and quickly filling three of my tables.

"I'll be right with you," I called to them. I set a coaster on the bar before the gentleman and grinned. "What's your poison?"

His lips curled into a strange, unsettling smile. "Surprise me."

I shook off the silly shiver and set five juice glasses before him. "How about a proper sampler then?" I asked. "Hot first, so it can cool." I filled the glasses from left to right and named the flavors as I went. "Cinnamon. Caramel. Fireside." I switched to cold jugs from the fridge. "Citrus and ginger, green apple." I went back to the glass with my new fireside flavor, dropped a handful of marshmallows on top, and browned them with my torch.

His cheek ticked, impressed, I supposed.

I did a weird curtsy. "I'll be back to see what you think."

I headed over to the tables crowded with women I didn't recognize. "Morning, y'all. What can I get you to start with?"

They ordered cider by the carafe, one caramel and one apple cinnamon, plus a tray of assorted sweets to share. Nothing easier than that order. I'd expected to test my waitressing and memory skills with so many in the group. "Be right back."

The man had emptied the three warm flights before I returned.

"What did you think?" I asked, turning one thumb up, then slowly down.

"Good," he said.

"You here for the big doings up at the fort?" I asked.

He nodded, selecting a glass of cold cider and holding it to the light for inspection. "Yep. Town's bigger than I expected."

"That's true," I said. "Our population may be small, but our geographical size is not. We're mostly farmers, lots of retired folks too. Some nature lovers live here for the river and national park access. They don't seem to mind the hour-or-more commute to wherever they work outside town."

"Others own shops on family farms," he said.

"Exactly." I filled the carafes for the ladies, then grabbed a tray for sweets.

"I saw a lot of cops over at the pumpkin patch the other day," he said, finishing the first cold cider selection. "There was supposed to be a car-crushing dinosaur, but the place was closed. Any idea what that was about?"

"The man who owned the pumpkin patch died," I said, the words attempting to lodge in my throat. "Crusher probably won't be back this season, but the reenactment won't be affected at all. I think that's mostly put on by out-of-towners."

He watched me, perhaps waiting for something more, but I wasn't saying another word on the topic. "I'm sorry about your loss," he said finally. "Your town's loss, I guess."

"Thanks." I arranged the women's sweets with newly shaking hands. The mix of regret and anxiety washed over me unbidden, and suddenly I was back in the street, staring at Mr. Potter's unseeing eyes in my truck bed, crowds of people whispering around me.

"Your sheriff any good?" the man asked, a testing look in his eye. "Makes all the difference if he is. Sometimes lawmen in small towns don't know what to do when tragedy strikes. They get out of practice. Lose their edge." He set the last empty glass on the counter with a small *thunk.*

I took a step back on instinct, that same strange feeling creeping along my skin. Instinct sent up red flags on the exchange, but I didn't know this man. It wouldn't make sense for a stranger to have killed Mr. Potter, and the blond outdoorsman before me looked nothing like the dark-haired, leather jacket–wearing fugitive whose mug shot was burned into my brain.

"There she is." Blake's voice cut through my internal meltdown and turned my head toward his approaching form.

"Restroom?" the man asked, low and curt.

I pointed without making eye contact, then rushed around the counter to greet Blake. I knew it wasn't fair to judge, and it was impossible to know what others were going through, but that customer had given me the creeps. He'd probably made the comment about lawmen losing their edge because he'd had a bad experience with the law enforcement in his own town. I couldn't let myself read into it. He'd had no idea I was being stalked by a fugitive and his comment had pushed me fifty yards closer to the cliff of insanity. How could he? Normal people weren't stalked by cop-killing psychopaths.

Blake opened his arms, and I ran into them, pressing myself briefly to his broad chest and allowing my rattled mind a moment to re-center.

"Hey!" I said, releasing him before the

hug became weird. "What brings you back so soon?"

"I think that's obvious. Don't you?" he asked with a gleam and a wink.

"No."

"Your cider is downright addictive." He strolled to the bar and helped himself to a stool.

I laughed, relieved. "Well then, what will it be today?"

The tables of women turned to watch him take a seat at the counter.

"Give me one minute," I said, lifting a finger as I ran for their carafes and sweets. "Hold that thought." I hurried the ciders and pastries to the women's tables.

Blake watched, swiveling on his stool to keep me in his sights. "My family's having dinner at Dante's tonight after the reenactment's first dress rehearsal. I thought it would be fun if you came," he said, turning to track me back behind the bar. "What do you think?"

My mouth opened, but words failed. I tried again, and failed again.

He patted the bar. "Take your time. I understand the invitation is incredibly complicated. Not everyone likes Italian food."

I stopped across the bar from him. "I

don't know."

He smirked. "You're going to eat dinner tonight, right?"

"Sure, but . . ."

"And Dante's is a good place to eat. We asked around, and that seemed to be the consensus for a family dinner." He rocked his head from side to side as if reconsidering his words. "It's also a bit of an ambush. It's been a while since we've seen Colton, and you know how hard it is to get information out of him. Plus, Mom wants to meet you. Accept my invitation and give her peace of mind."

"You want me to go so I can give you details about Colton?" I asked, then immediately laughed. "You realize he doesn't tell me anything either, right?"

Unless my life is literally in danger, I thought wryly. *Then he tells me the bare minimum at the very last minute.*

"My mom likes to meet our friends," he said, looking overly innocent. "You're my friend and Colton's. You're interesting, and local, and she wants to meet you."

I considered that a moment. It felt like a setup. I just wasn't sure what kind of setup or to what end. For that reason alone, I should've made a nice excuse and declined. Unfortunately, my incessant curiosity kept my mouth shut for a change. This was a perfect chance for me to get to know the people who'd raised Colton. Maybe even gather a little person-to-person insight on the man I'd grown so fond of for repeatedly saving my life. It was ridiculous that I needed a scheme or his mother to reach my goal. Most people talked to one another. Some more than others, but still. I'd never met anyone who hated to share as much as Colton did, and it irked me. What was his deal? His family seemed normal. Online at least, and his brother seemed fine. An extroverted yin to Colton's introverted yang.

"I'll drive," Blake said, still flashing his handsome smile. "I'll pay, and attire is completely optional."

"What?" I blustered, snapping my gaze to meet his.

He grinned. "Just making sure you were listening."

I consider him for another long beat, then gave up. "I'd love to join your family for dinner. Thank you for the invitation."

"Sweet," he said, lifting one fist in victory. "I told Colton you'd come if you were asked properly and given a little encouragement."

"I thought you said your mom wanted me to come."

His grin widened. "We all want you to come."

This was definitely a setup. Movement outside the open barn doors caught my eye. The blond man hadn't returned to his seat or paid for his cider, but he was putting distance between us now with long, steady strides.

He didn't lose a beat as he lit his cigarette.

CHAPTER TEN

The rest of my day at the shop was a blur. I threw myself into the work, trying and failing to get the strange man's face out of my head. I'd texted Colton to tell him about the encounter, then Googled images of Samuel Keller online. Keller had fair skin with a clean-shaven face and dark hair. This guy had been blond with tanned skin and scruff-covered cheeks. *It wasn't him,* I told myself. *Having a beef with law enforcement and smoking cigarettes does not make someone a fugitive or a stalker.* Regardless, he was a creep in my book. He'd stiffed me on his bill, and that ticked me off.

Colton didn't respond.

Blake left without ordering. He'd only come to convince me to join his family for dinner, then he'd headed out, satisfied by my acceptance and promising to pick me up at eight.

Now, it was seven-fifteen, and I stood in

front of my open closet doors, covered in a thin sheen of sweat from running home after work. The quarter-mile sprint wouldn't have fazed me five years ago, but the closer I got to my thirtieth birthday, the less it took to get me winded. It didn't help that I'd moved emotionally into full freak-out mode at a little after six, and my heart rate had been running double-time before I'd even closed the shop. I stared at my clothes, willing the perfect outfit for a likely ill-fated dinner to present itself. I had less than an hour to decide, then shower, blow-dry and curl my hair, tackle my makeup, and get dressed. I wasn't sure that was humanly possible.

What I really needed was a good reason to cancel.

What had I been thinking accepting Blake's offer? I'd agreed to go to dinner with Blake *and* Colton? *And* their parents? I didn't need food. I needed therapy.

My phone rang, and I leapt for it. "Dot!" I cried, answering in desperation. "Help!" I gave her the skinny on my big fat problem, and she agreed to be at my place when I got out of the shower.

Twenty minutes later, I rushed to let her in, wrapped in a towel with still-damp hair clinging to my shoulders, neck, and cheeks. "I only have twenty-five more minutes!" I hollered, rushing back to the blow-dryer waiting in my room. I bent forward at the hips and tossed my hair upside down before the mirror. I pushed the dryer settings to HOT and HIGH, then blew my hair into a frenzy.

"No problem," Dot hollered back, then went to stare at my pathetic wardrobe.

I wrenched upright several minutes later and set the blow-dryer on the vanity, then went to town untangling my dry but double-sized hair. "I'm a mess. This is a bad idea. What am I doing?"

"Take a few deep breaths," she said. "It's just dinner. It's not a big deal."

"Not a big deal?" I asked incredulously, raking the brush through my giant puffy locks. "Meeting Colton's parents is a huge, enormous deal."

"Colton's parents?" She swiveled at the waist to grin at me. "Not Blake's parents?"

"*Their* parents," I corrected, heat coursing over my cheeks.

"Uh-huh." Dot put her hands on her hips and evaluated me. "Maybe it's time you told the brother who's been chasing you around that your interest lies elsewhere."

"Maybe you should mind your own business," I suggested.

She smiled. "Now, what kind of a friend

would I be if I did that?" She turned her attention back to my closet and began flipping through the hangers. "Folks are talking about Mr. Potter everywhere I go, but no one can make heads or tails of what happened to him. Have you learned anything else?"

"Not really," I admitted. "I got a weird vibe from his wife when I visited, but that's almost to be expected. Grief is hard, and she's probably still in shock. I know I am," I said. I was also extremely thankful for Dot's change of subject. "I need to talk to Birdie and see if there was any discord between Mr. and Mrs. Potter that she's willing to share."

"What kind of discord?"

"I'm not sure, and it might be nothing, but Mrs. Potter stopped posting photos of him on her Facebook account a few months ago. It could be that something happened to create a rift between them, or it might just have been the timing. I imagine they probably both got busy around that time, gearing up for their fall business boom." I tossed the brush onto the vanity with a clatter and evaluated my hair in the mirror. The results were scary, which was why I normally let it all air-dry while I slept. Now, I'd have to wear it up. I opened a drawer and dug around for an elastic band. "I plan to talk to the Potters' neighbors soon. Nate Brumble made a few heated noise complaints online that I want to follow up on."

"Whoa," Dot interrupted. "Nate the butcher?"

I nodded as I secured my hair on top of my head with a tatty elastic band.

Dot turned to face me, and our gazes locked in the reflection of my vanity's mirror. A bolt of fear lanced her shocked expression. "Maybe I'm still shaken up from what went on this summer, but I don't think you should be upsetting an already-angry butcher. Maybe what you should do is listen to the sheriff this time and leave Mr. Potter's death alone."

I wet my lips and turned to face her. "Someone put him in my truck," I whispered. "A killer put Mr. Potter in my truck, and I drove away with his body as if nothing was wrong. We stopped for ice cream."

"I know," she said, her words coming more softly, matching mine. "But someone also attacked Sally. What if that was a warning from the killer? What if smashing pumpkins was just the beginning? What if you get hurt again?"

"I won't," I said. "I promise." I made the vow with as much confidence as I could muster, for her benefit and for mine.

Dot chewed her lip, debating.

I took the opportunity to change the subject again, this time in search of a topic that couldn't upset either of us. "Did I tell you that Hank's got a new mission?" I asked, letting a sly grin creep over my face.

Interest flickered in her eyes. "No."

I turned back to the mirror. Time was marching on, and I was still in a towel and without makeup. "He's running a one-man campaign to promote hunting."

"Hunting?" Dot's narrow brows furrowed. "Like deer hunting?"

"Like any hunting, I think." The mood lifted between us as I retold the silly tale. "So, basically, he wants more people to buy hunting licenses so the state doesn't begin making up the lost revenue by taxing companies like his. He's even made flyers. 'Real men hunt,' " I said, deepening my voice as I relayed the tagline.

"Oh boy," she said. "This ought to be good."

"It is," I assured, rifling through my makeup bag for bobby pins to hold the loose bun in place.

She laughed, then went back to digging in my closet. "Well, deer are a crash and boom population," she said. "On boom years, a lot of deer starve to death because there just isn't enough food sources to go around. During those times, hunting helps thin the herd, I guess. But there are also a lot of hunting accidents every year where humans are the casualties. Hunters shoot themselves and other hunters far more often than the news covers. It happened in Blossom Valley about eight years ago."

I tucked about a million bobby pins into my hair, careful that they held the style without becoming visible. Dot was right about the hunting accidents. I recalled several from my lifetime, the most devastating for me being the loss of our star high school running back. His dad mistook him for a deer and shot him on Thanksgiving. My friend didn't survive. His mom had a nervous breakdown, his parents got divorced, and three years later, his dad committed suicide on Thanksgiving. Awful.

"There must be other ways to raise money for our parks," Dot said. "I know! You could offer tours through town, visiting the sites of all your former crime scenes. Any place you've been hurt, located a body, or been abducted . . . be sure to include the hospital. You've been there quite a bit this year."

"Ha-ha," I said.

"Too soon?" she asked. "I can't help it.

I'm worried about you. I don't want you looking into Mr. Potter's death, even if Birdie Wilks thinks you should. You're my best friend, not hers, and she doesn't know how awful my life would be without you in it."

I blinked back the sting of emotion clawing at my eyes. "I'm not going to get hurt," I said. "At the moment, I'm going to dinner with two sheriffs and their retired parents. Unless I die of awkwardness, I will be one hundred percent fine." I released a long, shaky breath and slumped in my seat. "What was I thinking?"

The concern in Dot's eyes turned warm and comforting as she approached me. "You're probably thinking this dinner will give you an opportunity to get to know the sheriff a little better. He doesn't like to talk about himself, but a person's family tells you a lot about them. Literally and figuratively. Dinner with his folks will be eye-opening. You'll get a peek at where he came from. Meet the people who molded him into the man you like so much today. Watching him interact with them will tell you more about him too. Here." She passed me a black pencil skirt that hit below the knees with a peekaboo pleat on each side. The pleats were inlaid with black lace that

148

showed a hint of skin when I moved or otherwise stretched the material.

I pulled the skirt across my lap. "I bought this for a funeral," I said, working strategic tendrils of hair free from the bun. With any luck, the end result would appear carefree and enchanting instead of what it actually was, strategic and painfully executed. "I don't want to look like I'm going to a funeral." I plugged in my large-barrel curling iron to heat, then started on the makeup. "Maybe I should wear a dress."

"All you have are cotton sundresses and semi-formals. How do you not have a little black dress? You know what? Never mind. Put this on." She pulled a cream-colored camisole from my dresser. "I like the lace across the neckline. It's sexy, and it co-ordinates with the lace inserts on the skirt. Now, we just need a blouse or sweater that will show it off."

I stepped into the closet and shut the door while I put on my underthings and tugged the camisole over my head. I stepped into the skirt, zipped, then hurried back out to start my makeup. "This is hopeless. Blake will be here any minute, and I have nothing to go with this skirt. Unless I wear the black sweater I wore to the funeral."

"You aren't wearing a funeral outfit to

149

dinner," Dot snapped. "You worry about makeup. I'll figure out the ensemble."

I dragged an eyeshadow brush loaded with nude shimmer shadow across my closed lids, then swept midnight-black mascara through my lashes while Dot yanked tops from my closet.

She held blouses and sweaters against my back while I traced my lips with petal-pink liner and painted them in with clear gloss. I only bought makeup in shades that matched my skin, occasionally with a little shimmer, and none of it made a huge difference in my appearance, but I liked the effect. The products added a pleasant polish to my look, and I stood a little taller when I took the time to apply them.

"This," Dot said, holding a fitted cream-colored blouse up for inspection. "Leave your top two buttons open to show off the lacy camisole neckline and wear your thin gold chain with the golden apple charm."

I stared at the pristine blouse. "I'm going to get spaghetti sauce all over that."

She unbuttoned it and fanned it out like a bullfighter's cape. "Come on."

I threaded my arms into the snug sleeves, pre-rolled and buttoned at the elbows. "I don't know," I said, tucking the camisole into my skirt, then buttoning and tucking the blouse in with it. "What if I look like a school marm or a librarian?"

"Not with your figure and those girls," she said, nodding at my bosom. "Now, belt." Dot held a skinny black belt between her fingertips.

I looked down at my covered cleavage and admired the effect of the lace camisole. Dot was good. "A sexy librarian, then."

"Absolutely," Dot agreed. "I'll curl your hair."

I slid the belt through the skirt's narrow loops, then returned to my seat at the vanity.

Dot reached around me, dangling my delicate chain above my chest. She fastened the clasp at the back of my neck, and I adjusted the tiny golden apple against my collarbone. She was right. The combination of structured pieces looked elegant and understated. I liked it, and the makeup gave me confidence.

"Now for the finishing touches." Dot lifted the curling iron and wrapped a long strand of loose hair around it. "I like this look on you. It's very Jane Austen." She released the curled strand, and it fell warmly against my neck. Then, she moved on to the next. Piece by piece, she made each carefully selected bit of hair seem as if it had simply fallen loose. As if all my hair was made of perfect barrel curls, and I'd chosen to tie it up instead of show it off.

Dot stepped back to admire her work. "I'd say you look beautiful, but when don't you? At the moment, however, I'm willing to say you're glowing."

"It's the shimmer eyeshadow," I told her, standing to eliminate any wrinkles from my outfit. "I have the perfect shoes. New chunky-heeled pumps I can wear without falling down or twisting an ankle in, I think." I headed for the closet, kneading my shaky hands. "I ordered them online."

The ringing doorbell froze us in our places.

"I'll get that," Dot said. "You put on your safety heels."

I collected my new shoes from the closet while she headed for my door.

"Come in," Dot cooed. "It's so nice to see you again. You look great. How was dress rehearsal?"

"Back at ya," Blake's voice returned. "Dress rehearsal was really weird." He chuckled. "I'm glad to fill in for a friend, but I don't get the desire to re-create wars and other deadly events."

"Agreed," she said congenially. "Winnie's just grabbing her shoes. She won't be long.

152

Can I get you a glass of water or cider while you wait?"

"I'm good," Blake said.

I wobbled slowly toward the living room on my stiff and unforgiving shoes, unsure how to announce my presence.

"How's the goose?" Blake asked. "Still recovering from that run-in with a car?"

"He's going to be okay," she said a little sadly as I crept forward.

The pair came into view in my kitchen, smiling at one another. Dot was clearly thrilled he'd remembered her poor goose.

"Doc saved his life, but his wing won't be the same. He's grounded for life now and in need of a refuge. Luckily, I've arranged a temporary caretaker to protect him from predators and harsh weather."

Blake's expression went flat, and his face turned suddenly in my direction, as if he'd somehow sensed I was there.

I raised a hand hip-high and blushed. Caught listening in. "Hi."

He whistled long and slow. "Dang."

Dot smiled brightly behind him. "That's what I said."

Blake moved in my direction, then kissed my cheek in greeting. "You look amazing."

"Thanks." I tried to look more confident than I felt as I grabbed my handbag and stuffed my phone inside. "So do you." Blake had chosen simple tan khakis and a royal-blue V-neck sweater with a white T-shirt beneath. He'd have looked like a yuppie if it wasn't for his growing beard.

I hugged Dot, then gripped her shoulders in a quick you-are-my-hero-for-coming-here-tonight squeeze. "I'll call you," I said.

She smiled, clearly hearing the unspoken *and tell you everything.* "I'll walk you out. I want to check on Granny and Kenny Rogers."

Blake snorted. He lifted his eyes to mine, as one orange cat sniffed his shoes. "Is this guy Kenny Rogers or the other one?" He crouched to scratch Kenny behind his ears.

"That's Kenny," I said.

Dolly was curled on the back of my couch, oblivious to my raging anxiety and our guests.

Curiosity turned my gaze on Dot, who was already opening my front door. "You weren't talking about my cat," I said.

"Correct," she said.

Honk! a goose called from somewhere outside my door.

She smiled.

"Dot," I said. "What did you do?"

Blake strode through the door after her. "Was that the goose?"

154

I locked up behind us and followed my friends down the porch steps toward Granny's house. "Dot?"

Honk! Honk!

Blake lengthened his strides as we crossed the field. "No way!" he called.

Dot beamed at Granny, who was pouring a bucket of water into an inflatable kiddie pool. A goose wiggled his backside in the rising tide.

I balked. Granny was the one Dot said she'd found to keep the goose *for now*?

That goose was never going anywhere again, and we all knew it.

"Waddles," Granny cooed. "Here comes your guardian angel, Miss Dorothy Summers, with your new sister, Winona Mae Montgomery, and a very handsome stranger."

Blake shook Granny's hand and made a proper introduction while I processed the fact that yet another animal was living on our orchard. That made four new animal adoptions in a year. If Dot and Granny kept this up, we'd have to rename Smythe Orchard as Old MacDonald's farm.

My phone dinged, and I stopped short of greeting Granny to check the messages.

Colton had sent a text. I opened it, eager to see what had happened. It'd been hours since I'd told him about the alleged specter sightings near my home, which were probably nothing, and the man at the cider shop, which I hoped was nothing.

Did he look like this? Colton asked.

He attached a grainy surveillance photo to the message. I squinted at the screen as a follow-up text arrived.

This is the FBI's most recent photo of Samuel Keller.

I looked again, straining my eyes against the low-quality photo, but it didn't work. The man on the screen could've been Bigfoot or Granny for all I could tell. I took a steadying breath and responded.

Not sure. Photo unclear. Leaving soon. We'll talk at dinner.

Boo's familiar bleat caught my ear a moment later, and I lowered my phone to watch the goat approach. "You little stinker," I said. "You escaped again."

He tottered forward with a happy gait and made it into my reach before my phone beeped again.

Another text from Colton. The simple response sent my heart into panicked sprint.

What dinner?

I raised horrified eyes to Blake, who'd squatted before the kiddie pool, cheerfully splashing his fingers in the water.

"Does Colton know I'm coming to dinner?" I asked.

His steady blue eyes flashed up to meet mine.

"Did you tell him?"

Blake shook his head once, and my stomach knotted. "No," he said.

The goose honked.

Boo fell over.

I knew exactly how he felt.

CHAPTER ELEVEN

Dante's was the nicest restaurant in Blossom Valley, and the go-to destination for small-scale celebrations. Since there was always something to celebrate, the place was usually packed for dinner and later for drinks and desserts. I'd been there many times, and I'd never been disappointed. It was a light and airy venue with high beadboard ceilings and weathered reclaimed barnwood on the walls. Faux candles flickered on tabletops beside potted succulent plants and the music was always classical.

A hostess in a swanky black dress and heels led Blake and I through the crowded dining room. My toes screamed with the pinch of new shoes, and my nerves jangled with the anticipation of meeting Colton's parents. The hostess stopped outside a roomy nook with bank seating on three sides and a broad rectangular table at its center. Leafy green herbs hung in glossy white containers from a wall painted black with chalkboard-paint. The names of the plants had been scripted in loopy white chalk letters and little arrows indicated which names went with which herbs.

An older couple beamed and motioned to us from beneath the plants and whimsical fonts.

"Welcome!" the man said from his place behind the table. "We'd get up but it took us a while to scoot all the way in here." He patted the L shaped bench and laughed.

The couple had apparently worked their way along the bench at either short end of the table then around to the back.

"Don't worry about it," Blake said, sliding onto the seat. "We'll come to you." He scooted in the woman's direction, then snaked a long arm out to clasp my wrist and pull me down with him. He kissed the woman's cheek. "Mom, Dad, this is the lady I've been telling you about. Winona Mae Montgomery. She lives with her grandmother at Smythe Orchard, the family property where she grew up and now runs a cider shop."

"It's lovely to meet you," his mother said, reaching over Blake to squeeze my hand. "Your shop is in the big Mail Pouch barn, right?"

"Yes, ma'am," I said, releasing her hand before mine started sweating.

His dad saluted me from the other side of Blake's mother. "Hello. It's always nice to meet a friend of Blake's and Colton's."

I waved, then tucked my clammy hands under my thighs beneath the tablecloth.

Blake smiled at me. "Winnie, these are my parents, Mary and David Wise."

"We're so glad you came," Mary said, leaning forward, sincerity dripping from her words. "It's not often we get to talk to a woman our son is interested in romantically." She whispered the final word while performing a stage wink.

My cheeks heated, and I cast a sideways look at Blake, who'd stretched his arm across the seat behind me. "Um, I don't know what to say to that," I admitted.

David lifted his wife's hand in his and kissed her knuckles. "And she's just as beautiful as he said."

Mary looked near tears of joy.

"Told you," Blake said.

I imagined standing up calmly, then running out the front door. Maybe Dot had been right. Maybe I needed to confess to Blake that I already had a hopeless crush on someone else. I gave the door another wistful look, and Colton appeared, as if conjured by my desperate thoughts.

He moved smoothly in our direction without stopping at the hostess stand, as if he'd somehow known exactly where we were seated. I gawked openly at his confident strides, crisp white dress shirt, black slacks, and tie. His eyes were impossibly more blue than I recalled, and his cheeks more cleanly shaven. "Sorry I'm late," he said, pausing at our booth before looking me over slowly. He took a seat across from me at the long table, closer to his dad.

"We didn't mind waiting," his mother assured. "We all know you're busy, and it gave us a few moments to get to know Winnie. She's lovely. We're thrilled your brother had the good sense to invite her."

Colton's eyes narrowed on Blake, then slid to meet mine. "Winnie," he said gruffly, "you look beautiful." His lids shut briefly. When he opened his eyes again, the blank cop face I hated was firmly in place. "Have you ordered?"

Mary clucked her tongue. "There's plenty of time to order. We want to hear about your day, and your life here, and about your relationship with Winnie. How did the two of you meet?"

"He accused me of murder," I said, nervous energy pooling, then leaping from my

161

mouth. "Well, he accused me of conspiracy, maybe. It was my granny he accused, and me by default and proximity."

Colton rubbed his forehead while his parents frowned at him.

Blake laughed. "I knew it was a good idea to bring you," he said.

A server appeared with a tray of glasses and filled them with ice water. "Are you ready to order?"

Colton flicked his hand, and the waiter scurried away. I didn't blame him. I looked at the door again, dreaming of pulling the fire alarm or pretending to get an emergency phone call that required me to abandon ship.

Colton's eyes locked on mine, and for a moment I was certain he could read my mind. "Winnie has an uncanny way of falling into my path," he told his family, "specifically where local murders and crimes are concerned. I didn't know that about her when we met, so I'd assumed she was part of the problem. Now I know she's just a trouble magnet."

My jaw dropped. "Rude," I said through clenched teeth. "I'm not a trouble magnet."

He raised his brows in challenge.

I turned a syrup-sweet expression on his parents, hoping to make up for the terrible impression he'd just given them of me. "I was born and raised in Blossom Valley," I said. "I love my community, and I get a little protective of it. It's true that Colton and I cross paths quite often during his investigations, but that's only because I'm not sure what else to do when he starts looking up the wrong trees for killers. It seems reasonable to me that I should step in and help. After all, this is my home. I know and understand the people here, as well as the area."

David nodded, smiling at Colton. "She's plucky. I like her more every time she talks."

Mary leaned her head on her husband's shoulder. "Me too."

"Me three," Blake added.

Colton's frown deepened.

I pressed my lips together. This was officially the weirdest date I'd ever been on, and I'd been on some doozies. Night fishing. Planting potatoes. A driver's test.

Blake removed his arm from behind my head and twisted in my direction. "Speaking of your investigations, what did you think of that guy in the cider shop today? He had really blond hair and wore a ball cap low on his forehead. He was there when I walked in but made himself scarce pretty quickly. Do you remember him?"

"Yes." I perked up. "You do too?"

"Sure. He was . . . off somehow. I couldn't put my finger on it. I tried to follow him after he walked out, but he'd vanished."

"You tried to follow him?" That was why Blake had left so quickly.

He nodded. "Sure. It's my job to identify weirdos."

I kept forgetting that Blake was more than he seemed. Not a happy-go-lucky co-ed meandering through life. He was a sheriff. A trained lawman, and the carefree façade was only that. A façade. "Whoever he was, he didn't pay for his cider," I tattled to Colton, "and before Blake showed up, he made a snide comment about small-town lawmen losing their edge."

Colton stilled. His frame tensed. "You're positive he wasn't the man from the photo?"

"What photo?" Blake asked.

I freed my phone from my purse and presented the grainy surveillance picture to him.

Blake rubbed the sandy scruff on his cheeks. "Maybe."

"What?" I turned sharply in my seat and accidentally knocked our knees together. "How can you say that? The image is so blurry. How can you be sure that's not you or your dad or anyone else?"

164

"Because this guy has his keys and phone in his left hand. His right hand is just hanging there. So, what does that tell me?" He hitched his brows and waited.

"He's left-handed," I said.

"Yeah. Probably," Blake said. "And so was the man from the cider shop, which is why I said maybe. I saw that guy set down his last sample today, and I watched him pull a cigarette from the pack as he blew past us on his way out. He used his left hand both times. I know the picture isn't me because Dad and I are right-handed," he said with a wiggle of hand for emphasis. "Plus, this man's shoulders are rolled forward. He's hiding or has something to hide. Again, not us."

His dad nodded, despite the fact he couldn't even see the image from where he sat.

I recalled the man and the samples, replaying our brief exchanges in my mind. I concentrated on the hand he'd used to lift each glass. "He was left-handed," I said.

"Yep," Blake agreed.

I raised my gaze to Colton's flat expression. "And Samuel Keller?" I asked.

"Also left-handed," Colton answered, looking guarded and edgy.

My stomach pitted and rolled. "The man

was tan and blond."

Blake shrugged. "Hair dye and sun or a spray tan."

I forced myself to breathe. I'd spoken to my stalker. He'd sat in my shop, drinking my cider and probably thinking about how stupid I was. "He had facial hair and wore a plaid flannel shirt with jeans. He fit in. I thought he was here with the reenactment crowd."

Colton's jaw locked, and his gaze darkened.

"Why don't you have a bigger staff?" Blake asked. "The place has had steady traffic every time I'm there, but you're alone or there's just you and a little old lady behind the counter."

I tried and failed to formulate an answer. I couldn't force my mind and tongue to work together. My spiraling thoughts were going full speed around the realization that the fugitive who'd stalked me from afar last summer had boldly sat at my counter today. An arm's reach away. And he'd complained about the ineffectiveness of small-town lawmen. *My lawman.* I batted my eyes, trying harder to break the shock.

Colton stretched onto his feet and stuck Blake with a long, silent glare. "Excuse me. I need to make a call."

166

I stared at his retreating back.

"So, Winnie," Mary said, breaking the tense silence and drawing my eyes to hers. "We'd love to hear more about your cider shop. Do you make the ciders yourself?"

"Yes," I whispered, then cleared my throat a few times. Blake moved a glass of water in my direction, and I guzzled it. "Thanks," I croaked.

Mary smiled sweetly as she waited for me to pull myself together.

"The orchard produces three basic flavors of cider," I began the canned explanation through a tight throat. "I start with those, then add ingredients to create specialty flavors. I've been doing it since eighth grade Home Ec. You should stop by sometime. I'll set up a few samples for you, and I know Granny would love to give you a tour of the orchard."

Her eyes lit. "Absolutely."

David shot Blake a pointed look before smiling politely at me. "Our boys aren't always so intense. I hope they haven't ruined your evening."

I cast a dubious look in the direction Colton had gone. Intense was his defining characteristic. Wasn't it? "It's okay. It's been that kind of week," I said, turning back to David.

"Especially for you, I hear," he continued. "The boys were with you after you found that man in your truck. It must've been awful. They said you knew him?"

I fumbled mentally with the way he referred to Colton and Blake — two large, thirty-something county sheriffs — as "the boys," but plowed ahead. "Yes, sir. I knew Mr. Potter."

He shook his head mournfully. "I'm sorry for your loss."

Mary linked her arm in his. "Well, don't you worry. Colton will figure this out. Our boys are very good at what they do."

I nodded, overcome with emotion and the strange lure of gaining his mother's acceptance. "Colton has saved my life, you know? More than once."

Her lips curved with pride, and her eyes crinkled at the edges. "We know."

I flicked my gaze to Blake. According to him, Colton had never mentioned me.

"You've made quite the impression," Mary said, her smile growing. "Not an easy thing to do, but we've heard it all. 'Mama, she's smart.' 'Mama, she's funny.' 'She's loyal.' 'She's strong.' "

Blake pretended to cough, then drew a finger across his throat, indicating she should stop there.

She frowned. "Well, anyway." She sat back. "We're glad you're here."

My heart hammered. I loved that his parents approved of me, and that Blake seemed to like me too, but the knot in my gut had begun to tighten. Was I misleading him? His folks? Was I overthinking it all? Were we just great friends, and he knew it?

I looked over my shoulder to be sure the exit hadn't moved.

Birdie Wilks and her husband were at the hostess stand. She took notice of me staring and began to move in my direction.

I stood on instinct, then remembered my manners. I smiled at the Wises staring up at me. "Pardon me a moment." I caught Birdie halfway through the dining area and redirected her to the ladies' room, where I immediately checked under every stall for feet. "I'm so glad you're here," I said when the coast was clear. I'd been wishing for a hole in the earth to open and swallow me, but this worked too. I got away from the table for a moment, and I could speak privately to Birdie. "I need to ask you a question about the Potters."

"Shoot," she said, digging a tube of Mary Kay lipstick from her purse. "You look like a showstopper in that outfit," she said, watching me in the mirror. "Whoever the lucky man is, he might need a defibrillator by the night's end."

I tried to imagine that. If anyone needed resuscitating by the night's end, it would be me, thanks to the extreme awkwardness of our dinner party. "I'm actually here with Sheriff Wise's family," I said, knowing she'd find out eventually if she hadn't already recognized them somehow. "We met in town, and they invited me for dinner."

"Hmm. I didn't even see him," she said, painting her puckered lips in ruby red. "And I don't know where you've been hiding all those curves, but it ought to be a crime." She dropped the lipstick back into her bag, then used both hands to lift and adjust her bosoms. "I used to be shaped like that, but you can't fight gravity forever, kid. Embrace it while you can." She pulled a tissue from the dispenser and kissed it before tossing it into the trash.

I crossed my arms self-consciously and tried not to compare our figures in the mirror. I'd been gone too long already and needed to focus before the Wises thought I'd run away permanently. "Did Mr. and Mrs. Potter have some kind of a falling-out a few months ago? Some sort of rift that might've been ongoing?"

Birdie frowned. "Where's this coming from?"

"I'm not sure." I gave my best explanation based on the sudden lack of Facebook couple photos, and her shoulders drooped. She did know something! "Out with it," I told her. "I'm sure you want to protect your friend's privacy, but I can't help her if I don't know all the major issues that were going on in their lives. So, what happened between them?"

Birdie looked at the floor, then the ceiling, debating. When she finally looked at me, she said, "We think Jacob was having an affair. Hellen called him out on it, but he wouldn't come clean."

"So, the affair wasn't confirmed," I said. "She only had a suspicion."

"She knew," Birdie said. "A wife knows these things. We don't need proof. We can sense them, *feel* them." She pressed an overdramatic fist to her chest, like a local theater performer. "Right here, and Hellen knew."

I fought the urge to perform a slow clap for the performance, then realized I was cranky. I needed to eat and go home. This dinner had already been too much, and I hadn't even ordered yet. "Fine. Who was he seeing?"

Birdie squared her shoulders and hitched her chin. "You didn't hear it from me, but he was seen at Brittany Ann Tuttle's home on more than one occasion. After dark."

I blinked. "Brittany Ann?" She was at least fifteen years younger than Mr. Potter, barely older than me. Not to mention married with a home, land, and three small children. "How'd she have time for an affair?" I hadn't fully adjusted from adopting two cats a year ago.

"Lust," Birdie said. "You know how men can be."

I frowned. I understood what she was implying, but I was starting to feel bad for Birdie if these were the kinds of men she knew. "Have you told the police? Has Hellen?"

"No!" Birdie's expression morphed from somewhat superior to aghast. "Of course not," she whispered loudly. "That isn't the sort of thing you spread around, especially after the man's dead."

"This is exactly the sort of thing the police need to know. What if the affair is the reason he's dead? What if Brittany Ann's husband found out and put a stop to it?"

She blanched. "I hadn't thought of that."

I pressed the heels of my hands against my closed eyes and counted to ten. This night was too much. Too. Much.

My phone rang. I dropped my hand to remove the device from my bag. "Oh, it's the mechanic!" I accepted the call and listened closely while Birdie waited. My smile grew with each passing word. *No damage. Sheriff approved the release. No charge. Take care of that beauty.* "Will do!" I checked the time when I disconnected. "My car's ready, but Mr. Murphy's closing up shop in an hour," I told Birdie. "I have to go."

"What about Brittany Ann?" she asked.

"I'll visit her tomorrow. After I talk to Nate's wife. I got sidetracked from that today."

Birdie nodded. "Keep the affair quiet if you can. No reason to speak ill of the dead if there isn't any."

"I won't tell unless I need to," I said, wrenching the door open and stepping quickly into the hall. "Don't tell anyone else I'm helping you."

"Got it," she said with a satisfied smile. The expression went flat a heartbeat later.

I followed her gaze to Colton in the hallway.

"What's that?" he asked, peeling himself off the wall where he'd been lurking outside the ladies' room.

"Uh." My heart banged in my chest like boots in a dryer. "Um." I floundered for words, turning back to Birdie for help.

She let the restroom door close between us.

Traitor.

CHAPTER TWELVE

Colton watched me squirm, busted discussing a plan to continue my investigation, despite everything, and all because I had a curiosity that would not stop. Also, I had a deep innate desire to please older women. Whether that was because I loved and respected Granny so much, and the feelings transferred to all mother figures, or because my own mother had abandoned me, I couldn't be sure, and I probably didn't want to know. "Why did you agree to come here tonight?" he asked.

"Blake invited me," I said, a simple response to a highly complicated question.

Colton crossed his arms. "Yes, but why did you agree?"

My nose wrinkled. I wasn't sure why, but the question felt loaded, and I was already in enough trouble with him tonight. "What do you mean?"

His eyes tightened. "Why?" he repeated.

I lowered my gaze as a waiter passed with a tray of food in one hand and a bottle of wine in the other. When I returned my attention to Colton, he was staring. Waiting. "Because he asked," I said, truthfully. "Blake seems like a really nice guy. He invited me to have dinner with his family at a lovely restaurant. Why would I say no?" I tented my brows in challenge.

"Maybe because you just met him and you don't know anything about him," Colton explained flatly. "He could be a dangerous lunatic."

"He's your brother," I deadpanned. "Of course he's a lunatic."

Colton's lips quirked at the corners. "What did he say when he invited you?"

"What do you mean?" I frowned and scooted closer to him in the narrow hall, making room for another waiter and a busboy, both loaded down with plates and cups on trays and in tubs.

He waited, head angled low for a look into my eyes. The familiar scent of him enticed me closer, but I held my ground, tipping my head back only to return his gaze.

"Was it something he said that convinced you?" Colton asked. "Did you agree because you are polite? Or was it because he's so darn 'Tall, Dark, and Yummy'?"

I lifted a finger between us, prepared to argue, but not finding the words. I'd thought Blake was incredibly handsome when I'd first met him, but only realized later that it was probably because I thought Colton was drop-dead gorgeous in a know-it-all, overly masculine way and the pair shared a familial resemblance. Not that I'd utter any of that aloud this side of eternity.

Colton shifted, impatience knitting his brows. "Are you here as his friend? Are you here to meet my parents? Are you here looking for more information on Mr. Potter to share with Birdie Wilks?"

My jaw fell open. "Rude." I held my tongue until a pair of teens passed us on their way to the ladies' room. "What's going on with you tonight? Do you want me to leave? I can make an excuse and slip out. I don't want to ruin your visit with your folks, and they're only in town a few more days."

"No." Colton rubbed his brow, then the back of his neck. "You're right. I'm letting work get to me. It doesn't matter why you said yes to my brother. You did, and I'm glad you're here. We should probably leave it at that and get back to dinner." He motioned me toward the dining room with a dramatic swing of one arm.

I relaxed my stance and smiled back, not

quite ready to leave our little piece of hallway. "I agreed to dinner because I like Blake. I think he's fun, and I like you, but I don't know anything about you. I thought meeting your parents and seeing you interact with them would help me get to know you better. I thought tonight might tell me more about who you are behind the badge." My cheeks heated at the confession. "Heaven knows, you aren't offering up any details."

A parade of emotions passed quickly across his features as he processed my words. "You've never asked me for details."

I shrugged.

Colton rocked back on his heels, a sudden look of interest and wonder in his crystal-blue eyes.

"Stop gloating, or I'll leave."

He offered an apologetic smile. "Sorry. Don't leave. You just caught me off guard. That's all."

"Fine," I agreed, turning on my heels toward the dining area.

Colton set a broad palm against the small of my back as we walked, and I fought a goofy smile. I plastered what I hoped was a normal-looking expression on my face and kept my chin up, eyes forward. We parted ways at the table, under scrutiny of three sets of eyes. I reclaimed my seat beside Blake, and Colton slid onto the bench closer to his dad.

His mother looked startled. "What took you so long? The waiter came for our orders, and you weren't here."

"Sorry," I apologized. "I ran into a friend and got to talking. Colton saw me and waited."

"Oh." His mother's expression cleared. "That was nice."

His dad tapped a finger to the menu before him. "I'm having lasagna," he said. "My doctor says I should have a salad, but I want lasagna."

I lifted my menu and hid behind it.

Blake nudged me with his elbow. "Did you two finally get the chance to talk?"

"Blake," Colton warned from across the table.

"What?" he asked. "I've got a curious mind. You understand." He caught me in his sincere blue gaze before flicking it to his brother.

I nodded. I understood the power of curiosity better than anyone I'd ever met.

Blake returned his attention to Colton. "All right, let's circle back a minute. If there's a chance the man I saw at the cider shop was the fugitive you tried to put away, then Winnie's in danger. I think we need to address that."

Their mother gasped and pressed a palm to her chest.

Their father looked to Colton, who gave another definitive dip of his chin. "Why?" he asked.

Blake beat his thumbs against the table's edge. "Because he wants to punish Colton."

Their mother gripped her husband's hand and let her horrified expression move from Colton to me.

I longed to slide under the table, where I could have a proper mental breakdown in private. Unfortunately, it seemed my frame had gone rigid, and my limbs had turned to cement.

Their dad cleared his throat. "Sounds like any chance we had at a normal dinner is out the window. I guess we'll have a normal-for-us dinner instead." He offered me a polite smile, then switched his gaze from Colton to Blake and back. "Start from the beginning. It's been a while since I've heard the story of your fugitive."

"He was my informant," Colton began, retelling the tale of the man who'd ambushed him and killed his partner, then two additional officers more recently while escaping from a prison transport. Colton's testimony at the man's trial had cemented his fate. Life without parole in a high-security prison.

I listened through ringing ears and ordered a house salad when the waiter returned. When the order arrived, I dutifully pushed the chopped veggies around with my fork, too nauseated to eat anything.

When it was my turn to carry the story, I repeated the entire exchange I'd had with the man at my cider shop. The words had amounted to very little, but the Wises hung on every one.

Their voices mixed and mingled with the tinkling of silverware and white noise in the busy restaurant. Hashing possibilities. Forming theories on Samuel Keller's intent, itinerary, and next move. Their steady voices were secondary only to the whirring of panic in my head.

Colton's phone lit and vibrated on the table, where he'd left it in view. "I have to go," he said, checking the message. "Something's come up, but we can finish this tonight. I'll stop by to see you at the rental on my way home."

I snapped to my feet, eager to know what had Colton leaving in the middle of an important conversation, and desperate for fresh air before I collapsed from stress. "Me too. Take me," I said. "The mechanic called when I was in the ladies' room and told me I can pick up Sally." I looked at my watch, suddenly unsure how much time had passed and whether or not the body shop would be closed. "Please?"

Colton pressed his lips. He glanced at his phone, then back to my face. "Murphy's?"

I nodded, hoisting my purse onto one shoulder. I needed more than air. I needed to go home, warn Granny about the fugitive, then barricade my house.

"Blake?" Colton asked.

Blake waved a fork, unaffected. "Holler if you need me."

"Thank you," I said, dragging my gaze to each of the Wise family members still seated at the table.

They nodded our excusal, and Colton started for the door.

I hustled to keep pace as he crossed the parking lot to his truck. He beeped the door locks open before we reached the vehicle, then climbed inside and gunned the engine to life before I could get my seat belt in place. "What's going on?" I asked, bracing myself as we launched from the parking spot.

"My doorbell camera spotted Samuel Keller on the porch." He pressed his thumb

182

against his cell phone, unlocking the device, then handed the device to me.

A video of the man from my cider shop centered the screen, as crickets chirped in the background. He smiled and waved at the camera.

I gasped. "He knows he's being watched, and he doesn't care."

"He's getting bold," Colton said. "That comment he made to you about small-town cops being lax, tells me he thinks I'm losing my touch."

"Are you?" I squeaked, still gawking at the killer on camera.

"No, ma'am." Colton's tone was hard, his words firm and confident. "He's probably long gone by now, but I'm going home to see if he left a clue I can use to find him. Lucky for me, cocky usually leads to careless, and him thinking that I'm losing my touch is going to work in my favor."

I turned the phone off and put it in Colton's empty cup holder, distancing myself from the taunting image of a cold-blooded killer. "Maybe I need a security camera doorbell," I muttered, a new, crankier thought emerging as the previous one was voiced. "How does this guy know where you live when I don't?" It was probably the wrong time to be hung up on an irrelevant detail, and the answer was obvious, but why didn't I know where Colton lived? We were friends, weren't we? He'd been to my place dozens of times. As sheriff, he had to live in the county, but did he live in Blossom Valley?

"I'll have you over sometime," he said, "when a killer isn't potentially lying in wait for me to arrive." Colton hit the blinker a few minutes later, indicating a right-hand turn. Then we sailed into the gravel lot outside Murphy's auto shop.

Sally gleamed under the cone of security light.

The office door swung open a moment later, and Mr. Murphy appeared. He held a ring of keys over his head in one hand as he locked up behind him with the other.

I hopped out to greet him. "Thank you!"

"On the house," he said. "All she needed was a good scrubbing, and that was my pleasure."

I accepted the keys and said good night to Mr. Murphy, then hurried in Sally's direction, eager to be behind her wheel once more. No longer dependent on the Wise brothers or anyone else for rides. "Thanks for the lift," I told Colton through his open window. "Are you going to be okay on your own?" I asked, imagining Samuel Keller waiting in the shadows to ambush him. "Maybe you should call and ask your deputies to meet you at your place? Just in case."

Colton shook his head and rearranged his grip on the wheel. "I've got this. Drive safely so I don't have to worry about you anymore tonight. Keep watch for deer along the road, and lock up when you get home. Call me if you need anything."

Panic swelled in my chest once more, whether for his sake or mine, I couldn't say.

"I will."

Colton waited until Sally and I were on our way before leaving the parking lot. He tailed us down the county road as far as town. We split at the intersection past the Sip N Sup. I went east, him south, and that was that.

I pressed the gas pedal a little lower as Sally climbed hill after hill with ease. She hugged the inky asphalt curves, her headlights illuminating the dark road ahead.

Pairs of glinting green eyes lined the tall grasses and trees as I flew through the night. Colton had been right to warn me about deer.

Still, my thoughts roamed. Mostly back to Birdie in the ladies' room. I hadn't seen her come out, and I hoped she wasn't still in there, hiding. I wasn't sure what to make of her claim that Mr. Potter had been having an affair. If it was true, then the number of potential suspects in his death had increased. Mrs. Potter could have wanted to punish him for his infidelity. The other woman could have wanted to keep him quiet so her husband wouldn't find out. Maybe her husband had found out and wanted to punish Mr. Potter, though that seemed unlikely. Brittany Ann's husband didn't strike me as the murderous sort, *but then again,* I reasoned, *Brittany Ann didn't strike me as the adulterous sort.* Maybe anything was possible.

My instincts about people were usually on target. I wrinkled my nose, remembering instincts weren't perfect. I'd dated Hank for nearly five years.

I turned onto the orchard's long gravel drive a few minutes later and noticed a number of vehicles at Granny's house. She must've invited the ladies over for needle-pointing. A perfect turn of fate, because Granny's ladies were the ultimate resource for gossip in Blossom Valley. Assuming one of them knew someone who knew the Potters or Brittany Ann's family, I'd be in business. Facebook was good, but Granny and her ladies were better.

I parked Sally between our homes and

debated. I definitely wanted to run my evening past Granny and her stitching crew to see what they thought, but I preferred to do it in jeans and a sweatshirt.

I sent Granny a text message to let her know I'd be there in a minute to talk to her and her ladies about my night. Aside from gaining information on Mr. Potter's possible affair, I needed to tell her that Samuel Keller had been to the cider shop.

Granny responded immediately to let me know she was putting on a fresh pot of coffee. The tension in my shoulders eased instantly.

I took two steps in the direction of my home before I noticed a slow, waddling shadow moving in my direction. My heart rate sped at memories of being chased around parks and lakes by cranky mama geese as a child.

I picked up my pace, and so did the goose.

"Shoo," I said, motioning with my hands. "I'm not a fan, and I don't want anything that's yours, so go away." A bit of guilt pinched my cheeks. The goose had nearly been killed this week, and it would never fly again. Maybe the poor thing just wanted company, love, or a companion. I took another look at its tiny bear trap of a beak, then broke into a jog. "It's not you. It's me."

The goose honked and dove for my calves, flapping its good wing and trying to get a little air.

I squealed and leapt for my porch steps. "Stop! Bad! No!"

The goose craned its long, winding neck in my direction and made a horrendous goosey sound.

"Ah!" My fingers grasped the post at the end of my handrail, and I used the sturdy wooden anchor to throw me forward, like a pole vaulter jumping the short flight of porch steps.

The goose honked and flapped in the grass below, babying its injured wing.

I bent at the waist, puffing crisp autumn air and giggling slightly over the whole ordeal. Was this my life now? Dodging an adopted goose every time I left my porch? Would it be able to navigate the steps once its wing healed? I laughed at the ridiculousness of the possibility, contrasting it with my other problems. "We should be friends," I said, smiling more warmly at the goose moving away through the grass. "But it's not nice to bite or scare people. My heart can't take it," I muttered, confident the goose was no longer listening. "I'm under enough stress as it is."

I turned back to my house and screamed

at the silhouette of a man seated in the rocker beside my front door. His stillness sent a surge of panic through me, and I fumbled back down the steps, desperate not to fall or twist an ankle like the stupid women in horror films. No longer caring two figs about the goose and effectively scaring him back across the field with my outburst.

I mentally tallied the speed at which I could reach Sally before the man reached me, but he had the advantage, moving forward instead of backward and with the ability to leap from the steps to my side. I raised my hands to defend myself until my feet found solid ground, but the man didn't move.

A burst of cold wind lowered my arms and froze me in my tracks. The air lifted and tousled a sheet of paper attached to the figure's chest, and I realized, senses on high alert, that it wasn't a man at all. The figure was inanimate. A scarecrow had been removed from the fields and positioned at my door.

I crept forward, back up the steps, to read the message, which was obviously meant for me.

Stop asking questions.

CHAPTER THIRTEEN

I watched from the safety of my living room window as Colton collected the scarecrow and note. I sat on my knees like a child, turned backward on the couch to peer through the curtains at the porch, now awash in light. Kenny Rogers and Dolly had likely seen who'd delivered the threat, but they weren't talking, other than to demand more treats. I cuddled them to me, taking advantage of their snack obsession and nabbing squeezes while they munched. "This is no good," I told them. "This is where the snowball begins to gather mass and speed." First someone had smashed pumpkins on my car. Then a fugitive had visited my shop. Now Mr. Potter's killer had been to my home. The culprit knew what I drove and where I lived. So did the fugitive. Mr. Potter's killer probably knew everything about me. We were likely both residents of Blossom Valley, the world's most quintessential country town. There were folks around here who knew what I weighed when I was born. Finding my car or home was as easy as asking the next person you saw. I supposed that was how Samuel Keller had found me last summer as well.

Colton stuffed the bagged scarecrow into his truck, then headed for my front door. I scrambled off the couch to meet him.

"Hey." I pulled Colton inside and waved to Granny and her ladies, all lined up in her front window across the field. I'd waited with them for Colton to arrive, and they'd watched every move he'd made since. The curtains fell closed at Granny's, and I knew they knew I was okay. "I don't suppose whoever scared me tonight accidentally dropped their driver's license or other form of identification in the process."

"Afraid not," he said, hefting a messenger bag off his shoulder.

"What's that?"

"Laptop," Colton said, unzipping the top. "What's your Wi-Fi password?"

I shifted. "Why?"

"I thought I'd do a little work from here. I hate to leave you after that." He tipped his head toward my porch while liberating the computer from his bag. "Do you mind?"

"I guess not. Here, let me enter the

password for you," I offered. "It's a little long."

"Nah. I've got it," he said, taking a seat in the armchair beside my couch and positioning the device on his lap. "Shoot."

"Cider Boss for you," I said quickly, turning for the kitchen. "Capital C and B, the number four and capital letter U." I busied myself putting on a pot of coffee instead of waiting for his reaction to my goofy password that no one, besides Granny and Dot, was supposed to guess or need. I gave the filter an extra scoop of ground energy to work on because there was no way I'd be able to sleep tonight. Jangled nerves or not, I might as well make the most of my time with a caffeine pick-me-up.

Colton made himself at home in the living room, typing in the password I'd given him without comment.

"How'd it go at your house?" I asked. "Any signs of Samuel Keller?"

"One." Colton lifted his head and grimaced. "A photo. And a few colorful notes in the mud around my house. Probably drawn with a stick."

"How colorful?" I asked, my curiosity and quick tongue beating the only partially working filter in my addled mind.

"Mostly references to where I should go

and what I could do when I got there."

I laughed, and Colton swiveled on his seat to look at me. "You think that's funny, boss?"

"A little," I admitted, ignoring the blatant throwback to my goofy Wi-Fi password. "It's definitely juvenile. Kind of makes the big bad boogeyman feel a little more human. I was starting to think of him as something untouchable."

The human-shaped shadow from the tree line last summer had slowly become a twenty-foot-tall smoke monster in my imagination. Something capable of swallowing me whole and leaving no traces. Something uncontainable by authorities. Now he'd ruined the image. He'd provided a glimpse of his true self with those stick-drawn notes. Samuel Keller wasn't an uncontainable smoke monster. He was a petty, egotistical criminal who gained pleasure from taunting others. And I couldn't wait to see him in cuffs.

"He's not untouchable," Colton said. "He's cocky, and his ego is going to cost him."

I carried two mugs of coffee into the living room and set one on the end table beside Colton's chair. I took the other with me to the couch and brought my legs up, crisscross-applesauce. "Did you say he left a photo? Of what?"

"Us." Colton inhaled long and deep before releasing the breath just as slowly. He set his computer aside and shifted to remove his phone from his pocket. He tapped the screen, then started at the sight of the coffee. "Is this for me?"

I smiled. "Yes."

"Thanks." He handed the phone to me. "I took a picture of the photo before I sealed the original into an evidence bag."

I set my mug aside in favor of taking Colton's phone in both hands. A million ideas of what might await me on the screen raced through my mind. Who was *us*? A snapshot of Colton and Samuel taken when he was still Colton's informant? Or maybe something more recent, evidence of how much the predator knew and saw? Maybe something with Colton and his brother? My blood went cold as I realized Colton's parents were in town, and they weren't trained law enforcement like their sons. How easily could Samuel Keller reach them if he tried? Could Blake protect them while Colton chased Mr. Potter's killer and tried to keep me safe? Was Blake in danger too?

I turned my attention to the screen in my suddenly trembling hands. An image of

Colton and me stared back. I wasn't sure when it was taken, but we were in town, the frame tight on our torsos and faces. I was smiling, broad and wide, my head tipped back in an apparent burst of laughter, eyes pinched shut in the moment. Colton's smile was much smaller, the barely there hint at humor I'd come to appreciate on him. His eyes were trained on me. The image raised gooseflesh on my skin. His expression was one that every woman wanted to see when she met her man's eyes, but I'd never seen that look before now. I'd never expected to see it on Colton. "Wow," I uttered, stupidly.

Colton fixed his gaze back on his laptop and cleared his throat. "He's obviously fixating on you. You're not safe alone, so I think you should consider staying with me awhile."

I raised my eyes to him and gawked while I tried to knock the cuckoo off that suggestion. Stay with him? As in, at his house? "That is a very bad idea."

"Why?"

"Why?" I parroted. "Because I can't go shack up with the sheriff. What would people say?" *They'd probably be thinking hot dog! And lucky duck!* But they'd say other, ruder, more judgmental things. Especially at church. "Besides, Blake is staying with

195

you. Isn't he?"

"Blake can stay too. I have room, but if he doesn't want to, he can stay with our folks or get his own room until the reenactment is over. Despite his goofy, carefree, YOLO personality, my little brother really is a grown man."

"People will talk."

"I don't care."

I mulled that over. He clearly wasn't from a small town and didn't comprehend the damage a little bad press could do to a person. Some of Granny's friends still called the cobbler Up Chuck, because his name was Charles and he'd gotten sick in class as a middle-schooler. *Fifty years ago.* "I can't leave Granny," I said, realizing the most important reason I needed to stay. "She was hurt because of me last year, and I won't let it happen again. Besides, there's more than just one killer harassing me. Don't forget the nut who left me a note-wielding scarecrow. I need to stay here in case Granny needs me."

Colton bristled at the mention of a second killer on my tail. "Then I'll stay here."

I nearly swallowed my tongue. "You can't stay here. Same problem as the first. What will people think?"

He made a grouchy face. "That I'm trying

to protect you?"

I narrowed my eyes.

"Fine. I won't stay all night, but I'll be here, awake and in the living room, until almost dawn. Then I'll wait in my truck until I see you and your Granny have started your days before I leave."

"Fine," I echoed, stretching onto my feet. "Now, if you'll excuse me, I'm a nervous eater, and I didn't finish my dinner. I'm making grilled cheese. Would you like one?"

"I'd like ten."

I smiled, then went to town in my kitchen, preparing and serving the two best grilled-cheese sandwiches of my life, blissfully thankful for the quiet time. I'd needed to process Colton's wackadoodle proposals for my safety. Stay at his place? I'd never even seen his place. Let him stay here? I could think of at least four of Granny's friends who'd have immediate coronaries at the first wind of that gossip. Mostly because they wanted Colton for themselves, age differences be darned.

I ferried the plates back to the living room, warm scents of buttery bread and salty, stringy cheese filling the air. "I've officially decided I hate scarecrows," I said, delivering his plate to him. "Dot warned me they were trouble, and I'd argued." I retook my seat on the couch and bit into the pickle spear beside my sandwich. "I was wrong. Dot is wise."

"Don't go blaming the scarecrow," Colton said. "He didn't get there on his own or write that note. Scarecrows save crops, and they're fun to look at." He set his laptop aside and pulled his plate onto his lap. "Thank you. This looks and smells like heaven."

"Yeah, well, you haven't tried it yet," I warned. "Things aren't always what they appear."

"Amen," he muttered, sinking his teeth into the warm, melty sandwich. His eyes slid shut a moment later, and he groaned in delight.

I beamed, then scooped half of my sandwich off the plate. "It's mayonnaise," I said, answering his unspoken question. *How did I make it taste like nostalgia, childhood, and joy?* "I melt butter in my pan and spread mayo on the bread. I went a little heavy on the cheese too, but that's because I love cheese. It's American. The best kind for melting."

He looked at me as if I'd told him the meaning of life. "This is amazing."

"Mayonnaise," I repeated, this time with a wink.

"It reminds me of my grandma," he said, a twinkle in his eye. "She made the best grilled-cheese lunches with cups of home-made tomato soup for dunking. No one ever came close to sandwiches like those." He looked younger as he ate, more carefree, bopping his head with each bite.

"You were close to your grandma?" I asked, the answer already visible on his face and in his tone when he spoke of her. I instantly liked him a little more for it.

"She taught me to cook. She could make a meal out of nothing, probably because there were days when she'd had to. The skill served me well in college and in the military. Grandpa died when my mom was young. Grandma raised eight kids on nothing but faith, sweat, and determination. She made do with whatever they had. Nothing was wasted, and everyone worked. My mom and every one of her siblings can do just about anything because of Grandma's example."

I smiled. "I would've liked her. No gender-specific tasks. Girls keep house, and boys do the rest."

He barked a laugh. "At Grandma's house, if you had two hands, you were qualified for the job. Whatever it was."

"Yep. I definitely would've liked her." I took a bite of my sandwich and imagined meeting the woman who'd had such an impact on Colton.

"She would've liked you too," he said. "I was on assignment overseas when she passed. I didn't get the message until the funeral was done."

"I'm sorry," I said, feeling my spirits drop and the tug of grief waiting to pull me in.

Colton nodded. He raised his eyes to mine. "You have a big heart. It's one of my favorite things about you. You genuinely care about this town and the people. You're wholly devoted to everyone and everything you touch, especially your family. I like that. My grandma didn't raise me, but I can understand the bond you have with yours, and I have an idea about what the loss of your grampy must feel like. Grandma was one of the most influential and important people in my life to the very end, and in many ways, she still is."

Breath caught in my throat as I took in each of his precious words. Colton had never said so before, but he saw me. *Really* saw me. And he'd nailed the description to a T. I cared. Deeply. About everything, and it was wonderful and infuriating and exhausting, but true. Emotions rose hard and fast to the surface, both at his acknowledgment of who I was and at his mention of

Grampy. Grampy had truly been the guide for my path while he'd lived, and his words guided me still.

Colton stilled, looking a bit surprised at himself. He was finally opening up, and the only person more surprised than me was him. His mouth twitched, and a small smile edged its way across his face. "My grandma was pretty great."

"So are you," I said, my mouth moving again without a filter. I pushed the corner of my sandwich between my lips before I went on.

He traded his empty plate for his laptop and typed a few seconds before quitting again. "Back at ya."

Colton didn't say anything else until I'd collected his plate and carried it to the sink with mine. "As a member of law enforcement, I'm supposed to see frauds coming, but I've been burned on and off the clock," he said. "I don't let people in easily because doing that has bit me more often than I want to admit."

I turned to stare at him, still seated in the living room, eyes fixed to his laptop screen. "That's just proof that you're human, and that you chose to believe the best in those people. Whoever you're talking about specifically, they failed you. Not the other way around."

"I failed my partner when I trusted Samuel Keller."

I took a step in his direction. "Had he ever given you reason not to trust him before?"

"Not that I'm aware, but maybe I missed something."

"Probably not," I said. "I'm sensing there was also a girl."

"Why do you say that?" he hedged.

I stifled an eye roll on my way back to the couch. "Because there's always a girl. Everyone's got an epic broken-heart story by the time they reach our age."

He made a sour face. "Victoria."

I waited for details, ignoring the intense rush of dislike I felt toward a woman I'd never met. If he didn't go on, I'd understand. I avoided discussions about my time with Hank whenever possible.

"In hindsight, it wasn't all her fault," he said, taking responsibility for everything as usual. "We were young, and my expectations were too high."

"What happened?"

He stilled. "I've come to realize that being in a relationship with a lawman is tough. There's a constant level of distress for people who care about them. It's the same for people in the military, firefighters, and anyone else putting their lives on the line professionally. The job puts pressure on the significant other, and that adds stress to the relationship. I was with Victoria while I was in Clarksburg working on the joint task force. I was gone more than I was home, and most of what I did, especially where it related to the FBI, was confidential. There were only so many hours in a day, and when push came to shove, I chose the job more often than I chose her. So, she decided to find someone who had time for her when I didn't. I cut out early one day to surprise her and found some guy at her place, paying all sorts of attention to her."

I cringed. "That stinks."

He looked embarrassed by the confession, so I hurried on before he decided never to tell me another personal story.

"If Victoria wasn't happy with your relationship, she should've broken up with you, not cheated on you," I said. "Again. This was about her, not you. Cheating is selfish and cowardly, two things you are not."

"I trusted her," he said flatly, still trying to carry some responsibility.

"You are no more responsible for her behavior than you are for Samuel Keller's. Lots of people get life sentences in maximum-security prisons, but they don't all kill their transport guards and begin a revenge scheme on the cop who built the case against them. Actually," I said smartly, hoping to break his brooding funk, "I think it's quite pretentious of you to assume you are the puppeteer of all mankind."

Colton barked a short laugh. "Well, it's not as if I can control anything you do, so I suppose you're right about that." He deflated against the chair back, looking thoughtful. "I prefer to think there's something I could do differently to prevent negative outcomes. Otherwise I'm helpless."

"Human," I said, "not helpless, and for what it's worth, I like you, I respect you, and I want to maintain this friendship, but that isn't going to keep me from doing what I want to do. When I let my curiosity get me into messes, that's on me, and it has nothing to do with you."

"I really can't stop you from meddling in my investigations."

"Exactly," I said. "Except you should stop thinking of it as meddling. Think of it as helping. I know this place. You're still new here. That makes me an asset."

"It makes you something," he mumbled. "Rolling back to the topic of our exes, how's Hank doing?"

I tensed. "Fine. Why?"

"I saw him up at the fort passing out fly-ers. For hunting. He doesn't strike me as an outdoorsman, but he seemed pretty passionate on the subject. He even asked me to set up sting operations throughout the county at locations where satellite footage shows corn being planted in the woods."

"Can you do that?" I asked. "Wouldn't it be a huge waste of resources and manpower?"

"Yes and yes," he said. "So, I declined."

I smiled. The sting operation suggestion didn't surprise me. Hank was a dog with a bone. " 'Real men hunt,' " I said, recalling the goofy flyers. "So, Granny and I are going to get our licenses in the morning. We're meeting her needlepointing crew at the registration office, and Sue Ellen is taking a van load of ladies from her church later this week."

Colton sat a little taller, nose wrinkled. "All right. What am I missing?"

I explained the situation, then showed him a flyer I'd made to promote the registration event. I'd used a cartoon border of little deer, bass, turkey, trout, and pheasants around bright blue and gold words.

Keep WVA Beautiful.
Hunting license sales help support wildlife

Colton smirked. "You really do care about everything."

He set the flyer aside, concern troubling his brow once more. "What were you and Birdie Wilks talking about in the ladies' room tonight? I assume it had something to do with Mr. Potter's death, but I'd like to know the details. Please," he added with a congenial smile.

I appreciated the manners, so I told him everything.

"Brittany Ann Tuttle?" he asked. "Doesn't ring a bell."

"She's a sweet girl," I said. "My age. Three little kids. Nice husband. They attend most town events, but otherwise spend a lot of time at their home. They have several acres, so I imagine it's more fun out there than being in town anyway."

Colton's eyes lit as he reached for his laptop. "I'll see what I can find on her."

I grabbed my computer as well.

We typed in silence for a few quiet minutes, then I turned my screen to face him, Brittany Ann's social media up for view.

"Facebook?" He laughed.

"It's my number-one online resource," I said.

He typed again, bringing up the same page on his laptop, then he paused to scroll through her lovely family photos and read her silly, gushy praises for everything from a full night's sleep to a sunny day.

I followed along from my seat on the couch.

"See?" I said. "She's a delight, and I'm having a hard time imagining her cheating on her husband, especially with Mr. Potter, a man old enough to be her daddy."

"Mr. Potter was only fifty," Colton said.

"And Brittany Ann is thirty."

He grimaced. "All right." He rubbed his chin and typed some more. "Let's see what I can learn."

I craned my neck for a look at his screen, but my angle was wrong.

A moment later, he grabbed his phone and made a call asking whoever answered to run Brittany Ann and her husband through the system.

I mouthed the word *cheater,* and he grinned.

He finished the call, looking proud of himself. "Brittany Ann and her husband have clean records, but that doesn't mean they're innocent. Every criminal has a first offense, and some have many before actually getting caught."

"You think Brittany Ann could've killed her old-man lover? Why? Wouldn't it be more likely that his wife killed him for cheating? Or that Brittany Ann's husband killed him?"

He shrugged. "I'll find out."

"It's not fair you've got a whole crew of deputies and state tech support on your side. All I have is Facebook."

"You're not the sheriff."

I ignored his statement of fact, recalling I had something better than all the tech support in the world for this case.

I had Granny and her stitching crew.

CHAPTER FOURTEEN

I showered and dressed in a hurry the next morning, trying and failing to catch Colton before he left. We'd stayed up late, chatting about Blossom Valley and getting to know one another. It was nice, and I'd hated to go to bed, but eventually fatigue had won the battle. I'd woken to an empty home and Colton outside, working from his truck as promised, making notes with a pen and pad of paper pressed to his steering wheel. By the time I'd brewed a pot of coffee and poured a mug for him, he was gone.

The orchard had been open an hour before I finally stepped off the porch and into the sunlight with Kenny Rogers and Dolly at my heels. The day was chilly, and frost clung to blades of semi-frozen grass in the shade. My breaths lifted before me in little puffs of steam. The unseasonably warm days had ended. This was the perfect weather for a Fall Harvest Festival.

I smiled and waved at families tossing bean bags at apple-themed cornhole boards near the large white tent by the gate. The tent doubled as a ticket booth and a seasonal farmers' market, where Granny often greeted and mingled with guests.

Parents snapped photos of small faces peeking through cutouts in large wooden boards painted with barnyard scenes. One child was a smiling farmer, another his spotted puppy, the third, an apple atop the staggering pile.

Kenny Rogers and Dolly rampaged through the tall grass, hunkering then launching at one another before tearing off in a top-speed game of chase.

I slowed to watch Granny and Delilah load a group of guests onto the big hay-filled wagon for a tour of the property. Sue Ellen was perched on the tractor, twisted at the middle to watch the group's progress. I smiled. The fall festival was always a hit. Something about the last few moments before Thanksgiving put everyone in a strange state of anticipation. People were genuinely happy, and they wanted to seize the moments. It'd be time to carve the turkey before we knew it, then the rest of the winter would whip by and we'd land in a new year, cursing the way time flew. The happiest moments always passed too quickly.

I swallowed hard and told myself to stay in the moment. Make memories. Stop rushing through my life and pay attention to today. It was too easy to forget we weren't promised another one.

Delilah flipped the hinged step onto the full wagon and latched the small safety gate, then waved overhead to Sue Ellen, who gave a *whoop* before pulling away.

Granny was the first to turn back. She caught sight of me, and her smile brightened. "Winnie!"

"Hey, Granny." I closed the space between us and hugged her tight. "Looks like another busy day."

"Yep," she said proudly. "It's been a great year all around, thanks to your cider shop."

"I think your festival stands on its own." Always had. Folks came to the Fall Harvest Festival because they loved and supported Granny, plus it was a tradition, and Blossom Valley loved traditions. "I should probably fix up some flyers and take them with me into town. Try to spread the word to the tourists."

"Smart," Delilah agreed, jumping in on our conversation with ease. "You look lovely, Winnie. Where are you off to? Another big date?"

I gave my well-worn jeans and thermal shirt a long look. Definitely warm and practical. Lovely? Not so much. "I'm going to run some errands before I open the cider shop."

"Like what?" Granny asked, a little too innocently.

"I thought I'd visit some folks. Maybe deliver some cider and strudel." I returned her sugary smile, debating whether or not to tell her the whole story, but hating to drag her into my mess if I could avoid it. It wasn't as if she could join me, even if she wanted to. She had an orchard full of fall festival guests to tend to.

"Still pursuing Mr. Potter's death?" she asked.

"Maybe?" I hedged. "Why?"

Her sweet smile fell. "I know Birdie wants you looking into this thing," she said, taking my hand gently in hers. "I also expect you're feeling obligated to do as she asks, because she's your elder, and I taught you right. But respecting your elders is meant to show manners. You give them your seat when they need one or help them carry a package, maybe fetch them some tea. The rule doesn't apply to finding murderers or otherwise putting yourself in danger. Birdie

212

was wrong to have asked you for this."

"He was in my truck," I said, my mouth suddenly dry. "In Grampy's truck."

The goose honked nearby, and I stiffened. For a moment I imagined falling flat onto one side like Boo.

"There's Waddles," Delilah said, breaking the tension. "We looked all over for him earlier. Where have you been, little fella?"

I stepped back as the goose approached. "I think he's come to see me," I said, forcing my shoulders away from my ears. "He seems to turn up everywhere I go around here."

"Aw!" Delilah sang. "He likes you."

"Sure," I said. "He likes me like cats like mice."

Granny moved with me, refusing to be distracted from her question. "Who are you visiting today?"

"Hopefully Polly Brumble. It looks like Nate had a beef with the noise levels at the pumpkin patch, so I'm hoping to talk with his wife," I said.

Delilah's shrewd blue eyes widened. "Nate, the butcher?"

"His wife," I restated. "Nate left a few scathing reviews and ugly complaints online, and I want to know if she ever saw him get

213

mad enough to confront Mr. Potter directly."

Granny checked her watch. "I suppose Nate's at the butcher shop by now, and his wife's a doll. You should be safe on that mission."

"Excellent," Delilah said with a clap of her hands. "We'll stay here and get the festival games started."

I waved good-bye and headed for Sally before Granny changed her mind. I also wanted out of the way in case Delilah planned to use Granny's baked goods as prizes. I'd seen people trip their mothers at the church's cake walk to get their hands on one of Granny's pies.

Nate's house was adorable. I'd never paid any mind to it before, but it was loaded with curb appeal. A small white bungalow with a black roof and shutters. Two stout dormers overlooked the front yard, both with flower boxes in bloom. Mums in alternating purple and gold lined the walkway. A wreath of festive silk leaves with a broad scarlet sash and bow adorned the door.

I took the sidewalk to the porch, then rang the bell. A chorus of hound dogs bellowed in response. Several moments later, Nate opened the door.

I hopped back. "Oh. Hello."

He frowned at me while his wife struggled with four overzealous hounds, several feet behind him.

"Sit!" she called uselessly, being dragged closer by the second.

"Quiet!" Nate thundered, and the dogs fell still and silent, each taking an immediate seat where they were. Nate's gaze skimmed over me, thick brows furrowed over dark, deep-set eyes. "Sorry about the dogs. They just get excited. You know how that is."

"Sure." I glanced over his shoulder at Polly, debating my next move.

"What can we do for you?" Nate asked, rolling the unbuttoned sleeves of his dress shirt to his elbows. His attention lingered on the bag of cider and strudel dangling from my fingers.

"I'm Winona Mae Montgomery," I said, working up a smile and considering my options. Did I want to talk about Mr. Potter in front of Nate? No. Did I want to come back when it was just his wife and the Hounds of the Baskervilles? Also no. "Penny Smythe's granddaughter."

Nate's brows rose, and recognition lit up his eyes. "You're the one who found that pain in the —"

215

"Nate!" his wife scolded, her cheeks scarlet.

"Potter," he adjusted. "In the back of your granddaddy's farm truck."

"Yes, sir."

He sucked his teeth, expression stern. "You do it?"

"Nate!" his wife called again. "Stop."

He gave her a dismissive glance. "What? She came right to my doorstep, and I'm not supposed to ask the question on everyone's mind?"

His wife let her head fall forward, then turned on silent heels and dragged the dogs away with zero finesse.

"You think that's the question on everyone's mind?" I asked. "That doesn't even make sense. If I'd killed Mr. Potter, why would I load him up and drive him around in my truck?"

Nate crossed his arms and shrugged. "How'd he get in there, then?"

"I don't know!" I squeaked.

The dogs began to bark again, this time from somewhere distant and outdoors, probably the backyard.

"All right, then. Would you like to come in?" Nate asked.

"I don't want to keep you from work," I said. "You're usually at the butcher shop by

216

now. If you're on your way out, I don't want to hold you up."

"Nah," Nate stepped onto the porch, holding the door open for me to enter. "A lot of folks aren't in any mood to see me today, so I stayed home. I can't afford to lose business or my temper."

I chuckled nervously as I moved forward on autopilot, powered by generations of deeply ingrained Southern manners. "I hate to impose."

"Nonsense. I want to know what you know. Least I can do is offer you a seat and some coffee for your time. Polly will fix it for you once she motors back in here."

"I brought cider," I said, raising the gift bag in his direction and drawing the line at consuming anything a murder suspect offered me to drink. "There's apple strudel in there too, from my granny."

Nate took the offering with a smile. "Thank you kindly. Don't mind if I do."

I took one last look at Sally as he pressed the front door shut, then I focused on the room around me and the home's apparent layout in case I needed to make a run for it, and he was blocking the door. I was half Nate's size, but my desire to live made me about ten times faster than average in a crisis. Though I wasn't sure I could outrun the hounds.

Nate pointed to the couch, and I sat. The home's interior was as neat as a pin, decorated with items that had clearly been around the block a few times, and filled with giant dog toys. "What brings you by, Miss Montgomery?"

I attempted to clear my throat, but was unable to get the job done, I decided to just croak. "I wanted to ask you about the Potters. You're their closest neighbor. Aren't you?"

"I'm the only neighbor," he said, his expression softening slightly, as if he'd deemed me a friend instead of the enemy. "If that pumpkin patch had more people living nearby, things could've gone a lot differently. I could've started a petition or something to force him to keep the noise down. Instead, it was just my complaints against his beloved business."

"I see," I said. "That's tough. Your word against his."

Nate nodded. "Wasn't as if he ever tried to deny the noise. He just said there wasn't an ordinance during his hours of operation, and that was that. When the cops wouldn't tell him to keep it down, I tried airing the truth of it online, but people saw me as a villain. Out to pooh-pooh on their parade.

Now everyone thinks I'm the guy who hates fun."

And the guy who hated Mr. Potter, I thought, *and now Mr. Potter is dead.* "Is that why you stayed home today? People aren't happy you complained about the noise at Potter's Pumpkin Patch, and now he's gone?"

"No one likes a complainer," Nate said, "or a tattletale. Once word got out that I'd called the sheriff, folks started looking at me like I was a grinch trying to steal Christmas. Don't people understand I have to get up in the morning? I need to sleep, but Potter had local bands over there two nights a week, sometimes more, and fund-raisers. Don't even get me started on that car-crushing nightmare with the fire and the pumpkin catapult." He rubbed his stubble-covered cheeks. "It had to stop."

My throat tightened, and my stomach clenched. I wasn't sure if Nate had just confessed to murder, but if he had, my odds of leaving his house unscathed were nil.

"Sorry!" Polly called, hustling back through the kitchen doorway. She looked out of breath and more than a little worse for wear.

Outside, the hounds barked and howled. I bit my tongue against asking if the Potters

219

had ever complained about the yowling dogs that never seemed to quit.

"Why don't you pour us some of this cider?" Nate asked, handing his wife the bag. "And I'd like a little piece of that strudel." He dusted his palms together when she took the offerings, then turned back to me, dismissing her. "Potter was a real selfish piece of work. Him and his ever-expanding pumpkin patch. The darn thing's been encroaching on our property line for years. Growing every season, slowly making its way right to my front door, as if I wouldn't notice."

Polly returned to the kitchen and unloaded my offerings with a frown. Thanks to my angle on the couch and her reflection in the window above the sink, I had a clear view of both Brumbles. She upturned a trio of mugs and pulled a knife from the wooden block on her counter.

I returned my attention to Nate, curious about his new accusation. "Potter's Pumpkin Patch is partially on your property?" I asked, mentally tallying another reason Nate might've wanted Mr. Potter dead.

Polly laughed, but kept her head down and her hands busy, rinsing mugs and fiddling with the strudel.

Nate shot a dirty look at her back, then

turned serious eyes on me. "Not yet, but it was getting there. If I'd have given him another five years, he'd have been selling pumpkins off that couch." He nodded to the place where I sat, and his jaw set. "He was always taking more," Nate said, his voice coming low and gravelly. "My peace and quiet. My personal space. My land. Now my reputation, as if I didn't have good reason to complain! It was always more people, more cars blocking the roads, more noise keeping me up, and more trash blowing across the field. More. More. More! I was so sick of it."

I swallowed hard and popped onto my feet. "I should probably go," I said. "I've taken too much of your time already, and I just remembered Granny needs me at the orchard."

Polly grimaced from the doorway, a mug in each hand. "They were up to something over there."

"The Potters?" I asked, intrigued, but not enough to stay, and no longer interested in drinking anything the Brumbles served me, even if it originated from my place.

"Mm-hmm," she said, stepping into the living room with us. "Maybe making moonshine. Who knows what? They probably did their debauchery inside that corn maze no one can solve."

I dared a look through the window, following her gaze to the distant rows of corn. A shiver rocked down my spine. I hated the corn maze. I'd run off from Granny and Grampy in it once when the maze and I were both much smaller, and the experience had terrified me. There were black trash bags stuffed to look like massive creeping spiders stationed around corners, and ghosts made of sheets and dowel rods anchored among the stalks. I'd had nightmares for a year, and I'd never gone back into the maze. Whatever went on in there today was the Potters' secret to keep because even my curiosity wasn't strong enough to push me into the significantly larger and more elaborate maze today.

"No one wants to solve that maze," Nate said. "They go in because they want to be in, not out. They can stay in the maze all night. Party all hours."

"Are you sure?" I asked, trying and failing to imagine the Potters making moonshine and debauchery among the looming stalks of corn.

"Of course I'm sure," Nate said. "I'm not the sort of man who spreads lies and gossip or hearsay. I know what goes on over there, and I don't want any part of it. I've even got trail cameras set up all over my property to be sure none of those rowdy hooligans comes this way."

"Trail cameras?" Hank and his satellite imagery came to mind, but this was different. No trail camera could cover the kind of distance Nate was claiming, and it didn't seem likely that any camera could get a decent photo of what went on behind the closely planted stalks. I gave the window over the couch another long look. "You can see inside the Potters' corn maze from here?"

I turned back to evaluate Nate's expression and wait for his answer.

He gripped the back of his neck and let his gaze dart away. "I can't see inside the maze," he amended, "but I can see everyone who goes in."

Polly set the mugs on the coffee table and placed her hands on her hips.

I took another step toward the door. "I really should be on my way, but I do have one more question. If you don't mind." Nate and Polly exchanged a look but didn't protest, so I went on before I chickened out. "When was the last time either of you spoke to Mr. Potter?"

"We saw him the day he died," Polly said. "In town."

"Not at the pumpkin patch?" I asked.

"No." Nate scoffed. "We never go there. We had breakfast at the Sip N Sup, and passed him on the sidewalk. We exchanged howdy-dos, then I went to work and Polly headed home."

My heartbeat sped with intense relief. "You were at work when Mr. Potter died?"

Nate nodded. "I hadn't started yet, but I went outside when I saw the commotion. I recognized your granddad's truck and thought it might've broken down."

My mind raced. There would be witnesses to confirm Nate's story. If he was at the butcher shop while I was at the pumpkin patch, he couldn't be Mr. Potter's killer. I turned my eyes to Nate's wife. "And you were at home when he was discovered in my truck?"

She shrugged. "I suppose. I didn't hear about it until hours later."

"You were here when you heard the news?" I repeated, my heart rate increasing.

"Yeah," she said, her eyes widening with fire and challenge. "Alone."

My smile wobbled, then faded.

Maybe I'd been wrong to assume Nate was the only neighbor who had a beef with Mr. Potter, and maybe I really was standing in the home of a killer.

CHAPTER FIFTEEN

The cider shop was crowded by lunchtime as orchard guests made their way through the doors in search of a light snack or something sweet to tide them over. No one seemed to mind the standing-room-only situation, but I made mental plans to get another table or two into the space as soon as possible, at least until I could afford to expand into the loft above. Folks without a seat simply sipped their drinks and roamed the perimeter until a table opened. Meanwhile, they read old newspapers I'd collected from estate sales and the framed articles I'd hung on display, familiarizing themselves with Blossom Valley history. A few folks tried to buy my décor right off the walls, but I wasn't running a Cracker Barrel. Nothing in my shop was mass-produced or intended for resale. That was one of the things I loved most about my memorabilia: Everything I'd collected was as authentic, as original and irreplaceable, as the folks who'd owned them before me or those who were featured in the content.

I cleared empty plates and glasses from the counter as a trio of guests took their leave, replaced immediately by another wave of newcomers. "Welcome!" I said, motioning them to the empty seats before me. "Make yourselves at home. Menu's over the bar." I pointed to the mirror and smiled. "Let me know when you're ready."

I stepped aside to give them a minute, opting to tidy the display I'd made at the end of the counter. A brightly colored poster board encouraged folks to register for a West Virginia hunting license and help keep our state "wild and wonderful."

A pair of men in khaki pants and polo shirts stopped to give the sign a read. "Cider shops are drumming up hunters these days?" the taller man asked, looking first to his friend, then to me. "What's your gain? You're a fruit farmer, aren't you?"

"Yes," I said, "but license sales are down, and that money supports our Division of Natural Resources, which is important to me. Plus, hunting's a big deal around here. It's a long-held tradition, part of our local culture and who we are as a community."

The man nodded and rubbed his chin.

"My granddaddy taught me to hunt," he said, a little smile on his lips. "He taught me to track and trap. Respect nature. Eat what you kill and never waste. Probably why I don't hunt anymore. I haven't needed the food in years. Decades," he said with a humorless shake of his head. "Probably not since I joined the Air Force right out of high school."

His buddy grunted. "Time certainly flies, doesn't it?"

"You hunt?" the first man asked, looking my way once more.

"No, but my grampy taught me too. Half my high school missed class for opening day of deer season back then. They probably still do. Blossom Valley's big on traditions and not so much on change. Overall, though, the state's losing funds, and I wanted to raise awareness."

His gaze grew distant, caught in a memory, I supposed. "It's nice folks don't have to hunt for food the way we did as kids," he said. "You remember?"

His friend nodded. "Mama turned everything into jerky before we had a freezer. That or it got cooked and canned."

The men laughed, and I wondered briefly at their ages.

"I had no idea how poor we were," the

quieter man said.

" 'Cause we were happy. We didn't need things to make us that way. We just were. We had siblings, friends, a roof over our heads, and the big blue sky over that. Nothing but clean air and freedom everywhere."

I patted the display. "Well, if you have the extra money now, and want to help a good cause, you can pledge to buy a hunting license. I've got flyers with the office location where you can stop in and register."

The men smiled as they added their names to my list of pledges.

"Thanks," I said. "Cider's on the house. What'll it be?"

The quieter of the men handed me a business card. "How about twenty-five gallons of your best and a table at this week's reenactment? We're Bill and Jim, by the way. We fund the event every year, but this is the first we've attended in eons."

I took the card, then shook each man's now-extended hand. "Winnie," I said. "I'm confused. Are you placing an order or asking me to rent a table from you?" Did I even have twenty-five gallons of cider to spare? Granny had plenty in cold storage, but they were standard flavors. Was that what these guys wanted?

"We're offering you booth nineteen," Jim

said, nodding to the card in my hand. A number nineteen was scrawled in the top corner. "No charge. If you want it. I'd guess you're going to need twenty-five gallons to start."

Bill handed me a credit card. "How about we pay for the cider up front? Then you can donate the money you make on it to the DNR, or you could give a free cup to anyone who pledges to buy a hunting license. Whatever you think is best. We trust your judgment."

"Really?"

"Absolutely," he said. "We've been away from our roots far too long, and it's nice to know there are folks like you who still care about our home state and all the living things in it."

A bubble of gratitude swelled in my chest as I ran the credit card for twenty-five gallons of cider.

Two minutes later, I shook Bill's and Jim's hands once more, and they were gone.

Birdie passed them in the doorway before hustling in my direction. "Well?" she asked. "What'd you find out?"

I gave her a recap of my visit with Nate, Polly, and the hounds, then added, "He was ruder than I'd ever noticed at the butcher shop, and he seemed a little misogynistic.

He kind of bossed his wife around, but none of that makes him a killer. In fact, he says he was in town when we found Mr. Potter," I explained. "If his story's true, he couldn't have killed him. Mr. Potter died at his pumpkin patch, after I spoke with him and before I left."

"I'll ask around," she said. "Find out if he's lying."

"I wouldn't mind getting a look around the Potters' property, if Mrs. Potter won't mind. Nate seemed to think there was something going on over there worth checking out," I said, not wanting to elaborate or mention the corn maze in case Birdie told Mrs. Potter, and Nate was right about the debauchery.

"I'm sure she'll welcome you," Birdie said. "No one wants to name her husband's killer as much as she does. Now" — Birdie rapped her knuckles on the counter between us for dramatic effect — "what about Brittany Ann? Have you spoken with her?"

"Not yet, but I looked her up online, and she seems to be happily married. Not to mention a little young for Mr. Potter. I can't imagine her being involved in an affair at all, especially not with an old guy."

"Watch it," Birdie said. "I'm older than Jacob Potter was."

I cringed, mentally pulled my foot from my mouth, then lifted both palms in surrender. "I'm just saying, is all. Twenty years is a major age difference. Would you date someone my age?"

"Of course not," Birdie balked. "Who am I? Mrs. Robinson?"

I decided to let that go and work on another possibility. "Maybe he was secretly her father? The child of a young man's fling, covered up all these years."

Birdie looked at me as if I'd grown a second head.

"Sorry. I've been watching Granny's stories." Her term for daytime soap operas.

"Clearly," she said. "Brittany Ann's parents are from Pittsburgh. The family moved here when Brittany was eight."

"Right. I'll talk to her, but I'm not going to insult her by asking if she was having an affair. It's not my place and none of my business."

Birdie smiled. "Keep me posted." She hiked her big black purse high on one shoulder and brushed the tip of one pinkie against the corner of her mouth. "I'm headed out to the battlefield. The Marines are practicing in uniform today. I don't want to miss that."

"Enjoy." I grabbed two pitchers of seasonal cinnamon cider and went to check on the crowded tables. Cinnamon was the flavor of the day, which meant it came with unlimited refills. I'd invented the in-house promotion to encourage folks to try new flavors after I'd been forced to pour out several gallons of expired ginger and lemon cider last summer. Free refills on the flavor of the day meant expanding guests' palettes and turning over my stock before it aged out. I thanked my nearly completed business degree for that bright idea. Marketing Strategies 101 had been a brilliant and useful course. Unlike the Ancient European Art History class I was currently taking. Not that I didn't enjoy the content, but I wouldn't have willingly traded a thousand bucks for it, given a choice.

I topped off a couple of cups at a table near the entrance, and noticed Granny moving in my direction. She had a smile on her face and my old Radio Flyer wagon in tow behind her.

She hugged me and greeted several guests before hoisting the wagon into the barn and retaking the handle. I followed her behind the counter, eager to get my hands on her fresh-baked goodies.

"This all looks amazing," I said, emptying the wagon she'd purchased forty years ago for my mother. Grampy had repainted the wagon for me when I was a toddler, and it was probably on its fifth set of tires by now. I'd ridden miles around town in the little red rectangle as he walked, checking over his shoulder to see I was still there, happy and safe. When I was old enough, I'd pulled it many more miles on my own. Hauling picnics and fishing or swimming supplies to the lake at the far edge of our property. Farther than I'd wanted to carry my things. I'd pulled everything from blankets and sunscreen to battery-powered radios and Dot in my wagon, and I'd done it countless times. These days the wagon was on a singular parade route, moving from Granny's kitchen to my barn and back on a near-daily basis. Like today, the wagon was filled to capacity with Granny's mouth-watering baked goods, and I was champing at the bit to steal a bite of a turnover before they cooled.

"They're hot," she warned. "I just pulled them out of the oven and tucked them straight into these thermal doodads you bought me."

The thermal doodads were similar to what pizza deliverers used to keep the pies hot, and I'd found them for a steal online. Now, anyone lucky enough to be around for

Granny's delivery got the pastries hot from her oven instead of reheated in mine. I unzipped a bag and unwrapped a turnover immediately, then bit in. My eyes rolled back in my head and my lids fluttered as the warm, gooey center melted over my tongue. "Heaven," I whispered, crispy bits of pastry shell clinging to my lips.

"I had more when I left home, but folks kept stopping me on the way over here. I handed a bag off to Delilah to sell and reminded everyone else that when she ran out, they could get them up here with you."

I licked my fingertips, then took another bite.

"I saw Birdie up here earlier," Granny asked. "Any particular reason she flew out of here like her pants were on fire?"

"I think there might've been," I said with a mischievous grin. "Apparently the re-enactors are rehearsing in uniform today."

Granny gave a dramatic eye roll. "Men in uniform."

"Yep."

"Don't let Delilah hear about it," Granny said, "or she'll be nothing but taillights too."

Considering Delilah had been an army wife for forty years, that didn't surprise me.

I finished my turnover, then stacked the rest of Granny's pastries behind the counter with a wistful sigh. If only I could eat them all and not double in size. The weight gain would be completely worth it, but frankly, I couldn't afford a new wardrobe. My life savings had gone straight into opening the cider shop.

I forced my eyes away from the tempting treats and dusted my palms together. "Done."

"Great. Do you need more apples or cider up here?" Granny asked. "I'm expecting Harper any minute, and I don't have much to keep her busy. You know she won't leave until she's done something, and she doesn't know how to sit still."

I smiled. That was true enough, and it made Harper an excellent orchard manager, but not much of a conversationalist. "Sure," I said. "Send her my way with a load of cider. The men who finance the John Brown reenactment were just in here, and they bought twenty-five gallons of cider for me to give away tomorrow. A fresh cup to anyone who pledges to buy a hunting license."

"Nice."

"Yep, and they even gave me a table to use, free of charge." Most vendors paid upward of two hundred dollars for a table at the event. "I'm going to pass out flyers about the orchard while I'm there. If folks like the cider, they'll know where to buy more."

"Smart!" Granny said, turning her phone over in one hand. "Wait a minute." She pulled a pair of glasses from her coat pocket, settled them across her nose, then squinted at the screen. "That's Harper now. She's looking for me." Granny tapped her phone. "I'll tell her to load up the cider and head this way."

"Sounds good."

I greeted and rang out a small group of people who'd formed a line at my register while Granny responded to Harper.

I joined Granny in the doorway when I finished. Her gaze was fixed to Harper in the distance. She'd attached a mini-trailer to the riding mower, loaded it with cider, and was heading our way. The jugs jostled and bounced with every turn of the trailer's wheels. "Wow. That was fast."

Granny nodded. "She's a whirlwind."

"Hey, y'all," Harper hollered, parking the mower several feet away. She swung one short leg over the seat and dismounted with a little bounce. "Looks like your Fall Harvest Festival brought out half the town. No wonder you need more cider up here!" Her signature braid hung low over one shoulder, beneath a Mountaineers ball cap mounted on her head. She was tan from hours outdoors despite the lateness of the season and dressed in her usual jeans, muck boots, and flannel shirt.

I envied her zip and pep. I'd never been that way. Never mistaken for perky, I'd preferred listening to talking, and when I had something to say, it wasn't always filtered properly. I'd learned early, for example, that people didn't like to be corrected, even if they had no idea what they were doing or talking about, especially by a kid. And because I'd had a busy mind, my energy was spent inwardly more often than outwardly. Granny used to say I was an old soul, but in hindsight, I think she meant I was a strange child. I preferred libraries to concerts, and solitude to parties.

Maybe I had been a strange child.

Harper began to offload the gallons, and I took two from her hands. "Thanks so much for bringing these," I said, toting them to the refrigerator behind my counter while she and Granny hauled more to my walk-in refrigeration unit in the back.

I alternated between helping Harper and Granny and ringing up customers until the cider was all safely stored.

The minute we'd finished, Harper dusted

her palms and heaved a satisfied sigh. "I hate to run off so soon, but I've got to make a grocery run for Mama. She's expecting twenty-three for Thanksgiving next week, and we need to stockpile before company starts arriving."

Granny grinned. "We completely understand."

Granny often had a houseful for the holidays, though our guests weren't blood related. Granny liked to invite folks she knew would be alone otherwise, sometimes single people, sometimes older couples or single moms and their kids or folks whose spouses had to work. We didn't have any actual relatives in town, but we were never short on family.

Mr. Potter came to mind as I imagined Granny's kitchen stuffed with neighbors and friends. His neighbors were a little odd and had possibly been spying on him using trail cameras. "Before you go," I said, stalling Harper's exit, "what do you know about Brittany Ann Tuttle?" I leaned in close to keep my voice from traveling, then explained my reason for asking.

Harper's face crunched in disgust, her mouth turned down in a horseshoe. "He's old."

"Maybe love doesn't see age," I suggested,

glancing at Granny for input.

Granny frowned. "It's still weird, and I don't think that rumor is true." She put one hand to her lips for a moment, a gesture I recognized as her falling deep into thought. "Harper, did you see Sue Ellen when you were on your way up here?"

"Sure. She was helping Delilah unload a wagon of hayriders."

Granny nodded. "Be right back."

"I'll walk you out," Harper said, sliding off her stool. "Thanks for the cider, Winnie."

"Anytime." I lifted a rag and wiped the counter, then put their glasses in the dishwasher. I could only imagine what Granny was up to. Hopefully she planned to get some feedback from Delilah and Sue Ellen about Mr. Potter's alleged affair. I could use any reliable information I could get my ears on.

I filled a pot with freshly delivered cider while I waited, set it on the stovetop to heat, then collected a few ingredients from my shelves. I tossed a pair of cinnamon sticks into the pot, then added the zest from my oranges and a bit of real maple syrup for punch and sweetness. It was the same recipe I'd sent samples of to a national cider competition last summer but hadn't heard back about. Regardless of what the contest judges thought, cinnamon twist was my first and best-selling cider. When the shop began to smell like heaven, I covered the pot with a lid and set the temperature to simmer.

According to my watch, it was nearing five o'clock when my final set of customers left cash on the table and sauntered into the blazing sunset. I didn't close the shop until seven in the summer, but I'd been sliding that time back a bit each day, in keeping with daylight. As a general rule, once folks went home for supper, they stayed there this time of year.

I watched the fiery orange glow creep through my open doors, and a shiver ran down my spine. My barn had seen fire last winter, and the reminder chilled me to the core. A killer had been coming for me then too.

The lid on my pot began to rattle, and I jumped, spinning for a look behind the counter. I hurried in the pot's direction, suddenly eager to get home before dark.

"Well," Granny's voice sounded at my back, and I squawked in response.

"Good grace almighty!" I wailed, pressing a palm to my chest for fear my heart might escape. "You scared the bejeezus out of me."

"Sorry."

I took a beat to catch my breath, then

turned off the stovetop so my cider could cool. The flavors needed time to blend and set. I needed a minute to collect my marbles. "What's up?" I asked, sounding more breathless than I'd intended.

"I talked to Sue Ellen about Brittany Ann for you," she said, sounding confused. "I told you that was where I was going, didn't I?"

I nodded, though I couldn't remember what she'd said while my pulse was pounding so loudly in my head. "What did Sue Ellen say?"

"She said the Tuttles are members of her husband's church and quite a delightful couple as far as Sue Ellen can tell. Delilah agreed. She knows the Tuttles through friends and the card club."

"Okay." I leaned my elbows against the counter, considering the report and knowing both Sue Ellen and Delilah couldn't be wrong. Granny and her friends were excellent judges of character, and their abilities to see through people's pretenses was uncanny, superhuman almost. I'd often wondered if that skill came with age and experience because I could use a little more aptitude in that department. "So, Mrs. Potter was probably wrong about the affair, but something must've given her the idea.

It's not as if she picked Brittany Ann out of the clear blue sky as her husband's mistress. There has to be something to her suspicions."

"Exactly what I thought," Granny said, eyes twinkling. "Then Sue Ellen told me that Brittany Ann often helps retired folks at the church with their taxes."

"Taxes?" I let that rattle around in my head a minute before guessing what it meant. "Brittany's an accountant?"

Granny shrugged. "I'm not sure, but Sue Ellen says she seems to know tax laws, and considering the Potters owned a thriving business, it seems reasonable that Brittany Ann could've been helping Mr. Potter with his finances. It certainly makes more sense than assuming the two were having an extramarital affair. Honestly, I don't know why people are so quick to jump to that conclusion for everything. This isn't one of my stories, and even those have more complicated motives than just libidos at work. Like when that socialite came back from the dead to catch her husband cheating."

I nodded. This was why I'd wondered if Brittany Ann was Mr. Potter's love child. Too much television with Granny. Her "stories" had been on the air since before I was born, and she was right. Those shows were notorious for convoluted story lines.

I grabbed a washtub to collect dirty cups and plates and made my way through the ghost town of a dining area, clearing tables and imagining why Mr. Potter would've met with an accountant without telling his wife. None of the ideas I came up with made me think the Potters had a good marriage. In fact, it was possible that Mr. Potter was planning to leave his wife. Wasn't it? Maybe not for Brittany Ann, but for some other reason. Could that reason have been financial? Had he come into a windfall and not wanted to share?

My footsteps faltered as I reached the farthest table from the bar. A solitary cup stood beside an open pocketknife that had been jammed through a napkin and into the tabletop. Crimson sunlight reflected off the shiny blade, stealing my breath and making an already-terrifying scene feel intensely gruesome.

A one-word message had been scrawled across the red-tinted napkin. A threat that could only have been meant for me.

ENOUGH.

Chapter Sixteen

Colton made it to the cider shop in less than fifteen minutes. He was dressed in his personal version of a sheriff's uniform. Work boots, jeans, a jacket, and ball cap with the Jefferson County Sheriff's Department logo. His usual scowl was already in place as he strode through the barn doors. "You're having quite a week."

"I hadn't noticed," I said dryly, then turned to lead him to today's threat. "There." I opened a palm in the pocketknife's direction. "I'm certain the message was meant for me. I'm just not sure who left it." I crossed my arms to help support my failing bravado. "Enough," I said, reading the napkin aloud. "Enough what, do you suppose? Enough asking about Mr. Potter's death? Enough talking to you and your family about Samuel Keller? Enough drumming up hunting license registrants and support for the Division of Natural Resources?"

Colton raised his brow, snapping latex gloves onto his hands while I ranted. "Hunting licenses?"

I turned a pointed gaze toward the display at my counter. "Yeah."

"Get many names?" he asked, approaching the knife and note with an open evidence bag.

"A few." I took a seat at the next table to watch him work without getting in his way. "Granny and I got a bunch of ladies to register, and I got a huge order for cider from the men who fund the reenactment. They gave me a free table where I can give samples away and collect more names tomorrow."

He dropped the knife into an evidence bag and sealed it. "Nice."

I crossed my legs and bobbed my foot. "What do you think about the note? Any chance I'm wrong and whoever did that just wanted me to know they'd had enough cider?"

"Unlikely. Any chance you've installed a security camera in here?"

I barked a laugh. "I'll be able to afford security cameras right around the time pigs fly and Boo spends an entire day on all four feet." The truth of it stung. The cider shop did well for a new business, and I'd financed

245

most of the barn's renovation with the sale of two Mustangs, but I'd poured my life savings into it as well. Now my comforting, hard-earned nest egg was gone, and I had more bills than I'd ever known, plus another semester of college tuition to pay. "Maybe I can run over to the Radio-Shack and buy one of those teddy bears people use to spy on their babysitter."

"You need more than a nanny cam. You need a GoPro camera mounted to a helmet that you never take off. At least then I could review the footage and know who was seated at this table today."

"It was really busy for a while," I said. "Mostly tourists I didn't know."

He tapped his phone screen, sending or receiving messages, I wasn't sure. "I think this message is from Potter's killer. I know Samuel Keller was in here the other day, but the message doesn't make any sense coming from him. Can you remember anyone who sat at that table this afternoon? Or the one next to it?" he asked, taking the seat beside me. "Maybe that person will remember who was there right before or after them."

I searched my fuzzy mind for faces and names from the day. "Most folks stop at the bar to order, then they find a seat, and I don't see them again until they come up to pay. I don't always take drinks into the dining area, so I don't necessarily see where they sit, especially when it's packed in here." *Except today,* I thought. *Today I'd been giving refills.* I closed my eyes and searched my mind for those moments when I'd been looking for the red-rimmed cups I'd used to help identify my cider of the day. I could hear the white noise of voices and laughter, feel the heat generated from the crush of bodies in the space, the weight of my pitchers in each hand. But I hadn't really looked at the guests. I'd been concentrating on the red rims. Frustration twisted in my core. I'd been here when the lunatic was jamming a pocketknife into my table, and I hadn't noticed a thing.

"It's okay," Colton said, probably reading my expression.

I opened my eyes, a little surprised to feel the weight of unshed tears hanging there. "I was right here."

Colton set a big palm between my shoulder blades. "It's okay. We'll figure it out. I'll run the knife for prints, then ask around to see if there's anything special about it. Maybe I can learn where it was purchased and how long ago. I might even find the purchaser that way."

"That's pretty optimistic."

He removed his hand from my back, returned it to his lap, and smiled. "Thanks. I've been told I'm kind of a downer, so I'm trying to think more positively."

"I don't think you're a downer."

"No?" His voice hitched with challenge.

"I'd agree that you can be unnecessarily intense at times, and grouchy on occasion, but I suppose the former is a hazard of the job and the latter is often my fault."

Colton's lips twitched, fighting a smile. "You're not wrong."

A small laugh bubbled up from my chest, and I leaned against his side, allowing the strength of him to support me. "I talked to the Potters' neighbors today," I confessed.

He leaned away from me, forcing me to sit up straight. "You what?"

My chin inched up on instinct, and my shoulders squared in defiance. I was setting the tone here. Not Colton. I'd chosen to tell him about the visit, and I wouldn't allow him to think he was bullying the information from me.

We locked eyes for a long beat before he relented his air of superiority. "What happened?"

Satisfied that he'd eased up on the angry face, I told him about the strange couple,

248

the trail cameras, and the obnoxious hounds.

Colton pinched the bridge of his nose when I finished. "I'll follow up with the Brumbles. Anything else I should know?"

"I think Mr. Potter might've been planning to sell the pumpkin patch or leave his wife," I said.

Colton's hand fell away from his face. "Why?"

"Mrs. Potter told Birdie that she suspected Mr. Potter was having an affair with Brittany Ann Tuttle. But when Granny asked around, Sue Ellen told her that Brittany Ann helps folks at church with their taxes. I don't think Brittany was involved romantically with Mr. Potter. I think she was helping him with his money somehow."

"I'll talk to Brittany Ann too," he said. "Meanwhile, I'm going to agree with the table-stabber. Enough already. You've got plenty to keep you busy here and with the Fall Harvest Festival. So, I'll take over the questioning of our citizens," he said, pressing a palm to his chest, "and you make the cider." He turned a pointed finger in my direction.

"Fine."

Colton stood. "Good. Now, we're done here. Can I walk you home?"

"Why not?" I loaded a few jugs of cider into the wagon. I didn't expect to rest tonight, so I might as well use the time to work on my anniversary flavor while I was up.

Colton checked his watch before taking the wagon's handle. "I've got a meeting with the coroner and crime scene team at seven. I'm buying dinner, and we're putting in some overtime, but I'll swing by here to check on you later."

I locked up the shop and turned to join him on the old dirt road back to my place. I wanted to tell him I would be fine. That I wasn't afraid to be alone or in need of a babysitter, but that was all lies. "Okay."

We moseyed toward the orchard in companionable silence. Colton's cruiser was parked in the lot with our other guests. The fences were lined in twinkle lights, and the open space was filled with folks enjoying the festival. Scents of hot cider and cocoa sweetened the crisp evening air, and the ashy hint of a distant bonfire sent nostalgia over me like a tidal wave. These short autumn days had always been my favorites. Bundled in sweaters and caps, cheeks pink from the wind, heart warm from the company. Country music piped through the speakers at the big farmers' market tent, and I hummed along to a tune I hadn't heard since high school.

The warm feelings subsided slowly as the festival-goers came into better view. They all seemed too happy. None of them knew a killer had been here tonight, at my shop, on this property, maybe even mingling anonymously among them.

Then again, maybe one of them was the killer.

Thirty-five minutes later, I was on Brittany Ann Tuttle's doorstep. I'd promised to stop questioning the citizens, but my house had been too still and my imagination too busy. A little wind had rattled my kitchen window, and I'd decided to take a drive and clear my head.

Somehow I'd wound up on the curb outside the Tuttle home.

Since I was here . . . I knocked.

The rambling farmhouse was old with chipping white paint, but it had a distinctly happy vibe. The walkway was lined in well-manicured flower beds and neatly cut grass. Tiny bicycles lay in the drive alongside abandoned balls, bats, and a pile of sidewalk chalk. A pastel-colored stick figure family of five welcomed my arrival. A tire hung from a rope in the giant oak out front, and a white swing swayed lazily on the covered porch.

The front door opened a moment after I knocked, releasing sounds of music and laughter into the night. A man in his early thirties greeted me with a smile. His sandy hair and beard were neatly trimmed, but in evident disarray. A toddler in a cape and diaper clung to his back, chubby arms wrapped around the man's neck. A pre-schooler in a tiara and tutu gripped his leg as she looked me over.

"Hello," he said, resting one palm over the toddler's hands at his neck, and the other atop the strawberry-blond princess at his side. "Can we help you?"

The princess curtsied deeply and raised a wand. "I believe I can help you," she said sweetly. "Have you come to bring me a puppy?"

I grinned. "No, sorry, no puppy."

Her tiny form straightened, and she stood tall once more. "That's okay. Do you like hot dogs?"

"I do," I said, shifting my glance from her to the man. "I'm Winona Mae Montgomery. I live at Smythe Orchard with my granny."

"Welcome," he said. "We love the orchard. We were just there last weekend for the festival."

"Five minutes," a woman's voice called from deep within the home.

The man swung the door wide. "Come on in. We're just about to have dinner."

"I don't want to intrude," I said. "I didn't realize the time." Truthfully, it was after seven, and I was surprised the little ones weren't getting ready for bed, but what did I know about children? I'd grown up on a farmer's schedule, so I'd been thankful to sleep in once school started.

"No intrusion. There are plenty of hot dogs for everyone," he said with a wink.

I stepped cautiously into the front room, taking in the colorful surroundings. Toys covered everything in sight, and the woman's voice had begun to sing the alphabet song.

"I'm Frank," the man said, offering a hand. "This is F.J., Frank Jr., and Celeste, our little princess."

"Mama!" The princess released Frank's hand to curtsy again, then bolted away. "The apple lady is here!"

Frank Jr. buried his face into his daddy's neck.

"Brittany Ann's in the kitchen. Did you come to see her about the orchard?" He turned for the long hallway down the home's middle, and I followed.

The kitchen was at the other end of the hall, bright with white cabinets and a blue-checkered floor. A baby sat in a highchair, kicking his feet and patting the tray. His lips were smeared in orange goop, pureed carrots, if the baby food jar on the table was any clue.

"Brit, this is Winona Mae Montgomery from Smythe Orchard," Frank said, making the introduction.

"Hi," I said as brightly as I could manage, wishing I hadn't crashed the family's dinner.

Brittany paused to consider me while Frank ushered the older children to the dinner table alongside the highchair. She rubbed her hands on her apron and tipped her strawberry-blond head over one shoulder. "Hi. Did we have an appointment?"

"No," I said feebly, unsure where to go from there.

Her brows knitted. There was kindness and sincerity in her voice and expression, despite the fact I'd arrived unannounced and so far without explanation. I felt instantly awful for even listening to the rumor about her and Mr. Potter. "Did I order something?" she asked, moving her gaze to the nearly forgotten bag in my hands.

"Oh!" I lifted the gift in her direction.

"No, I just wanted to bring you some cider from the orchard. There are a few turnovers in there too."

"Thank you." She accepted the offering warmly, though still clearly and understandably baffled by my appearance.

I tried to imagine myself in her shoes, singing the alphabet to a baby while making dinner for a brood. It was an image I'd never had the pleasure of seeing at my own house, *Granny and Grampy's house.* I'd longed for my mother all my life, but I'd never imagined myself as a mother. The sudden weight of it pressed hard against my chest. Could this be me one day? Cooking and singing and becoming the thing I'd once wanted for myself? Would I do a good job? Make my family happy?

Frank kissed his wife's cheek, then ferried bowls and plates to the table.

I didn't know any adulterers, but I couldn't imagine they came from happy, laughter-filled homes like this one.

"We love Granny Smythe's apples and pastries," Brittany Ann said. "Are you going door to door with freebies, or did something else bring you by tonight?" She tipped her head toward the table, indicating I really should join them.

"Honestly, a friend asked me to talk to

you about Mr. Potter," I said. "I can come back another time."

"Nonsense." Frank handed me a prepared plate. "The more the merrier, right, guys?"

The princess and Frank Jr. sang out, "Yeah!"

I took the plate with a laugh. Frank had cut one end of the hot dog in a deep X, creating four long, skinny "legs," then spread those over a sea of macaroni and cheese and painted a ketchup smile on the top half of the hot dog.

"Tonight, we eat octopuses," Frank said in a pirate-like voice.

"Octopi," the princess corrected.

"Thank you," I said again, feeling wholly humbled as I lifted one of the apple slices Frank had fanned out around the macaroni sea.

Brittany set a pitcher of water in the table's center, then poured everyone a glass.

The princess took my hand. "Say grace! Say grace!"

I closed my eyes and gave silent thanks for people like these, who loved one another and their children. For folks who stayed the course and didn't run. And for folks who'd invite a stranger into their home for octopus hot dogs just because that stranger rang the bell.

Frank took the kids away after dinner, and Brittany Ann led me to the back porch, where we could talk privately.

The rear porch was impossibly more inviting than the front. Another porch swing. A pair of rockers. Hanging baskets of mums in every color.

We each took a rocker and a minute to breathe.

"I recognize you," Brittany Ann said. "Now that I've had a minute. You helped find out what happened to your neighbor after she was killed. You got shot."

My stomach clenched with an onslaught of unwelcome memories, and the scar tissue seemed to burn along my side. "That's right."

"How are you?" she asked, her thoughtful gaze traveling over me.

An emotional mess, came to mind. Along with words like *paranoid* and *nosy.* But the truth was that I liked helping find Mrs. Cooper's killer, even if I'd gotten hurt as a result. "I'm okay."

"Is that why you're here now? Trying to find justice for Mr. Potter?"

"Yes."

Brittany Ann nodded. "I see." She sipped her water, then watched me, a pensive expression on her pretty face. "I suppose someone found out I was seeing him and assumed the worst."

"Something like that," I said. "But you were helping him with his taxes?"

"No," she said earnestly, then paused before speaking again. "What I'm going to tell you is between me and you. Okay? I'm only telling you because I think you mean well, and because you helped your neighbor when she needed someone to find the truth for her. Mr. Potter deserves that. He was a good man."

"He was," I said, "and I'll do what I can, but I'll also get help from the sheriff if I need it."

She nodded again, this time chewing her lip.

"Why were you seeing Mr. Potter? Was he having financial trouble? Was his business failing?" The questions seemed insane given the wild popularity of Potter's Pumpkin Patch and Nate's accusation that the Potters were expanding, but what else could it be?

"Yes and no," she said with a reluctant frown. "Mr. Potter was having financial trouble, but not because his business was failing. He brought his books to me for review when they weren't adding up the way he'd expected."

"I don't understand," I said.

Brittany Ann looked at her hands, now twined on her lap, then raised a tentative gaze to mine. "Mr. Potter suspected his wife was skimming money from their business."

CHAPTER SEVENTEEN

I woke to the sound of a text notification just after sunup the next morning. Colton let me know he was leaving his post outside my front door. Granny and her ladies were setting up to open the orchard, and Colton was headed home for a few hours of rest.

I took my time getting ready, too exhausted to move any faster, then I went to Granny's for breakfast.

She met me at the door with a mug of coffee and a smile. "You're just in time!"

I accepted the offered mug and climbed onto my favorite chair at the table. A spread of breakfast pastries, breads, and sweets filled the center. I helped myself to a chocolate croissant.

A muffled commotion filtered through the house, accompanied by the occasional cuss word and followed with a round of prayers and giggles. The sounds were nearly masked by a festive holiday tune pumping from

Granny's thirty-year-old boom box on the countertop.

"What's going on?"

"Hank and the ladies are bringing my kitchen tree down from the attic," Granny said. "I love this part. It always feels like the official kickoff for the holidays, don't you think?"

A series of thunderous bumps rattled the walls and elicited more cussing from Delilah, whose voice was clear now that the commotion was getting closer. Hank laughed, and Sue Ellen followed up with another round of prayer.

Granny peeked into the living room, where the staircase would soon deliver our friends.

"All right!" Hank's voice arrived before his face a few moments later.

Granny stepped aside as the tip of a six-foot faux fir squashed through the doorway behind him.

"Things weren't looking good for a while, but we made it." He dragged the tree to the window and hoisted it upright on the far side of the room. "Here?"

"Perfect," she cooed.

Granny's kitchen tree had been handed down to her from her mother long ago, and while Granny and Grampy had always chosen a live tree for the front window in the living room, her mama's fake tree had been the first official decoration of the season all my life.

Sue Ellen and Delilah rushed in to tug and arrange the branches, which had been squashed flat during storage and the commute downstairs. They pulled and twisted, working each branch. When they finished, the tree would be full and fat, its central support post hidden from view.

"Looks good," I told him.

"Beautiful as always," Sue Ellen agreed.

Delilah didn't look convinced. "Looks like it's been stuffed up in that hoarder's paradise of an attic you have upstairs, if you ask me. But it'll be gorgeous with a little time, lights, and ornaments. Did you bring the ornaments?" She swung her gaze to Sue Ellen, who blanched.

"I thought Hank had them."

Hank gaped, openmouthed. "I was carrying a six-foot tree. Where did you think I put the ornaments?"

Sue Ellen shrugged.

"I'll get the decorations in a minute," Granny said, patting Hank's cheek on her way to help her friends. "You're a good boy, Hank. I don't care what anyone says." She winked at me behind his back and kept going.

"Can you stay for coffee?" I asked.

"Sure," Hank said, a hopeful gleam in his eye. "I'd like that."

I pointed to the machine on the counter. I was glad to offer, but not awake enough to serve.

He filled a mug, then joined me at the table. "Does it seem like it should be Thanksgiving in a few days to you? I might be getting old, but I feel like we just had Christmas."

Sue Ellen clucked her tongue, then stood back to appraise the tree before going at it again. "It's felt like Christmas for me since Labor Day. We've been filling holiday-themed needlepoint orders for months."

Delilah nodded. "We can't keep up with the demand."

"Are you selling your work at the festival?" I asked. "Under the tent?"

Granny peeked around the tree at me and pointed to a lidded tote near the door. "Sure. We take orders and sell our stock. Which reminds me. We need to replenish soon."

Hank eyeballed the container of completed needlework. "Do you finally get to needlepoint some nice things now that

Christmas is coming?"

I smiled. Granny loved to needlepoint but hated how many orders she received for rude or obnoxious pieces. I thought they were funny, but she thought the craft was a dying art that should be preserved the way she'd learned it, with delicate rows of flowers around Bible verses. Unfortunately, folks these days wanted delicate rows of flowers around goofy and contrasting words like COME BACK WITH A WARRANT.

Granny heaved a sigh, then eased out from behind the tree. She exchanged looks with her ladies, who both failed at hiding their smirks. "I've been doing a lot of movie quotes this year," she said. " 'Son of a nutcracker.' 'Cotton-headed ninny muggings.' 'You'll shoot your eye out.' You know the ones."

Delilah beamed. "I've been doing surprise-faced gingerbread men with broken legs and the words, 'Oh, snap!' It's funny because it's the sound his leg probably made when it broke and the thing young folks say when something is truly delicious."

Hank hiked a brow.

I shook my head silently, warning him to leave it alone. "Well," I said instead, after finishing my croissant and coffee, "I should get moving." If I didn't leave before

Granny's crew started hauling decorations from the attic, I'd be in for a day of untangling twinkle lights, and I had too many other things on my plate already.

I set my empty cup in the sink, then tossed Granny and her ladies a few air-kisses on my way out, feeling full and caffeinated. "See ya, Hank," I called over my shoulder.

A brisk slap of air smacked my face as I moved onto the porch and peered across the field between our homes. "Where are you hiding, Waddles?"

I turned nervously in search of Granny's new rescue goose, then made a break for it.

I stalled my pace a few strides from my home when Colton's cruiser caught my attention, moving slowly up the lane in my direction.

He parked beside me and climbed out with a frown. "You'll never guess who I just talked to," he said, hands braced on his hips as he approached. "I'll help you out. It was Brittany Ann Tuttle. She was completely floored to see me. Turns out I'm the second person to ask her about Mr. Potter since dinner last night. Crazy, right? You want to guess who the first person was?"

I shook my head. Negative.

"You sure? You shouldn't need any help with this one."

I pursed my lips, then pulled them to one side. I was busted. Again. And I knew from experience that whatever I said next would only make him grumpier.

Honk!

I yipped and spun in search of the dreaded sound. *Waddles!*

Granny's goose sped through the tall grass like a torpedo locked on his target. *Me.*

I fled for my front door, taking the steps two at a time before Waddles's long, telescoping neck and bruise-making beak could reach me.

Honk! Honk!

I ducked inside, then peered out through the window in my door. Waddles might not be able to fly up the steps with his injured wing, but he could hop if he wanted, and I wasn't going to stand around and tempt him to figure that out.

Colton strode past the goose, who'd stopped at the bottom of my steps, and knocked on my door.

I eased the door open to let him in, then shut it tight behind him. "That goose wants to kill me."

Colton's lips twitched. "Let me help you take your mind off of it. Tell me what you were doing at the Tuttles' place for dinner. More specifically, I'd like to know what you learned while you were there. Might as well see if the story she gave me today matches up with whatever she told you last night."

I released a long breath, thankful Colton wasn't too angry, then headed for the kitchen. "How about something to eat or drink while we talk?"

Colton waved me off. "No thanks. Just the talk today, I think."

I stopped short and redirected myself to the couch. Colton took the chair, angling to face me. I spilled what I had, then waited for the verdict. Had Brittany Ann told us both the same tale?

Colton stretched back onto his feet when I finished and turned for my door.

"Well?" I asked.

"Well, what?"

"Did her stories match?"

Colton examined me carefully. "They did, but since you're pushing, I've got to know. Why did you go to see her? I'd just asked you to leave this alone, and you'd agreed. Then you went back on your own word as soon as I left." He heaved a long, tired sigh. "I don't like being lied to, Winnie. You get away with a lot because you've got a big heart and good intentions, but the cute factor has worn out on you playing private detective. And to be honest, I'm having a hard time justifying a friendship with some-one I can't trust."

"What?" I pressed a palm to my gut where his verbal hit had landed.

Colton opened my door.

"No. Wait!" I leaped in his direction, grab-bing wildly for his hand. I caught his wrist with my fingers, and he pulled to a stop, ap-praising me with those sharp, soulful eyes. "Look. I know I have a problem. I don't want to be this curious. I just want to understand why and how things happen. I want to fix problems and help people. I can't stop myself. I know I need a support group, but that sort of thing doesn't exist."

"Then start one," he said, pulling free from my grip.

"I'm sorry." I turned my eyes to his, mean-ing the apology deep in my bones.

Colton ran a big hand through unusually mussed hair, tension leeching from his expression. "I'm working around the clock to find Mr. Potter's killer and keep Samuel Keller away from you. I can't do anything else. Not even babysit you while you're off on your amateur missions of shenanigans and tomfoolery."

"Hey," I snapped. "Unfair."

He expelled a dark chuckle. "Hardly. You have an uncanny way of getting into a killer's clutches, and frankly, I can't deal with that again." His phone buzzed, and he gave the device a cursory look, then groaned. "I'm supposed to have narrowed Keller's coordinates by now so the marshals can set up a capture. Instead, I'm here having this conversation with you. Again." His face screwed up as he tapped the phone screen, presumably responding to the message.

"Did you say 'marshals?' " I asked, my brain hurrying to catch up. "Like US Marshals?"

"Marshals capture fugitives," he said, pulling his attention from the phone briefly. "Small-town sheriffs aren't supposed to have to deal with this. Small-town sheriffs don't normally bring cop-killing lunatics with them when they accept the office." He tucked the phone back into his pocket. "For once, I'd like to spend a few days settling neighborly disputes, maybe a domestic issue here or there, a drunk and disorderly, something *normal.* Not another murder/fugitive doubleheader." He opened his arms like an airplane before letting them drop back to his sides.

"I'm not trying to make your job harder," I said, feeling a boulder of guilt roll onto my chest. "I can't sit here and do nothing with a local killer and a fugitive circling me. That's not who I am."

When he didn't respond, I pressed on. "Did you hear anything from the lab about the knife left in my café table? Were they able to get prints?"

"The knife belongs to one of the re-enactors. I tracked him down, but he says he lost the knife in the national park during an informal rehearsal."

I considered that a moment. "Did you check to see if that guy had a connection to Mr. Potter? Saying the knife was lost, then stolen by a killer to be used for a threat at my shop seems convenient."

"I'm looking into it," Colton said, his grouchy expression returning. "You need to stop."

I raised my palms in surrender. "How about we call a truce on this argument, and I promise to try?"

He rubbed his forehead and muttered something about never winning. "Did you ever hear back from that magazine contest you entered last summer? *Cider House* something-or-other?"

"*Cider Wars,* and not yet." Though it seemed to me that the winners would've been notified by now. Since I hadn't received a call or an email, I could only assume I wasn't one of them.

"Well, how's your anniversary cider coming along?" he asked when his eyes met mine once more, clearly looking for something to keep me busy.

"Terrible," I admitted. "I get in my head and overthink every ingredient until it's all wrong. I need a taste-tester." I dared a broad smile and waited.

"Does the job come with some of your granny's turnovers or apple fries?"

"I do believe it does."

And just like that, Colton was staying a while longer.

CHAPTER EIGHTEEN

I put a sign on the cider shop door letting folks know they could find me at the re-enactment until two, then I loaded Sally's back seat with cider, sweets, and flyers. I packed a stack of promotional materials for the orchard as well as educational and motivational material on West Virginia's Division of Natural Resources and hunting license registration.

I cranked Sally's windows down to enjoy the brisk and beating wind. I wouldn't be able to drive without the heater much longer, and I treasured the feel of fresh air against my skin. I pumped up the volume on my favorite song and crooned along, loud and off-key, but mostly just happy. There were a few things in my life I could do without at the moment, like a cop-killing stalker and a second murderer making threats, but other than that, I wouldn't change a thing. I thought of Granny and her ladies setting up the kitchen tree. My healed relationship with Hank, and my thriving cider shop. Colton's acceptance of me for who I was and his priceless input on my recipes this morning. True friends like Dot. A strong community. And the indescribable beauty all around me. Lurking killers or not, my life was exceptional.

I pressed the gas pedal a little lower as Sally floated around endless sweeping curves and sailed over the magnificent stretch of road between mountains. Anticipation fluttered in my stomach as I made the final turn toward the state park. Sally's gleaming white paint and historic beauty earned lots of attention from passersby and lookie-loos. Locals waved or honked. Visitors simply stared. I understood. Sally was a sight to behold.

Traffic crawled to a stop near the entrance to the John Brown fort and reenactment site. Vendors were already setting up for the day, and folks in period costumes greeted each car with a smile. I handed over my table number information and parking fee to a woman in a high-necked gown and bonnet, then I motored into the grassy field doubling as reenactment parking.

Folks streamed in all directions from their vehicles and through the designated area beyond the trees.

I gathered my things and hurried to find my table.

Twenty minutes later, I'd covered Table 19 with a red-and-white-checkered cloth, arranged baskets of fresh apples at the corners on top and on the ground near the legs, then lined flyers and promotional materials down the center. I created a display of Granny's sweets along one edge of the space and set plastic sample cups for cider along the other. I moved around to the front to snap a picture for Granny and admired my work.

A familiar and contagious spout of laughter broke through the white noise and busyness around me and spun me on my toes. Dot stood several yards away, cheeks rosy and smile wide as she spoke with a couple I didn't recognize. The blonde was petite, tan, and beautiful, leaning against a man who was better fit for a billboard than a Civil War reenactment. I hurried in their direction, eager to see Dot and fixing to tell her how much I appreciated her giving Granny that mean old goose.

"Winnie!" Dot called, catching me in her sights before I arrived.

I threaded my way around knots and clusters of tables and people getting set up for the day. "Here she is now," she told the couple. "My lifelong friend and maker of the best apple cider on earth, Winona Mae Montgomery. Folks around here call her Winnie." She turned her smile to me then. "This is Lacy and her husband Jack. They came all the way from New Orleans to support a friend in the reenactment. Lacy owns a pet boutique and makes treats for pets." Dot let her jaw hang open in exaggerated awe. No wonder she was having so much fun. She'd met a woman who could teach her new ways to spoil every animal in West Virginia. With baked goods.

"Nice to meet you," I said.

Dot pointed to the unreasonably handsome man. "Jack's a —" she paused, then puzzled. "I guess I didn't catch what you do."

He extended a hand in my direction. "I'm a Jack of all trades."

I evaluated his stance, the tight expression on his brow, and the tension in his tone and jaw. "Are you a lawman?" I guessed. "A marshal?" Were they here to capture Samuel Keller? Was *he* here? I craned my neck for a look in every direction, seeking signs of lurking shadows and glowing cigarette embers.

"She's good," Lacy said, impressed.

"Very good," Dot said. "Winnie's solved two local murders in a year. She's working on another one now."

Jack made a strange noise in the back of his throat, then shot his wife a pointed look. "We should go. I promised Henry I'd meet him." He looked to me with a strange curiosity and caution. "I'm not a marshal, just a man on vacation."

"Wait. Wait." Lacy tugged his hand where he urged her along. "How well do you know the local homicide detective?"

"Sheriff," Dot supplied. "And better all the time."

Lacy laughed heartily, as if I'd missed out on a colossal inside joke.

Jack's expression broke as he watched her, and he smiled, pulling her into his arms and kissing her head as they walked away.

"Your turn," Dot said from behind Doc Austin's Adopt-a-Rehabilitating-Animal booth. She pushed a clipboard in my direction. "Would you like to sponsor a rehabilitating animal? Doc Austin donates his time and provides the facilities, but rehabilitation is expensive and can be a very long process."

I examined the table and displays. A white linen cover with a large red plus sign at the center. Doc Austin's veterinary practice logo on the side, along with the street address and phone number to his office. Dot had arranged photo books, testimonial accounts, and informational materials in the center. She'd also brought a set of large glass cookie jars with animal treats. Bones in one. Kitten treats in another. A third with some sort of birdseed. "If I sponsor an animal, are you going to expect me to keep it when it's healed?"

"No." She grinned, and I knew she was lying. "I'm only here to encourage folks to help reduce costs and save lives by pledging a onetime donation or monthly sponsorship." She opened a thick scrapbook and pointed to the sad, sickly faces inside. "Just ten bucks a month can make an enormous difference to these guys. Like him." She tapped a photo of a mangled snout on a pathetic-looking pig.

"What happened to him?" I asked, heart sinking and unable to pull my eyes away.

"He was the lost truffle hog those Northerners brought down here hunting mushrooms last summer, then couldn't find before they left. He got his snout caught in a bear trap, nearly ripped it clean off. A hiker found him a few weeks ago and called it in to the ranger station. We came and picked him up. Doc removed the trap and has been working on rebuilding his damaged snout. The hog should live, but he won't be hunting mushrooms anymore. Too much olfactory damage." She tapped her nose for emphasis, then handed me a pen.

I pledged ten bucks a month and signed my name. Then I scanned the other sponsors on the list. My brows rose as I read the line above mine. "That couple from New Orleans just donated five thousand dollars and a year's supply of Grandpa Smacker pupcakes and tuna tarts. I thought Grandpa Smacker made gourmet jelly."

Dot spun the clipboard for a closer look and gaped. "Oh my goodness! Five thousand dollars! I have to find them and thank them!"

"Go," I said, flipping her BE BACK SOON sign.

"I won't be a minute," she said, already darting past me into the crowd.

I headed back to my table.

Blake was sampling the cider when I arrived. His Civil War–era Marine uniform was adorable on him. The navy jacket emphasized his broad shoulders and lean body, but I especially liked the small red plume on his hat.

"I hope you registered for a hunting license," I said, sliding into place behind the booth. "That cider is a ploy for convincing folks to register."

He grinned. "I always register." He tossed the empty sample cup into a nearby waste bin, then leaned his palms against the checkered cloth between us. "I came here to settle a score."

"What score?"

"I invited you to dinner, but you left before you finished. The way I see it, I still owe you a meal." He straightened to his full height and smiled. "What do you say?" Blake swept one arm out to indicate the row of food trucks and county fair vendors on his left. "Anything you want. On me."

I laughed. "You don't have to do that. It wasn't your fault I didn't finish eating," I said. "I'm the one who took off."

Blake seemed to consider this a moment. "Let me buy you a giant turkey leg, and I'll consider us square. I'll even tell you everything I know about the man who says he lost his pocketknife on the battlefield but you found it at your cider shop."

My feet were immediately in motion. I inhaled the scents of a half-dozen food vendors as I led the way to the Leg Man truck, then waited while Blake ordered two Stout Ladies, sauce on the side, and two sweet teas.

"Thank you. You really didn't need to do

this," I said as we stepped over to the pickup window to wait. I put on my widest smile. "Now, tell me everything you know."

Blake grinned. "I talked to the missing knife guy last night. He says he's never been to your shop, and he wouldn't go there because he doesn't like cider."

My jaw sank open. "Excuse me? That's ridiculous. Everyone likes cider."

"Apparently not this guy." He tucked a few bucks into a tip jar shaped like a turkey when our order arrived, then accepted the legs and teas being passed across the counter. He gave one of each to me. "The pocketknife was a dead end. How's your investigation going otherwise?"

"Not well." I rolled my eyes. "Your brother yelled at me about it today. Apparently I'm not a very good friend because I can't seem to mind my own business."

Blake bit into his giant drumstick, head bobbing in understanding. He watched me while he chewed. "I can see how that would frustrate him," he said eventually.

I shot him a sour look, then used my fingertips to peel the skin off my turkey before digging in. "I'm not trying to tick him off, you know? He acts like my every move on this is a personal affront, but it's completely not. I'm not even thinking about him when I'm asking questions. I just want the answers."

"Hit me," he said. "Maybe I can help."

I sighed. "How do we know the pocket-knife guy isn't lying? His were the only prints on the knife. Why should we believe him? He obviously lied about not liking cider."

Blake laughed. "An excellent point. But seriously, I think he's just some guy from Vermont who loves reenacting important events from the past. It's what these people do," he said, motioning around us. "They're history buffs, and I doubt any of them has a secondary reason to be here. Especially not something deep and nefarious like murdering a pumpkin farmer and threatening a cider maker."

I took another big bite of tender, juicy turkey and chewed.

Blake nudged me with his elbow. "Come on. We should get back. They'll want me on the field soon, and you've got cider to share."

I fell into step beside him, my thoughts caught in an endless loop of unanswerable questions. The most basic query being the most infuriating: Who killed Mr. Potter? A disgruntled neighbor? A thieving wife? Someone else? Why?

Maybe if I couldn't stop asking questions, I could at least learn to be more stealthy about it.

"Isn't that your ex?" Blake asked, pointing his drumstick ahead of us.

I followed his gaze to Hank, positioned beside a table with stand-up posters and wide, waving banners declaring the importance of registering for a hunting license. Hank was in fatigues, something I'd never seen him wear before, and likely wouldn't again. He'd probably purchased the ensemble exclusively for this occasion, the way other people bought costumes for Halloween. Hank smiled at a man collecting literature from his table and a young boy aiming an orange plastic rifle at a deer statue meant for target practice.

Blake locked his arm with mine and towed me in Hank's direction. "Let's say hi."

I dragged my feet on my way to the table, unsure about Blake's motivation. He and Hank hadn't exactly hit it off before. "Hi," I said as the man and child moved away. "Your booth looks good. Are you getting many registration commitments?"

"A few," Hank said, his gaze moving swiftly to the man at my side, then to our tangled arms. His jaw set. "Hello again, Blake."

"What's up?" Blake wondered, congenially.

"I think you're supposed to be on the field," he said, tipping his head in the general direction of the other reenactors.

The crowd around us had begun to thin. Vendors had taken their places behind long, decorated tables. Folks in costume had circled up near the fort, which would soon be seized for the South.

"I'm on my way," Blake said. "I owed Miss Montgomery a proper meal after ours was interrupted the other night." He lifted the massive turkey leg, as if Hank might've missed it. "Then, of course, I wanted to stop by and say hello to you."

"Of course." Hank sucked his teeth.

I held my breath, not knowing where the conversation was going and praying it wasn't somewhere embarrassing for me.

Hank lifted his chin. "How tall are you, man?" he asked, evaluating the difference between them. There weren't many men taller than Hank in town, and while, like his dashing good looks, he had no control or influence over the height of his lean six-foot-one frame, it was, nonetheless, a source of pride.

"Six-two."

Hank frowned. "And what do you do for

283

a living?" he asked, nearly glaring at Blake's borrowed Confederate uniform costume. "When you aren't pretending to be a bad guy from the eighteen-hundreds?"

"I'm the Marion County sheriff."

Hank rolled his head dramatically in my direction. "I suppose he already has a hunting license."

"Every year since I was fifteen," Blake said with a proud smile.

Hank considered him a moment. "But you're Sheriff Wise's brother."

Blake nodded. "Guilty."

Hank chuckled. He turned his charming expression to me. "Anything I can do to help with your investigation?"

"Nothing I can think of." But it felt good to have so much support on the matter, especially while I was still feeling guilty over the heated discussion I'd had with Colton this morning.

"I can talk to folks for you when they stop at my table today," Hank offered. "Maybe even keep you company on your next outing." He frowned. "What is your next outing?"

"I'm not sure," I admitted. "According to Birdie Wilks, Mrs. Potter suspected her husband had been seeing another woman, but that turned out to be false. Now I'm wondering if I should talk to Mrs. Potter about the allegation and set the record straight."

"All right," Hank said. "That makes sense. I'm here if you want company."

Blake pulled his phone from one pocket and stepped away from me. He tapped the screen a few seconds before putting the device away and flashing a bright smile. "Looks like you're right, Hank. The men are looking for me. See you later, Winnie?"

"Sure."

Blake patted my shoulder before breaking into a jog. "Take Hank with you if you do anything stupid," he hollered, then vanished into a sea of Civil War soldiers.

I packed up my cider and sweets at half-past one. The reenactment had ended and was set to begin again at four for the afternoon crowd. Meanwhile, the soldiers and their costumed entourages mingled with the visitors and grabbed lunch from the food trucks. I took the initiative to beat the exiting crowd out of the park, then headed for the pumpkin patch. I wouldn't likely make it back to the cider shop by two as planned, but anyone who beat me there could enjoy the Fall Harvest Festival while they waited, and I wouldn't be long.

I left Sally on the curb outside the Potters' house and went in search of Mrs. Potter when she didn't answer the doorbell. It was strange to see the pumpkin patch empty. The property had been crawling with people for weeks, then with friends and law enforcement on my more recent visits. Now there was no one. No laughing children climbing bales of hay. No couples sharing lemonades. No music piped through hidden speakers or car-crushing dinosaurs wowing a crowd. Just me and a distant squeaking sound I guessed to be an old wagon or wheelbarrow, hopefully being operated by Mrs. Potter or someone who knew where I could find her.

I followed the sounds to a small figure in the distance.

Mrs. Potter was in the picnic area, taking down decorations from the festival. She pulled a brightly painted gourd-shaped sign from the earth and dropped it onto the pile behind her. A small flatbed wagon, like the ones folks used to haul their pumpkin selections, was now covered in a stack of fall-themed signs and end-of-the-season décor.

"Hello, Mrs. Potter," I called, announcing myself before I got close enough to startle her.

She wiped her eyes on her sleeve, before

turning to look me over. "Winnie." She nodded in my direction, then lifted the handle on her cart and moved in the direction of the next sign.

I followed.

"Have you gotten any ideas about who killed my husband yet?" she asked, her voice thick and croaky.

"Not yet, ma'am," I said, "but I'm working on it."

An unexpected shiver rocked down my spine as I recalled the recent threats made to me by that killer. Obviously, I was close to knowing who it was, or I had gotten close at some point and spooked the killer enough to warn me off. I just didn't know when or what I'd done precisely that had started the threats. If I knew that, then I'd have a much smaller suspect pool. As it was, my pool included the entire town. None of the clues I'd followed had led anywhere, and considering I'd been parked in Timbuktu when Mr. Potter was killed, anyone could've come along, knocked him off, and loaded him into the back of my truck.

Mrs. Potter wrenched another sign loose from the dirt and chucked it roughly onto the pile.

Tension rolled off her in thick, oppressive waves, stealing my breath and making me reconsider my visit. But I couldn't do that. I'd come all the way to the pumpkin patch to tell her what I'd learned. More than that, I wanted to see her reaction when she heard.

I decided to lead into my news with a little small talk. "Hard to believe the season is over already."

"The season is over forever for me," she grouched. "This farm was his dream. It was never mine. Now the whole place is filled with awful memories. His death. Frantic phone calls from folks in town when his body was discovered. The sheriff and his team sweeping the land for clues to Jacob's murder. I can't stay here." She wiped her eyes again and turned away, back to the next sign. "I'm selling, and I'm moving. I don't want to be here anymore."

I tried to gauge the full reason behind her tears. Was it grief alone? Or did I detect a bit of guilt in there as well? Shame, maybe? For what? Killing her husband? Stealing from him? Something else? Or maybe it was my imagination, and there was nothing there except the grief.

"You can stop looking into it," she said sharply over her shoulder. Her red and swollen eyes pinned me briefly in place. "Just stop whatever you've been doing. I don't want to know who did this anymore. I just want to move on. I want this to be over." She yanked another wooden sign from the ground, then turned to face me with it. "You should probably go now."

I imagined her taking a swing at my head with the oversized cartoon crow in a straw hat and bandana, and I stepped back as she tossed it clattering onto the pile. "Okay," I said, keeping my distance. "I didn't mean to bother you. I only dropped by to tell you I spoke with Brittany Ann Tuttle."

Mrs. Potter's eyes widened. Her lips pressed into a thin white line, and her cheeks went scarlet. "What did she say?"

"Mr. Potter was making regular trips to her place, but it wasn't what you think. They met there for privacy and discretion. Her husband knew. He helped with the kids while she went over your pumpkin patch's financial records."

Mrs. Potter's brows pinched, and her gaze darted nervously.

"Brittany is an accountant, Mrs. Potter, or she was, briefly, before having kids. Now she helps folks from her place, during off-hours when her husband is home."

Mrs. Potter's jaw went slack. "What are you saying? He had her doing his books? I do his books!"

I grimaced. "I know, and that's probably

why he didn't come to you when he noticed the numbers weren't adding up. He wanted confirmation before making any wrong assumptions."

Her arms crossed, and her stance widened. "He thought I was stealing?" she seethed.

"You were in charge of the books," I pointed out. Immediately regretting my big mouth, I added a hasty and too-late "Sorry."

Mrs. Potter stepped forward, and I retreated another foot. "I was not stealing." She spat the words as if they were filth. "I slacked off a little recently. Sure. What else could I do? I'm only one person, and this is our busiest time of year. He was too cheap to hire enough help, so I had to step up. *On everything.* I barely have time to eat or sleep or think from September through November without this place encroaching on it. And he was doing what? Double-checking my work? It must've been nice to have the time to spare. Then he snuck off behind my back so he could smear my name without having the guts or decency to confront me first?"

I took another step back. "Um."

"You know what? Get out!" she screamed. Her face flushed beet red and streamed with sudden tears.

My heart rate hitched, and my body

whirled on autopilot.

"Get out! Get out!"

I ran full-speed until I reached the safety of Sally's interior, then locked the doors and peeled out without looking back. I passed a large red pickup truck on the corner and said a quiet prayer for whomever was inside. If the driver planned to check on Mrs. Potter, he or she might wish they hadn't.

I fixed my eyes on the road and concentrated on putting more distance between myself and the angry widow.

Maybe Colton had a point. Maybe I should stick to cider making.

CHAPTER NINETEEN

The scare Mrs. Potter gave me lasted the rest of the day. I concentrated on my work at the shop, had dinner with Granny, then went to bed early with the lights on. I woke with the sun the next morning, feeling strangely refreshed and newly motivated to work on my anniversary cider flavor.

Colton had given me a lot of good feedback during his sampling session, and I'd fallen asleep contemplating ways I could incorporate the advice into something new and delicious. The biggest epiphany I'd had at night was the realization that my anniversary cider didn't have to become a year-round best seller. It could be something seasonal. Something special.

I'd opened the shop at Christmastime, so it seemed fitting that the anniversary flavor feel festive, and I homed in on that. I also recalled from my early marketing courses that making a product available for a limited time increased its demand and perceived value. I wouldn't charge more for the special flavor, but I would make it available only in the month of December. Furthermore, I could add to the uniqueness factor by doing a special print run for the labels and feature a holly wreath or set of sleigh bells beneath the name.

I cranked up the volume on my favorite radio station, now playing only holiday music until Christmas. Then I gave the contents of the pots on my stove a stir. Sweet scents of apples, cinnamon, brown sugar, and molasses wafted into the air, accented by a note of crisp cranberries. I danced around the island in fuzzy-socked feet, singing into my wooden spoon and feeling happy, hopeful, and ten years younger. It was barely breakfast time, but today was a great day.

A jolt of enthusiasm punched through me as Granny and her ladies appeared outside my window, and I hurried to the door.

"Hey, y'all!" I called, running into the frigid air. "Where're you going?" The words lifted before me in little clouds of steam and ice crystals. "You want to come in for some hot cider?"

The trio changed directions in a turn as precise and uniform as any high school

293

marching band and headed up my steps. "Good morning," they called, declaring appreciation for the invitation and their happiness to see me.

I waved them inside and closed the door behind us. "I'm so glad you're here. Let me get you some cider."

"No, thank you," Sue Ellen said, stalling my pace to the stove. "It smells like heaven in here," she continued, "but we just finished breakfast at Penny's, and I'm fit to bust."

Delilah rubbed her flat stomach for effect. "It's true. We're headed up to the fort. We made biscuits and gravy for the soldiers, militia, and Marines."

"Rain check," Granny said. "Do you want to come with us to the fort?"

"There are lots of men in uniform," Delilah said. "They're all real nice too. I gave my phone number to the man playing General Lee last night when we went out to meet the cast, and he called right away."

"Meet the cast?" I asked. "There was a party to meet the reenactors? That's new."

Delilah nodded. "It's the first year they've done it, but it was a hit. So many folks come into town for this every year that the mayor thought it would be nice to celebrate them. It was a huge potluck with a local band."

"They strung lights through the tree limbs," Sue Ellen added, "and made a big bonfire in the clearing. It was lovely."

"I'm sorry I missed it," I said. "I had no idea, but I got a good night's rest and had a very productive morning." I hooked a thumb over one shoulder, indicating the simmering pots on my stove. "I think I finally nailed down the anniversary cider flavor I've been struggling with."

"Sounds like you had a great night too," Sue Ellen said. "We didn't get any sleep. Delilah insisted we pull an all-nighter making biscuits and gravy from scratch while she talked to General Lee."

Delilah huffed. "I helped, and we had to work all night. How else could we make enough for everyone? We have to feed a literal army."

"It's a pint-sized militia and some men in a fort," Sue Ellen said. "We didn't have to make so much."

"Well, we had to finish the needlepoints," Delilah said, a look of triumph rising on her brow. "Or at least *I* did after *you* fell asleep."

Granny exhaled deeply, then shot me a look that said she'd heard this conversation before. "I suppose we ought to go before it all gets cold," she said, redirecting her ladies.

I smiled. "Another time then."

I kissed Granny's cheek, then went to open the door for her again. "What were you needlepointing all night?" I asked.

Delilah pulled a fabric square from her pocket and passed it to me. "I goofed this one up along the bottom, but you get the drift."

I spread the fabric across my palm. A small version of John Brown's fort stood tall and proud at the center. The year of the original battle was stitched in red alongside the current year above the fort. The words BLOSSOM VALLEY, WEST VIRGINIA were stitched below the picture. "These are really neat. Everyone is going to want one."

"I hope so," Granny said. "We're going to price them cheap, then donate all the money to the local food bank."

"Great idea." Granny's number-one passion was people, specifically making sure they were fed, and I respected that to my core. In fact, it gave me an idea of my own. "Maybe I should make the sales from my anniversary cider go to the same cause."

Granny's eyes lit, and she wrapped me in a warm embrace. "Do it," she whispered. "I think that would be wonderful."

"Bye, Winnie. Come on, you two," Delilah called from halfway across the field. "Gravy's getting cold."

Sue Ellen stopped to roll her eyes at Delilah, then hugged me good-bye. "That gravy is piping hot in my thermal totes. She's just in a big fat hurry to see General Lee again. They were up talking half the night. That's the only reason she stayed awake to finish the needlepointing."

I smiled.

Delilah called again, and the other ladies hurried to catch up.

I headed back inside, still smiling. It was nice that Delilah had met someone. Now that my heart had healed from the bruising Hank gave it, I thought I might like having someone to talk to like that again. Openly and about anything. I had Dot, and I wanted her in my life forever, but she wouldn't always be enough. The truth was, despite my train wreck of a mother and never-met-him father, I'd had an example of a perfect marriage in front of me all my life, and I envied it. I wanted what Granny and Grampy had. I'd be crazy not to.

Of course, with love comes loss, and no one wanted that. I could still recall in vivid detail the way Granny had folded in on herself after Grampy died. There had been days when I'd worried she wouldn't pull out of it, and I'd be alone. A selfish fear, yes, but the loss I'd experienced was so deep already, I didn't think I could bear another.

My thoughts ran back to Mrs. Potter as I turned off the burners on my stove to let the pots cool. She'd been so angry when I'd seen her last. Erratically so. A side effect of her recent world-altering grief, no doubt. Yet I'd run away when she ordered me out. Maybe I should've offered her a hug or come back later with a peace offering. What had I expected her to do or feel? I'd delivered awful news to her already-broken heart and pushed her over the emotional edge.

Mrs. Potter was right to tell me to leave her husband's death alone. She didn't need an inept amateur investigator. She needed a friend.

A fresh spark of hope and determination ignited inside me, and I knew what I needed to do.

I grabbed a jug of cider and a pumpkin roll from the refrigerator, then slipped into my coat and shoes. I wouldn't stay long or ask her a single question, but I wanted to let Mrs. Potter know she was cared for, and that I was there if she needed anything at all.

The red pickup I'd passed on my way out yesterday afternoon was in the Potters' driveway when I pulled in. The license plate was personalized and issued in another county. RUN FST. Probably a family member who'd come to stay and look after her for a few days.

I rapped lightly on the door, hoping not to wake her and prepared to wait.

The door sucked open, and Mrs. Potter leaned dramatically against the frame. A heartbeat later, she jumped back, looking horrified. "Oh my!" She clutched her nightgown and gaped openmouthed at the sight of me on her porch. "Winona Mae! What on earth are you doing here?"

I lifted the cider and pumpkin roll in her direction, confused by her odd nightgown. It wasn't a nightgown, exactly. More like the top half of a red plaid pajama set, but it was far too big to be hers. The hem hung nearly to her knees, and I realized she must be sleeping in her husband's nightclothes to feel close to him again. "I'm not here to stay," I said. "I just wanted to bring you a little something and be sure you knew I was here for you if you needed anything. Granny too. Just holler."

She nodded, cheeks pale as she accepted my offerings. Her gaze darted over my shoulders. "Thank you. I'm going back to bed."

"Okay." I gave a little wave, then turned

and ran smack into the bare chest of a man carrying a pile of cut firewood. "Oops!" I called, reaching to steady the wood before it fell.

The man looked past me to the open door where Mrs. Potter stood, still frozen, in a shirt that matched his bottoms perfectly.

"Oh," I said, as my brain caught up with the scene unfolding before me. "Wow. I did not see that coming," I whispered, as much to myself as to the man. "I'm so sorry. Pardon me."

I covered my eyes with one hand, then split my fingers far enough apart that I could see where I was going as I hurried away.

Apparently the red pickup didn't belong to a family member who'd come to comfort Mrs. Potter last night. At least I hoped she and the man weren't related. I certainly wasn't going to ask.

I really needed to stop visiting this house.

CHAPTER TWENTY

The cider shop was inviting by day, but it was downright enchanting at night. Dot and I had strung rows of small round patio lights from the rafters for a wedding last summer, and I'd never taken them down. They gave the exposed, high-pitched ceiling an almost ethereal look. Not quite like the night sky, because there were thousands of stars to be seen outside, but the illusion of something magical, nonetheless.

Seeing Granny's well-dressed kitchen Christmas tree glowing festively in the window had put the urge to decorate under my skin as well. When the barn grew empty around suppertime, I couldn't ignore the itch any longer.

I packed up the fall-themed décor, then dragged tubs and boxes of Christmas items from my storage room in back and started turning the cider shop into a winter wonderland. I hung lanterns with flameless candles from each of the support posts, then wrapped the posts in holiday greens. I set boughs of holly on windowsills, tied them with wide velvet ribbons, and sprayed the bottom of each glass pane with faux snow. The real stuff would be here soon enough, but I enjoyed the effect in the meantime. I arranged poinsettias at the corners of the bar and drew a border of blue and white snowflakes around my giant menu mirror to replace the multicolored leaves.

The tables were my favorite part of the transformation. I'd planned their apparel for months, in anticipation of our second annual Christmas at the Orchard event. Each table was draped in a new scarlet or silver cloth and topped with a leaded-glass bowl. Fake apples and real pine cones were piled high in the bowls and sprayed with silver glitter. The overall look screamed tidings of great joy.

I bebopped my way through the work, singing along to "Jingle Bell Rock" on CD and enjoying the faint sounds of distant laughter from the Fall Harvest Festival going strong outside. Part of me tensed at every burst of wind against the barn doors or window frames, but I chose to stay in the moment and out of my head.

When my phone buzzed with an incoming

text saying Colton was there, I hurried to meet him at the door.

His cheeks were pink from the biting wind, and his sheriff's jacket was zipped to the top. He pulled gloves from his hands as he watched me.

"Thank you so much for coming," I said quickly, getting the prerequisite small talk out of the way. Satisfied, I jumped right in. "What did you find out about the pickup outside the Potter place?"

He tucked the gloves into his coat pockets, not bothering to return the greeting or smile as I locked up behind him. "You texted me to ask me to run a license plate for you without explanation. Why would you do that?"

I lifted a palm. "Do I question your reasoning when you ask for warm apple fries?" I asked, ducking behind the bar to retrieve the plate of flaky pastry–covered apple slices from the warmer where I'd prepped and placed them for this exact moment of resistance.

I delivered the plate to the counter and set a side dish of melted caramel sauce beside it, then shoved the duo gently in Colton's direction.

He moved to the counter and dipped a fry

into the caramel sauce without taking a seat. "Talk."

"I saw a truck I didn't recognize outside the Potters' place. Twice. And the vanity plate was from another county, so I wondered who it belonged to."

"What were you doing at the Potters' place?"

I frowned. "I upset Mrs. Potter yesterday when I told her what Brittany Ann said about her, so I went back to apologize and let her know I wouldn't look into Mr. Potter's death anymore. I just wanted to be there for her if she needed anything."

Colton stared. "But you're still looking into his death. That's what this is about, isn't it?"

"A little."

"Knock it off," he said, taking another fry, then a seat at the counter. "Quit. Leave it alone. Keep your promise to me and to her. Just stop."

A wave of disappointment rushed over me, and I felt the whine building in my chest before it oozed slowly off my lips. "I can't." The words dragged on until I started to laugh. Because it was true. I had a problem.

Colton held my gaze, unimpressed and not laughing with me.

"I can't help it," I said, my mind working faster now. "I think I'm on to something that's worth looking into, and I need your help. Stopping now could mean the killer gets away."

He pinched the bridge of his nose. "You realize I'm the county sheriff? That my men and I are currently conducting a professional investigation into this matter?"

I poured him some cider to go with his apple fries. "I do."

"Yet you persist. I'm sure I'll regret asking," he said, "but please go on."

"Thanks." I unloaded the entire tale. The intense way Mrs. Potter had responded to the news of her husband's suspicion she was stealing. About the red pickup that arrived as I was leaving and about how it was still there this morning. Then I told him about the pajamas.

"And they each had on one piece of a matching set?" he asked, polishing off the fries and caramel dip. "You're sure?"

"I can't be positive," I admitted. "I didn't ask or check the tags or anything, and maybe they're siblings? Best friends from childhood? I don't know, and I didn't see him get out of the truck, so maybe it's not even his pickup, but it sure seemed like something worth looking into. I mean, what if that guy was tired of his girlfriend being married and got rid of the husband? Or what if he's married to an heiress with a prenup and Mr. Potter found out about the affair and threatened to tell and ruin his take on the money?"

"I need to talk to your granny about the amount of daytime television she lets you watch."

"Valid, but what if Mrs. Potter wanted out of her marriage to be with this guy except she didn't want to give up her half of the business she's helped build? The way I see it, this possible affair changes things. Right?"

Colton let his head drop forward a moment. When he lifted it, he took out his phone and began to tap the screen. He put the phone to his ear, looking wholly exhausted. "I need to run a plate."

I stifled a smile as I cleared his empty plate and glass. From there, I went to put away the now-empty storage tubs littered around my shop. It seemed rude to eavesdrop.

Colton climbed off his stool a few moments later. "They're looking into the truck's owner. Preliminary reports show no priors." He gave a long, appreciative whistle as he scanned the room, apparently noticing the change for the first time. "You do all this yourself?"

"I did."

He turned in a small circle, taking it all in. "Well done."

"Thanks." I smiled, hoping he wasn't too mad at me for persisting on a mission I'd vowed to cease.

"Would you say it's closing time yet?" he asked. " 'Cause I could use a ride back to the sheriff's department."

"It's been closing time," I said with a wave of my hand, indicating the complete lack of guests. "Why do you need a ride? What happened to your cruiser?"

"I left it at the station. The crime scene team finished with your truck, so I signed it out for you."

My heart leaped. "You brought my truck home?"

"I knew you'd want it back as soon as possible, and the impound lot was closing. I didn't think you'd mind giving me a ride back to the station."

I threw my arms around him in a quick hug, then went to grab my coat and keys. "Thank you so much." The truck was old and used hard like a farm truck ought to be, but it was Grampy's, and I loved it. He'd saved it from the junk pile before I was born, and he'd spent years collecting the parts it needed to run again. I'd logged countless hours at his side beneath the hood when it had gotten closer to completion. The truck represented a lifetime of my memories. It represented Grampy, and it was a touchstone to my life before his loss. "Let's go."

I kept my eyes peeled as we made our way down the old dirt road toward my home, where Colton parked my truck, mostly for signs of Waddles, but also for Samuel Keller or Mr. Potter's killer.

"What are you thinking?" Colton asked. "I thought you'd be happy, but you seem on edge."

"I'm happy." I smiled at him in the moon-light. "I'm just looking out for Waddles."

He laughed. "I used to have a rooster who chased me like that."

"Really? What'd you do?"

"I ran," he said, the words hitching with remembered fear. "I hated that rooster, and he only picked on me. I can probably thank him for my position on the middle-school track team and my endurance today. That rooster was a jerk."

"What was his name?" I asked, enjoying the image of Colton being chased by a bird.

"Romeo." Another little laugh burst free. "Mom named him that because we had so many chickens. Only one rooster."

"No wonder he was always in a bad mood," I said. "Image how long your to-do list would be with a dozen wives."

Colton laughed louder then. "No, thank you."

We walked in smiling silence, our breaths puffing white in the cold night air. Our footfalls in sync against the hard ground.

"Hey," he said eventually, looking down at me from the several inches of height between us. "I'm sorry I said you weren't a good friend. It's not true. You're a great friend."

"It's okay," I said. "I know you're under a ton of pressure. Eventually you have to let off a little steam."

"Not on you." He turned an intense, almost-alarmed look my way. "Never on you. I was wrong, and I don't want you to think otherwise."

I nodded, struck with warmth and affection for him.

"Blake says I expect too much of people. That I think if others don't behave the way I want them to, then it's a betrayal. He also says people are people, and trying to force them to fit my mold is wrong. Even if I'm right. He didn't add that last part, I did."

I slowed my pace for a better look at him.

He was opening up to me again. "Do you think Blake's right about you?"

"Maybe." Colton's lips twitched, fighting a smile. "Probably." He began to walk faster, and I kept pace at his side. "Blake's always been better with people. More patient. Less critical. More likeable."

"I don't know," I said. "I like you just fine."

"Yeah?"

I nodded.

He swung his attention forward once more, pulling his clear blue eyes away from mine. "Blake likes you too," he said. "He thinks you're interesting and fun. Says you're made of good stock."

"Does it bother you that Blake's been hanging around me so much since he got here?" I asked. "Not that I think you'd have any reason to be bothered," I blurted, trying to take back the idiotic implication that Colton could be jealous of anything having to do with me. "I just don't want you to get the wrong idea," I said, backpedaling further.

"What idea would that be?" he asked, a mischievous grin on his handsome face.

My cheeks heated until I was sure they glowed from internal fire. How did I keep making it worse? "I don't know. Nothing.

Never mind."

"Well, I don't mind. Blake's a good companion for you right now. He's a lawman like me, but without a fugitive trying to get to him, and he's ex-military, so he's trained to defend you if the need arises."

My stomach tightened at the reminder I was in constant danger. "Right."

A few paces later, Grampy's truck came into view, gleaming in the porchlight outside my home.

"You washed it," I said, impressed and unexpectedly emotional as I rushed to run my palm along the cold metal fender.

"I know the truck means a lot to you," he said simply.

"Thank you," I whispered past a growing lump in my throat.

"Anytime." He handed me the keys and headed for the passenger door. "You know Blake's interfering."

"In what?" I met Colton inside the cab and started the engine with a breath of relief. The truck was fine. I was fine. Colton was here, and I was safe.

"He's evaluating you. I don't normally keep friends, and I've mentioned you more than once, so he's curious."

I nearly choked on the concept as I navigated down the long lane away from the orchard. "He hasn't been hitting on me?" I asked, laughing. "He's trying to decide if I'm good enough for you?"

Colton laughed too. "I think so, yeah. Are you disappointed?"

"I'm relieved," I said honestly, then frowned. "He told me you'd never mentioned me."

Colton gave a low groan of laughter. "Untrue, and exactly the reason he's spending so much time with you. I'm not big on details, so he's trying to get information through other means."

Suddenly all the awkward things that had been said between Blake and his folks at dinner came rushing back to me. Their son thought I was kind and funny and beautiful. Their son talked about me all the time. Their son was interested in me, *romantically.*

Their son Colton.

I turned to face him on the dark country road a mile or so outside the orchard. I was thankful for the dark night and the new moon to hide the heat crawling across my cheeks. Thankfully, there weren't many streetlights along the road for another quarter mile or so while I settled my racing heart.

His heated gaze caught mine in the dark cab and stole my breath.

Before I could look away, two blinding headlights flashed into existence and morphed into one broad beam outside his window. A massive truck plowed into Col ton's door a heartbeat later, sending us into a spin.

Colton's head hit the glass an instant before his limp body jerked in my direction, head and arms flinging uselessly against my side and shoulder.

"Colton!"

My ears rang, and my vision blurred as the impact set us on a new path. I gripped the wheel tightly as we careened off the pavement and through the frozen grass toward a massive tree at the edge of a drop-off. "Colton!" I screamed again, frantic and afraid.

I jerked the wheel with everything I had, desperate to avoid the tree and save our lives, but my wheels passed the drop-off's edge, and we began to roll.

"Winnie," a deep and unfamiliar voice warbled softly nearby, pulling me up through the clutching darkness. "Winnie," the voice cooed, deep and foreboding.

I dragged my heavy eyelids open, forcing them to make sense of the nonsensical sights before me. Grass at eye level. A window frame. No glass. A hillside on its head.

A pair of brown work boots took shape outside the broken window.

My head throbbed as I worked to keep the boots in focus.

"Ah, you hear me now, don't you?" the voice taunted. A small orange glow landed beside the boots and was quickly snuffed out.

Beside me, Colton groaned.

I rolled my head in his direction. "Colton?" His arms hung overhead, as did mine, I realized.

We were upside down. Inside Grampy's truck. Held fast to the seat above by our safety belts, something Grampy had added despite their inauthenticity. A trickle of warmth curled over my cheek and onto my forehead. I swiped at it. Not tears. Blood.

"Winnie," the outside voice cooed. "Are you still with me?"

I turned back to find a familiar face hovering outside my broken window. The man from my cider shop crouched low over his boots, peering into the ruined truck. "Nod if you can hear me."

I nodded.

"Good. You're going to be okay this time," he said. "Just a few cuts and bruises. Nothing that won't heal. It's your boyfriend who'll hurt the longest. Bruised egos take time." He chuckled at the remark. "I need you to pass along a message for me, okay?"

I blinked through fresh hot tears, unable to nod or respond. Too horrified by the truth of what had happened to form words. Samuel Keller had attacked us, and we'd never seen him coming.

Nowhere was safe. Not home or work.

Not even while I was moving along the county road at fifty miles per hour.

With Colton at my side.

"I want you to tell Sheriff Wise that I did this," he said coldly, the inflection of his voice scraping ice shards down my spine. "I want you to tell him I won't stop coming for you until he stops hunting me. Tell him this is his last warning, and if I have to act again, the next time your truck rolls it will be over a cliff."

Colton groaned and cursed, the word coming slow and slurred. Apparently he'd woken in time to hear the message I wasn't sure I could've passed on.

The next time Samuel Keller struck at me, I wouldn't survive.

Colton unlatched his seat belt and fell onto the ceiling with a thud and a curse. He kicked the door open and crawled into the grass. A moment later, he was on his feet, running wildly toward the truck that had sent us rolling. Its blinding lights drew back, then spun away as our assailant piloted his vehicle back onto the road.

Colton fired his weapon as the truck roared away.

I released my safety belt and broke into sobs as I crashed onto the ceiling then crawled out through the shattered window. I knew. Even before I saw. The truck's frame was twisted, the metal mangled and bent.

I'd survived Samuel Keller's attack tonight, but Grampy's truck had become a casualty.

Along with my heart.

CHAPTER TWENTY-ONE

It was after midnight when we finally made it home from the hospital.

Colton collapsed onto my couch with a groan of pain. "I still don't have my car."

Thankfully, Owen had seen our headlights shining in the darkness on his way to visit Granny and stopped to help. He'd gone to fetch her when the ambulance arrived, then drove her to the hospital to be with me. They'd delivered Colton and me back to my place, and neither of us had thought to complain. His car was usually here.

"Just sit," I said, carrying two bottles of water to the seat beside him. "Drink this and be still. You shouldn't drive anyway after whatever they put in our IVs for pain." I knew it was powerful stuff because I didn't give two hoots what anyone thought of him sleeping it off here.

"How did I let that happen?" he asked, cracking open his water and looking utterly

317

disgusted. The tone and expression nearly broke my heart.

"You didn't *let* anything happen. You can't control people," I said, sounding a lot like his brother. "You're not all-seeing or all-knowing. You're just a guy with too much responsibility on his shoulders, and you'll be miserable forever if you go around thinking it's all on you to handle alone."

He flicked a weary gaze to me, then set the water aside. "Isn't it? I'm the sheriff. I swore an oath to serve and protect the citizens of this county, and I'm doing a downright awful job. I should be fired. I brought a cop-killing maniac to Blossom Valley. I'm not a protector. I'm a menace."

"You're human," I said, "and you absolutely did not bring Samuel Keller here. That's absurd. It's like saying you caused him to kill your partner or run us off the road. It's just not true."

Colton pulled his gaze away and dropped his head forward. He braced his elbows against his knees and locked shaky fingers at the back of his neck. His silence said what he wouldn't.

"It is not your fault." I scooted closer and set a gentle palm against his broad back. "I can see you think it is, but honey, it's just not."

He released the grip on his neck, but didn't lift his head or face me. "He killed my partner, and now he's trying to kill you. What if I can't stop him?"

A charge of determination pushed through my veins where terror should have been. My spine stiffened, and I tugged hard on Colton's shirt, forcing him upright and back against the couch until his eyes caught mine. "Listen here." The warm and comforting tone I'd been hoping for came out sounding more like my old baseball coach when we were down in the last inning. "This is crazy talk. It's a bunch of mess, and you don't have time for it. You're letting Keller get into your head." I scooted forward and placed a palm against his cheek. "That's exactly what he wants, and we're not giving it to him. We're going to find that creep, and you're going to arrest him, or shoot him, I don't care which right now, though that might change in the morning. Regardless, you're going to let me help you, even if that just means you promise to come here for dinner and respite once a day so you can refuel. Running yourself down isn't the answer, it looks more like a form of personal punishment, and you've got to stop that. It's not helping."

Finished ranting, I leaned against his side

and rested my cheek on his chest. "We're in this together, and we're going to turn it around. Keller thinks he's got us scared, but all he's done is tick us off."

Colton's arm fell protectively around me. He tipped his cheek against the top of my head. "You've got a nice way of believing in me."

"It's 'cause I know you," I said, "so I also know we're going to be just fine."

I woke to footfalls and hearty whispers in my kitchen. Bright streams of sunlight filtered through the window and onto my face.

Granny and her ladies were covering my countertops in a breakfast spread big enough to feed me for a week. Kenny Rogers and Dolly were circling Granny's ankles and meowing their best for one little, tiny taste of any of it.

The hot, buttery scent of scrambled eggs and the salty, greasy smell of my beloved bacon, made my mouth water. My stomach sang along with the cats.

I sat upright with a wince, and the previous night returned to me in full force, bringing a deluge of unbidden tears to my eyes.

"Oh, sweetie," Granny said, taking notice at once and hurrying to my side. "You're okay now. We made you breakfast. All your favorites."

"Grampy's truck," I said, half-choking on the words.

"Shh, shh, shh," she sat beside me and curled me close in her arms. "That was just an old truck, baby girl. I don't care about that, and neither would your grampy. In fact, I wonder if it wasn't his hand that protected you last night when things could have been so much worse."

I sobbed freely then, at the thought of Grampy looking out for me from above. I mopped my face with a wad of offered tissues until the tears ran dry, then pulled myself together. "Thanks."

Granny kissed my head. "You be still. I'll fix you a plate."

Granny headed back to the kitchen, and Delilah moved into view. She set some letters and a package on the coffee table. "I brought your mail."

"Thanks." I wiped my eyes and nose, then leaned back against the couch. A new thought pulled me up straight, causing my head to ache and spin. "Where's Colton?" I turned on my knees for a look outside the window. "Did you see him leave?" His cruiser wasn't there, but it never had been. I'd been driving him to the station when

Keller hit us.

"I believe his brother came for him at dawn," Granny said.

Sue Ellen brought me a cup of coffee, then sat on the chair beside my couch. "My friend Margie works the front desk at the sheriff's department, and she said a pair of US Marshals arrived just after seven this morning. They're hunting that man who ran you off the road last night. She said she'll do her best to report back anything she hears. She's not usually one to eavesdrop or gossip, but she says she'll make an exception this one time, on account of you nearly being killed and all."

Granny's face was pale. "Good. Thank her for me."

The ladies stayed for a long breakfast and plenty of good girl talk. No one said a word about Colton sleeping over, which I appreciated, since I was traumatized enough by last night's crash without being made to feel I'd done something unseemly on top of it. Delilah told me all about her General Lee actor, whose name was really Dilbert Maloy, and Granny admitted to accepting a formal dinner invite from Owen, something she'd been putting off and dancing around for months. I knew why she was avoiding the date, but I was also certain Grampy would approve. Sue Ellen talked of her husband's congregation and the wonderful things they were doing in the community. Slowly, I filled my stomach with hot, delicious foods and recharged my batteries with heaping helpings of love, hope, and coffee.

Exactly the combination I'd needed.

I hugged them each good-bye when Granny couldn't put off opening the orchard any longer, then I went back to sleep.

I woke for the second time around noon, thankful Delilah had volunteered to run the cider shop for me. I didn't have it in me today. Instead, I took a hospital-issued ibuprofen the size of my head and chased it with a bottle of water. Then I bumbled into my bathroom for a long, blasting hot shower. I stayed until my skin was pruney and the painful twisted knots of tension in my neck, back, and shoulders had given up the fight. I supposed the pain pill helped.

Forty minutes later, I was dressed, restless, and finishing a reheated second helping from Granny's breakfast buffet. She'd taken Kenny Rogers and Dolly with her, so I had no one to talk to, and I nearly dove on the phone for company when it rang.

Seeing Dot's number on the caller ID put an instant smile on my face. "Hello?"

"How are you feeling?" she asked. "Because everyone in town's talking about that crash, and it's got me worried about you all over again. Folks say it's a miracle you both survived without a lengthy hospital stay."

"I'm fine," I assured her, "but to be fair, Grampy's truck was a bit of a tank." My throat constricted at the correct use of past tense. "They don't make them like that anymore."

"True, and speaking of historic vehicles. Since you're feeling fine, how would you like to take Sally for a spin?" she asked. "Maybe bring a hungry friend some lunch?"

"Of course. Where are you?" Much as I hated the thought of getting behind the wheel again so soon, I needed to get out of the house before I climbed the walls, and it seemed unlikely Samuel Keller would hit me again already. Plus, the marshals were in town now. Surely, he knew that and was hiding under a rock somewhere.

"I'm at the fort," Dot said as a round of musket fire erupted. "I'm manning two tables, and I left my purse at home."

I smiled against the receiver. "No problem. Give me thirty minutes."

Dot had the BE BACK SOON sign up on both tables when I arrived. She'd erected a pop-up chair between Dr. Austin's wildlife rehabilitation table and an informational/

educational table for the national park. "Thank goodness," she said at the sight of me. "My stomach is making more noise than the Marines invading that fort. I was half-asleep when I left home today. I walked off without my wallet or water jug. Thankfully I had my keys and cell phone. Then again, I guess I couldn't have gotten here without my keys." She yawned. "I didn't get home from the hospital until after midnight. You know that. You were there. How was your night after that?"

"Okay. I slept in today, and Granny made me breakfast. Thanks for keeping me company at the ER. You didn't have to do that."

Dot flung an arm around my shoulders. "Of course I did. You were nearly killed. Where else would I be?"

I leaned my head onto her shoulder as we headed for the food trucks. "Colton blames himself for the accident."

"Of course he does. If brooding were a sport, he'd be a gold medalist, hold the world title, and have a crown. Did you set him straight yet?"

"I tried," I said. "I haven't seen or talked to him today, so I don't know if it took."

"Well, don't hold your breath or blame yourself if it didn't. He seems to be a bit of a hardhead if you ask me."

I snorted at the truth in her appraisal. Colton's unyielding pigheadedness was one of the things I respected most about him. As someone who suffered from the same affliction, I knew it was both a blessing and a curse.

Dot and I ordered southwestern grilled chicken salads from the Fork in the Road food truck, then carried them to a quiet picnic table with a little dapple of sunlight to counter the biting wind.

Dot dug into her meal with gusto, moaning and bobbing her head as if she hadn't had second breakfasts already like I had. She tucked the same hank of wild auburn hair behind her ear every few minutes, but the wind just raked it loose again.

I was thankful I'd thought ahead to braid my ponytails and tug a knit cap down to my ears.

I smiled and nibbled my way through the best parts of my salad, unable to really eat again so soon. Still, there was always room for a little seasoned chicken, sweet corn, black beans, and those brightly colored crunchy strips.

"Let me ask you something," Dot said, when she took a break on the salad and reached for her water. "Maybe this isn't the right time, and you're completely over it, but it's making me nuts, so I really want to ask."

"What?" I grinned, curiosity fully piqued.

"Mrs. Potter accused her husband of having an affair, all while she was the one having an affair of her own. Talk about projecting her own issues onto others." She widened her eyes and took a swig of water. "That's crazy, right?"

"I thought the same thing at first," I admitted. "Like, maybe she really had been skimming cash so she could afford to leave her husband and be with the other guy."

"And?"

I gave a sad smile. "I don't know. All I have on the boyfriend is the county his truck is registered in and the fact that he has no priors. Also, he's got a sturdy frame. He didn't even drop the firewood when I crashed into him like a clumsy moron."

"Maybe Mr. Potter's death was a tandem effort," Dot said, turning back to her salad. "Love is a powerful thing. So is anger. If Mrs. Potter was falling for the firewood guy and mad at her husband because she thought he was cheating, those things could have become a dangerous cocktail for rash behavior."

I stopped to truly consider the possibility of Mrs. Potter as a killer. I'd tossed the theory around more than once without ever really taking time to ponder whether she was even capable. "Mr. Potter was hit over the head with a shovel while loading my truck," I began. "I guess anyone could've done that. There's no reason to assume he was overpowered or that he fought back. Someone shorter and not as strong could easily have administered the fatal blow. Heck, he could've even known she was there and just kept working. He had no reason to fear turning his back on his wife."

Dot dropped her fork and napkin into the empty salad container, then drained her water. "Could've been the boyfriend too. No one would've recognized him, and Mr. Potter had no reason to think anyone wanted to harm him."

I nodded thoughtfully, imagining both scenarios and trying to put myself in Mr. Potter's shoes each time.

"I guess what I'm trying to say is that I wouldn't go back to the Potters' house if I was you," Dot said. "If we're right, and Mrs. Potter or her boyfriend were behind Mr. Potter's death, and they now know that you know about their relationship, they have good reason to want you silenced."

"Pft," I said, stretching onto my feet. "They're going to have to get in line."

"That's not funny," Dot said. She offered a small, sad smile. "I'm sorry your life is so insane right now. Remember how dull it used to be?"

"Not really," I admitted. My life had always felt frantic, filled with work and school and helping around the farm, plus after-school clubs and sports teams in high school and extra hours helping Granny with her food bank distribution as an adult. It wasn't in my DNA to be idle, so I never had been.

Recently, my busy life had simply become more perilous and less entertaining.

"Walk me back?" Dot asked, tossing her trash into the nearest bin.

I shrugged and snapped the lid onto my salad. I'd have to finish it later when my appetite returned. "After you."

We wound our way back to the tables, dodging happy families and kids with plastic guns and foam swords. "How'd you do with your table the other day?" she asked. "Get a lot of donations or hunters registered?"

"Quite a few, actually, and I sold a ton of cider to folks who didn't want a free cup for registering for a license. I made enough that way to send the DNR a check for two hundred dollars."

Dot lifted her hand to give me a cool high

five. "Is it crazy that I feel a little guilty for leaving the table to eat?" she asked as her tables came back into view. "What if someone came by to sponsor a rehabilitating animal while I was off eating salad and concocting theories about things that weren't my business?"

"You had to eat. People understand that. Besides, if they have a heart like yours, they'll be back," I said. "How's the truffle hog doing?" Images of the poor thing's severely damaged snout had cropped up in my mind a dozen times since I'd seen the gruesome photographs.

"He's stable," she said. "Doc's got him doped up to keep his activity level low while his snout heals a little more. He's eating on his own and putting back some of the weight he lost while stuck in that trap. He's got a lot of big adjustments ahead of him. He's going to need someone with patience to take him on, and hopefully not someone looking to take him to market. He's a big boy, but he's had a hard enough time already."

"Good grief." My stomach coiled at the thought. "Who would rescue a rehabilitated pig just to take him to market?"

"You'd be surprised, especially since our adoptions are so affordable, and hogs bring good money at the county fair."

"I wouldn't mind making a donation specifically for him," I said, a related thought pressing immediately into mind. "Haven't you been able to reach his owners? Those mushroom hunters were looking for him before they went home last summer. Someone ought to let them know he's been recovered, and he's badly hurt."

"How?" she asked, eyebrows high. "He doesn't have a collar and tags like a lost dog or cat might, and it's not like his people left any contact information. And honestly," she continued, "since I took up training with Doc Austin after my shifts at the park, I've barely had time to sleep, let alone pursue the band of New England mushroom hunters who abandoned their pig."

"Sorry," I said, realizing too late that I'd overstepped and hit a nerve. No one loved animals like Dot did, and I'd practically accused her of neglect. "What I meant to say was, maybe I can reach out to the mushroom hunters and let them know what's happened to him. I'll ask around and see if someone remembers the name of their group, then I'll look them up online."

Dot nodded, her expression warm with emotion. "Thank you. I really appreciate it. I know Kenny Rogers will too."

I laughed. "I'm glad to help."

I could use the distraction from my other problems, and it would be nice to dig up a lost pet's parents. The task might even be enough to keep me from digging into Mrs. Potter's boyfriend.

CHAPTER TWENTY-TWO

I swung by the Sip N Sup on my way home and asked Reese if she remembered the name of the mushroom hunters' group that had come through this summer. She did, so I found them online while I drank a cup of coffee at the counter. I called and left a message with my name and phone number before leaving a big tip for Reese.

I loved the idea of reuniting a lost and traumatized pig with his owners, but my progress was stalled until someone returned my call. By the time I got home, my thoughts had returned to Mrs. Potter. I climbed onto my couch with my laptop and scrolled through the people on her friends list until I found the man I'd run into.

According to her social media account, the guy's name was Rex Stover. Rex was a marathon runner who spent a lot of his time sharing about it on his page. He was divorced. Once. Seven years ago. He had two grown kids and worked at a steel mill in the next county. His local criminal justice website confirmed Rex didn't have any prior arrests. That could either mean he was an upright, law-abiding citizen or that he was a really good criminal. And even perfect citizens broke bad sometimes. Had he?

I tapped my fingers against the edge of my laptop, willing myself to leave it alone.

A creak on my porch set my muscles to spring. I calculated the amount of time I needed to reach Louisa, my baseball bat, in the corner near my door before an intruder had time to break in.

I relaxed by a fraction when someone knocked.

I set my laptop aside and tiptoed to the window for a peek. Killers probably didn't knock, but I couldn't be sure.

Blake waved, already looking in my direction when I pulled the curtain back an inch. "Hi, Winnie," he called through the glass. "How y'all doing?"

I opened the door and motioned him inside. "How'd you know to catch me peeking?"

"Please, you aren't fooling nobody." His smile was mischievous. "What were you doing when I got here?"

"Nothing." I moved in front of my laptop

and pushed the lid shut.

"Then why are you looking so guilty?"

"That's ridiculous." I smoothed my hair and shirt. "Can I get you something to drink?"

"No, ma'am," he said with a wink. "But look here. I brought us some desserts to share." Blake fell onto my couch and rested a white bag on his lap. "How are you feeling? You look rough," he said. "Did you sleep?"

"Yes. Twice. But thanks for your brutal honesty." I took a seat beside him and pulled my socked feet onto the cushions with me. "Why are you here with desserts instead of at the fort? What are you up to?"

"My part was done. I die early every time." He exaggerated a sad face. "I didn't have to stick around because we aren't doing another show tonight. So, I caught a shower and a change of clothes, then hit up the Belgian waffles food truck on my way over here."

"I didn't see a Belgian waffle truck when I was there," I said, leaning closer and inhaling the sweet scents of powdered sugar and fresh-baked cinnamon-vanilla batter as he opened the bag.

"Dessert trucks don't come until dinner. You missed them the other day when you left early too." He handed me a paper boat with a taco-shaped waffle, a rich, sandy-colored cream clinging to its pockets and ridges. "It's a vanilla waffle with a cinnamon and ginger spread. Try it while it's still hot. You're going to love it."

I lifted the warm waffle to my nose and inhaled deeply. "Oh my goodness."

"Right? Bite it," he said, taunting, as if the request was a dare.

Sweet and savory flavors burst in my mouth as the creamy spread melted across my tongue. I chewed the soft shell slowly, reverently. My eyes closed unintentionally, caught in the moment.

"Uh-huh," Blake said. "That's what I thought. Now that you're all blissed out and sugared up, why don't you tell me what you were looking up on your laptop when I arrived? It wasn't the weather, or you wouldn't have closed the computer so fast. Plus, you had guilt written all over your face."

I opened my eyes and set my paper boat aside, moment ruined. "Buzzkill."

He grinned. "But I'm not wrong."

"Did Colton send you to keep an eye on me?" I asked. "Or are you just here to finish your evaluation?" I hiked one brow in challenge.

"He told you about my evaluation?" Blake

asked, a small smile tugging his lips. "Well, what do you know?" He rubbed his chin as he considered it. "Did he tell you I approve?"

"I think so," I said, trying to recall Colton's exact words. "He said you thought I was fun and interesting."

"Anything else?"

"He said you weren't hitting on me. You were just looking out for him." I fought the blush that wanted to rise. The last thing I wanted to discuss with Blake was the fact I'd thought he was hitting on me.

"I'm hitting on you a little bit," he said. "You just aren't biting."

I shook my head in exasperation. "Goof."

"What? It's true. And while I'm a little disappointed that you don't flirt back, I think I know why."

"Really?" I asked, wishing I hadn't started this conversation. "Do you think it's your inflated ego or your inability to take anything seriously?"

He lifted his waffle and took another bite. "It's Colton," he said as he chewed.

I looked away, knowing he'd see through me if we made eye contact, probably even if we didn't. I collected the laptop and opened it again, then set it on his knees. "I ran into this guy at Mrs. Potter's house."

I told him the entire awkward tale, then about the talk I'd had with Dot and our suspicions over what Mrs. Potter's affair could mean to the case.

"You could be on to something," he said. "Divorce is expensive. I don't know what half of their farm is worth, but there would be a lot less to split after they paid two lawyers for a few months of their time."

"Mr. Potter thought she was skimming," I said. "Maybe he was right. Maybe she was stocking up to run away with Rex."

Blake set the laptop aside and turned his full attention to me. "Maybe. I'd rather talk about how you're really doing. You say you're fine, but you were in a near-deadly crash last night and you were threatened by a killer. You can't be well. Keeping yourself so distracted that you don't think about what scares you most isn't going to help you. All the bad memories and feelings are going to resurface one way or another. The thing about not dealing with your damage now is that you won't get to choose when you deal with it later. Sometimes all it takes is a song on the radio or a certain scent to bring it all down on top of you, probably at the most inopportune time."

I didn't like the sound of that. "What do you know about it?" I asked, hoping he was

338

only trying to scare me into letting it out now.

"I was a POW briefly," he said.

My jaw sank open. "I'm sorry. I didn't know."

He waved a hand dismissively. "It was nothing like a lot of soldiers have gone through, but it was enough to steal my sleep, my wife, and darn near my sanity."

Divorce is expensive. He'd said the words in regard to the Potters, and it hadn't occurred to me that Blake might've had personal experience with the statement. I pressed my lips together, unsure what else to say.

"I think you should consider sleeping at your granny's house or letting Colton in at night. I could crash on your couch, if you want, but you need to do something. You shouldn't be alone. Safety in numbers and all that."

I didn't have the heart to point out that Colton had been with me when we were run off the road and nearly killed. Not being alone hadn't stopped that from happening. So, there was no way I was staying with Granny and putting her in the lunatic's path. "Maybe I should get a room somewhere for a while," I said. "Samuel Keller knows where I live, and he could use Granny to get at me, even if I'm not sleeping at her place. Maybe a temporary relocation is the answer. At least until the marshals can get Keller."

"Have you thought of staying with Colton? He's got plenty of room."

I pursed my lips, hoping my cheeks wouldn't turn scarlet at the idea of sleeping over at Colton's. "I can't," I said. "He's new here, and most folks don't know him yet. If people knew I was staying there, they'd talk. I don't want him getting a bad reputation before people have had a chance to get to know him."

Blake screwed his face up, then burst into laughter.

A pair of headlights flashed across my front window, then blinked out. I froze, mouth open and ready to tell Blake what I thought of being laughed at.

Blake pushed onto his feet before I could reach the window for a peek. "That's my relief pitcher," he said, going to open my front door.

Colton moseyed inside. "Thanks. Everything okay?"

"Yep." Blake extended a fist to his older brother, and they touched their knuckles together.

"This was a babysitting mission?" I asked.

Blake smiled. "Yeah, but I brought desserts. You can't be mad at that."

I crossed my arms. "Yes, I can. I asked you if Colton sent you, and you said no."

"No," he said, head shaking. "You asked, but I didn't answer."

Colton pushed past his little brother. "You'd better take off before you get either of us in more trouble."

Blake laughed, waved, and made his way out the door, bouncing jauntily down my steps.

I locked up behind him, then sank back onto the couch. "I appreciate your intentions here, but I don't like being treated like a child."

"I'm not treating you like a child," Colton said. He took a seat in the chair across from me, his feet planted wide and forearms resting against his thighs. "I'm treating you like you're important to me."

My heart stopped momentarily, then kicked into a sprint. "Oh." I tried to look cool. "Okay, well, did you or the marshals get a bead on Keller today?"

"Not yet. They're canvassing with his picture. They hit about half the town today. They'll finish up tomorrow. Now folks will know who he really is when they see him. He won't be able to blend in anymore, can't

341

eat at local restaurants or shop at local businesses without being recognized. The marshals left his photo with as many folks as would accept it. Hopefully they hang them on their refrigerators and behind their business counters until his face is committed to the whole town's memories."

"Did anyone recognize him from the picture?" I asked.

"A few. He's going by the name Stephen now, and he's been here long enough to shed the black leather and sports car he was so fond of. Folks say he drives an old Ford and regularly wears jeans with a ball cap and barn coat. Unfortunately, no one knew where he's staying. We're also looking for a truck matching the description of the one that hit us. He couldn't have gone far with that much front end damage, not without being noticed." Colton patted his knees, clearly ready to change the subject. "What's in the package?"

I followed his gaze to the little stack of mail Delilah had delivered to me this morning. "I don't know." I moved toward it slowly. "I wasn't expecting anything."

"Check the return address before you touch it."

I leaned over the large bubble mailer, suddenly worried it was a bomb, a dead rat, or someone's finger. "It's from *Cider Wars,*" I whispered. The cider magazine where I'd mailed samples of my products last summer. "What if it's about the contest?"

"Open it," Colton said, moving to stand beside me. "Here." He pulled a pocketknife from his jeans and passed it my way. "Grand prize winner gets a national ad campaign, right? Placement in stores across the country?"

I nodded, unable to speak as I worked the knife beneath the envelope's flap. I didn't need to win to be thrilled. I just needed to know I was up to par. Good enough. Up to snuff.

I needed an attagirl. Bad.

Inside the box was a stack of magazines and a letter. "Congratulations, Winona Mae Montgomery," I read slowly, "your Sweet Cinnamon cider is *Cider Wars* magazine's third place winner."

I covered my mouth with one hand and felt the rush of tears and legitimization flood through me. *I'm good enough. My cider is good enough.*

Colton tugged the letter and magazines from my hands, then pulled me to him as he continued reading the letter. "We're thrilled to offer your cider temporary placement in one hundred and twenty participating stores throughout your region. Additionally, a full-page ad featuring your product has been created and placed in next month's issue of *Cider Wars* magazine. A check for one thousand dollars will be sent separately in the coming weeks. Meanwhile, please accept these early copies as our gift to you. Congratulations, and thank you again for entering the *Cider Wars* Challenge."

"I did it," I whispered.

Colton tossed the magazines onto the coffee table and folded me into his embrace. "Yes, you did. When all the craziness dies down around here, I'd like to help you celebrate."

I pulled back for a look into his blank cop face. "I'd like that," I said. "Very much."

Then Colton lit up the room with a magnificent smile.

CHAPTER TWENTY-THREE

I opened the cider shop early the next day and offered free samples of my Sweet Cinnamon cider to everyone I saw. I'd carefully removed the one-page ad from *Cider Wars* magazine with a craft knife and adhered it to a board and mat beside the also neatly removed cover before framing the pair. I stood the frame on the counter near the register where everyone would see it, then arranged samples on a tray marked AWARD-WINNING CIDER. PLEASE HELP YOURSELF.

The *Cider Wars* win had buoyed my spirits in the extreme. It felt like foreshadowing. A preview of good things yet to come, and I needed more good things. Being stalked simultaneously by two killers had become a real bummer.

I rolled my shoulders and pressed my fingertips against the bunching muscles along the back of my neck. I'd taken the

345

mammoth ibuprofen with breakfast as prescribed, but I was sorer today than I had been yesterday, and the pain was slowing me down.

Harper arrived at eleven sharp, my usual opening time, and sidled up to the counter with a smile. "This place looks amazing. It's like Christmas threw up in here."

I laughed. Not the exact look I'd been going for, but I knew what she meant. "Thanks. Our second annual Christmas at the Orchard is right around the corner." I handed her a stack of half-sheet flyers. "Help spread the word?"

She accepted the papers with her usual pep and vigor. "Will do. I just finished up the mailing, bill paying, and stock inventory at the orchard. Anything I can help you with while I'm here?"

"Not really, unless you'd like to sample my finally finished anniversary cider, or" — I paused for dramatic effect — "my award-winning Sweet Cinnamon cider, which just took third place in the national *Cider Wars* magazine competition."

"Shut. Up," she said with appropriate awe and enthusiasm. "Come here!" She leaned across the bar and threw her arms around my neck. "Congratulations! That's fantastic!"

"Thanks," I said, slipping free of her hug to pass her a sample. "I needed something positive to happen, so I'm really holding tight to this."

She took the sample cup, but her smile fell. "I heard about what's been going on with you. The crash. The truck. The fugitive." Her eyes widened. "What on earth?"

"I know." I took a few minutes to fill her in on the details she'd missed and to correct the ones she'd heard but were incorrect.

"I guess we're never really safe," she said, her voice just above a whisper. "It's hard to hide today, especially if someone's determined to find you." Her far-off gaze made me wonder if she, like Blake and his divorce comment, was speaking from experience. She slid off her stool and offered a warm smile as she patted the counter. "I guess I'll get going and leave you to it. Give me a call if you think of anything you need. I can be back here in a jiff."

"Okay. Drive safe," I called, but Harper was already gone.

Business was steady through lunch, though nothing like it had been on the day the pocketknife had been jammed into my table. I was thankful for the extra time to talk to folks about their families, the weather, and whatever was on their minds.

I heard all about the reenactment and the associated mixers with the actors. People shared their traditions and plans for Thanksgiving dinner. Many bought multiple jugs of my specialty ciders to serve with their meals.

The vibe in the air was electric and charged with positivity in anticipation of good things to come. It was just what I needed. My day got even better when I noticed Mr. Potter's farmhand, Wes, at a table with the newspaper.

"Hey, there," I said, sidling up to him with a smile. "Welcome to my cider shop."

He looked up, apparently stunned by my presence for a moment. Then, the proverbial light bulb flicked on. "Hey! Sorry, you caught me in another world for a minute." He tapped the newspaper.

"No problem." I tucked my order pad into my apron pocket. I wouldn't need it to remember the requests of one guy. "Wes, right?"

He nodded, and a little smile formed on his troubled face. "How'd you remember that?"

"I work at it," I admitted. "I was a waitress for a decade before opening this place. Plus,

I like the idea of knowing folks by name. I think it feels good to be remembered, and I like making people feel good. Can I get you started with a couple free cider samples?"

He agreed, and I went to grab a pair of cups from the service counter. One Sweet Cinnamon cider, and one anniversary sample.

When I returned with the drinks, I noticed a pen on the table with his newspaper. "Working the crossword?" I asked, craning my neck as I set the cups beside the paper.

"No. Looking for work," he said, turning the paper in my direction. "Unfortunately, no one wants my kind of help right now. There isn't much demand for farmhands in Blossom Valley this time of year."

My stomach sank as I recalled Mrs. Potter's rant about the farm being her husband's dream and not hers. I hadn't given any thought to what that would mean for those depending on the pumpkin patch for a paycheck. "You were let go at the Potters' place."

"Mrs. Potter is selling," he said. "She promised me a good reference for whoever buys the farm, but that doesn't help me today or for Christmas."

"Well, at least tell me what I can get you for lunch. Whatever it is, it's on me. You're going to need your energy to make all those new employment contacts."

He smiled. "Okay." His gaze rose to the giant mirror behind the bar where I'd scripted the daily menu. "Ham and cheese sliders? And tater tots?"

"Good choices. You like apple fritters?"

"Yeah." He tented his brow, an odd look of hope in his eye. "I hope the folks I contact about work are going to be this nice."

"I think most folks are quite nice," I said truthfully. "I hope they'll surprise you."

"Me too," he said.

I chewed my lip, debating the thing I wanted to say next. "Do you think Mrs. Potter's decision to sell so soon has anything to do with her boyfriend?"

Wes's mouth opened, and his cheeks went red. He dipped his head and leaned in my direction. "You know about that?"

I gave a sad smile. "Do you think Mr. Potter knew?"

"I don't think so. He never said anything if he did."

I thought of the last time I'd seen Mr. Potter and how, at first glimpse, he'd seemed to be fuming. "He was mad the day he died," I said gently. "Not at me, but about something that happened before he saw me.

He came around the edge of the barn with a scowl, and I could tell he was upset when we spoke, but he covered it pretty well."

Wes frowned. "I didn't know."

"Could he have fought with his wife?"

"Maybe," Wes said. "We were swamped that day, and I was going in every direction. I barely slowed down before the sheriff came. Then everything stopped."

"Did you ever meet the guy Mrs. Potter is seeing?" I asked. "Rex?"

Wes's eyes widened. "How'd you know his name?"

"I ran into him when I went to check on Mrs. Potter. It was awkward."

"I bet."

"Is he nice?" I asked. Rex wasn't traditionally handsome, or rich if the social media photos of his house were any indication. But he had to be something if he'd enticed a married woman into an affair.

"I don't know him," Wes said. "I only saw him around. He paid a lot of attention to Mrs. Potter, and she liked that. He helped her carry things and do stuff around the market area. He complimented her too. At first he just hung around listening while she complained about her life. Then he started showing up more and more. By September, his truck was around all the time, but I rarely saw him. Later I saw less of Mrs. Potter. I figured they snuck off together, and I spent a lot of time hoping Mr. Potter wouldn't accidentally run into them somewhere."

"Wow," I said.

Wes blew out a long, exhausted sigh. "Yeah."

I excused myself and went to prepare his food. I doubled up on the meat per sandwich and added two extra sliders to the standard order size. Then I filled a bag with apples and other Smythe Orchard produce for Wes's mama and ferried it all back to him.

His mouth opened at the sight of the sandwiches, a bowl piled high with tater tots, extra desserts, and a full grocery bag to go. "Whoa. You did not have to do all this."

"I wanted to." I set a page from my order pad on the table beside his food. My number was written across the paper. "You can call me if you need anything. Your mama can too."

His jaw set as a storm of unexpected gratitude rubbed against his pride.

"One more thing about the Potters," I said. "Then I promise to leave you in peace and get back to work."

He dropped a tater tot into his mouth and nodded.

"Did anyone besides Mrs. Potter have access to the money from the farm? The register till, for example?"

He drove a napkin over his lips as he swallowed the first gulp of food. "Mr. Potter," he said. "Just the two of them. Why?"

"No reason. Eat up, and remember what I said. Don't lose my number."

I headed back to the counter, the conversation with Wes circling in my mind. Mrs. Potter had been seeing Rex for months. Probably since she'd stopped posting photos of her and her husband on social media. And I couldn't help wondering if the debauchery her neighbors claimed went on in the corn maze was actually Mrs. Potter with her boyfriend.

The barn door slid open, and a gust of icy wind whirled inside, followed closely by three Wise men and one Wise woman. I beamed at the sight of them.

"Beautiful!" Mrs. Wise exclaimed, darting her gaze around the barn, then taking a long moment to appreciate the soaring rafters. "Amazing."

Her husband waved to me, then joined her in a slow circle around the perimeter, taking in my Blossom Valley paraphernalia.

Colton and Blake headed for the bar.

Blake sat first and rested his joined hands in front of him. "I hear congratulations are in order. Third place in a national cider competition? Nice work. Smart judges."

I beamed.

"So, where is it?" he asked. "I want to try this very famous award-winning cider that my brother can't stop talking about."

I glanced at Colton, who groaned as he fell onto the stool beside him. "Ignore him. How's your day?"

"Better now," I said, setting two full glasses on the bar, then filling two more for their parents.

Mr. and Mrs. Wise took the stools beside their boys, and I distributed their ciders.

"I'm so glad y'all found the time to stop by," I said, sincerely. "It's an honor to have you here. Can I make you something to go with the cider? Light lunch? Something sweet?"

Mrs. Wise waved me off, then sipped the cider and sighed. "This is heavenly. How many flavors do you make?"

"Several," I said. "I'm always trying new recipes. I keep what works and try not to talk about the ones that don't."

"Smart." Mr. Wise finished his cup and smiled. "It's fabulous. A perfect balance of sweet and tart."

"That's the orange zest you're tasting," I said. "It works well with the syrup and cinnamon."

Mrs. Wise examined the framed magazine pages on the counter. "Delightful and sweet, just like the cider maker herself."

Blake chuckled. "Wait till you get to know her better."

Colton shook his head and grinned, but didn't protest.

I spent the rest of the day wondering how Colton would describe me, if it wasn't as delightful or sweet.

That was a mystery I wanted solved.

CHAPTER TWENTY-FOUR

Colton slept in his truck again, but he came in for breakfast with a little coaxing, which was nice.

He sipped his coffee and watched me carefully as I plated the scrambled eggs and biscuits. "I have some good news."

My hands froze, and my heart caught mid-beat. "You caught Potter's killer?"

"No, but I did transfer my daily duties to a set of deputies I trust so I can shadow you until all this is over. Now you won't have to worry about being in danger."

"Shadow me?" I asked, understanding the meaning and not liking it at all. It sounded a lot like babysitting.

"Exactly. So, what do you want to do today?" he asked.

I went back to filling the plates and delivered them to my small table. "Honestly, I'd like to find out where Samuel Keller is hiding and turn him over to the marshals. Or

we could figure out who killed Mr. Potter."
I took the seat across from him and bit into
the corner of a piece of buttered toast.

Colton made a sour face, then lifted his
fork to shovel eggs.

"Did I tell you Mr. Potter's farmhand,
Wes, was in the cider shop yesterday?" I
filled Colton in on my conversation with
Wes, and he frowned.

"It's a shame that he and his mama's
livelihoods are wrapped up in this mess."

"It is," I agreed, then narrowed my eyes.
"Why aren't you telling me to knock it off
and go make cider?"

He kicked back in his seat, amused. "I'm
a lot less concerned for your safety now that
my entire focus can be on maintaining it."

I mulled that over for a moment, then
decided to test him out. "Then I guess the
first thing I want to do is take some more
produce and pastries to Wes and his mother.
What little I had on hand at the shop
yesterday doesn't seem like nearly enough.
I've got lasting things in my pantry here,
like soups and spaghetti sauces, that will
keep until they need them."

"Sounds good."

"And you're just going to ride along?" I
asked.

He chuckled. "Absolutely not. I'm driving. You didn't do so well the last time we hit the road together."

I headed for my bedroom to change. "Funny," I called over my shoulder.

I rubbed some ChapStick on and brushed my hair while Colton finished breakfast. I hit my lashes with the mascara wand and called it good enough. The dropping temperatures would pink up my cheeks, so no need to bother with blusher. I hurried back to the kitchen and packed two paper grocery sacks full of foods from my pantry, freezer, and fridge. Lastly, I grabbed an oversized barn coat and zipped it to my chin. "Ready," I said. "Get the door?"

Colton took the bags from my arms and tipped his head in the direction of my door. "I'll carry the bags."

"Because you're the man?"

"Because my arms are longer, and you have to lock up. I don't have a key."

I eyeballed him as he sidled onto the porch with two overflowing bags and a smirk. "Good answer."

"It's not my first rodeo."

I preferred not to think of his past rodeos, so I didn't ask.

We secured the bags on the floorboards in the back seat of his cruiser, then climbed into the front.

"Do you know where this guy lives?" Colton asked, buckling in behind the wheel.

"Not exactly, but I bet you can find out," I said, trying to look as sweet and adorable as possible.

Colton groaned, then made a call to dispatch, who found Wes's name on one of the reports made the day Mr. Potter died and traced his address from there. "Anything else?" he asked, pulling onto the main road.

"Nope," I said, feeling powerful at the thought of an entire day with Colton at my beck and call. That wasn't what he'd called it, but I thought there was room for interpretation.

The day was cold, probably the coldest this season, and frost clung to the grass along the roadside despite the brilliant sun. Deer milled in fields and near the barren tree lines. I thought of our recent push to register an army of hunters, and I silently wished the deer luck.

The homes outside my window became smaller and older, then fewer and farther between. They moved from unkempt to dilapidated within a mile, then with more trash on their porches and lawns.

I knew the area well. Granny and I made produce deliveries to a nearby church and daycare almost weekly.

Dirty children lined the edge of a precipice near a curve so sharp and steep we nearly had to stop to navigate it in the cruiser. The kids held sticks in their hands, tiny mudballs speared to the ends.

"What are they doing?" Colton asked, watching the children in his mirror after we passed. "Should they be so close to the edge?"

"Probably not, but they're slinging mudballs," I said. "It requires a good view of the gorge or it's no fun."

He wrinkled his forehead at me. "What?"

"Those little mudballs will sail on forever if you've got a good stick, and you can trail them a long way this time of year with the leaves down."

Colton cast me another quizzical look as the road grew narrow and the broken pavement turned to strictly rock and dirt.

"You never slung mudballs?"

He slowed to let a handful of chickens cross the road. "No."

I shook my head. "We've got to change that." I squinted at the numbers on passing mailboxes until we reached the end of the road. "I think that's it," I said, peering up at a small, neglected home on the hillside. One of the numbers was missing from the mailbox, but I was certain we'd arrived.

Colton rocked his cruiser to a stop in the makeshift drive, which amounted to a bare spot in the grass. We climbed out and collected the groceries.

"If you have any questions about my family, you can ask me," Colton said, taking up the strangely difficult subject for him once more, as we crossed the porch. "They all have plenty of questions about you."

I loved the open invitation, but I couldn't bring myself to get started. Asking a barrage of personal questions just felt wrong and rude. "How about if there's anything you want me to know about your life, you just tell me?" I suggested, giving the home's front door a heavy rap. "Whatever it is, I'll want to know because you wanted to tell me."

He frowned.

"Coming!" a woman called from somewhere inside the home, successfully ending our conversation. A moment later, the door swung open, and a woman with disheveled hair and smeared-on lipstick squinted into the daylight. She leaned against the open door as if it was the only thing holding her upright. "Can I help you, sheriff?" she slurred, eyes fixed on Colton's badge.

"Mrs. Watkins?" he asked. "Wes Watkins's

mother?"

"That's right." She groaned and pushed away from the door, leaving it open as she wandered back into the dimly lit home. She gathered her cigarettes and a lighter from the TV stand beside a worn-out recliner and lit up. "Well, don't just stand there," she rasped. "Come on in and tell me what Wes has done."

Colton and I exchanged looks. We stepped carefully into the home and set our bags on a coffee table lined in filthy ashtrays, toppled beer cans, and unfolded laundry. I took a seat on the couch, but Colton remained on his feet.

"Wes hasn't done anything," I said. "We met last week, and I wanted to bring you both a few things. I'm Winona Mae Montgomery, by the way," I said, realizing too late that I hadn't introduced myself. "I live at Smythe Orchard."

"I don't suppose you got any hooch in those bags?" she asked.

"No, ma'am." I looked around, desperate to make small talk, but not sure what to say. "Is Wes home?"

"He's never home," she groused. "He's always working. Always leaving me here by myself." She collapsed onto the recliner in a heap, dislodging a mangy black cat and about six pounds of loose hair. Her head lolled, and her lids drooped. "I'm always alone."

Colton tipped his head toward the door, and I stood, unsure what else to do. "We can see ourselves out," Colton said. "Have a good day."

I paused in the doorway and gave the sad, sleeping woman another long look. How long had her son been caring for her? He said he'd quit high school because his mother was sick, but she wasn't sick in the way I'd imagined. Wes's mother was a drunk. And like too many others, she'd let her kid carry that burden. My heart ached for him and all the kids like him. And frankly for all the women like her, because surely no one wanted to be like that or feel like that. Yet, she did. "Will you let Wes know we came by?" I asked, projecting my voice to rouse her.

"The minute I see him," she said, her eyes opening briefly before slowly closing once more. She'd set her cigarette in the ashtray by her side with a dozen other finished ones, burning its way out while she fell back asleep.

Colton stepped back through the door and snuffed it out.

Wes's mother didn't even notice.

■ ■ ■ ■

Business was slow back at the orchard. Granny had erected heaters under the tent, where she kept a register, prepackaged sweets, and produce. She was reading a book about raising geese and considering closing up for the day when I went to open the cider shop. I thought she should. Everyone needed a day off once in a while, and the continuously falling temperatures had put a stop to the festival fun.

"I guess the reenactment wrapped up just in time," Colton said, making himself at home on a stool at the bar. "It was fairly warm until yesterday."

"Things have a way of working out," I said, moving to the business side of the counter.

"The town's going to feel empty tomorrow."

"It was a much better turnout than usual. Whoever's kid had tournaments and forced the thing back a few weeks did us a favor. I bet some of our local businesses will finish their year in the black thanks to this." I soaked a rag in the prep sink and wrang it out. "This means your family's headed home. How are you feeling about that?"

He shrugged. "Blake's got work, and my folks are becoming a couple of vagabonds since retirement. They've decided to travel down the coast, after one of the reenactors said they were from Savannah. I swear my folks are like those co-eds who backpack across Europe, only Mom and Dad are in their sixties and have money."

I laughed. "So, nothing at all like co-eds who backpack."

"I guess they're on a permanent vacation."

"Isn't that what retirement's for?" I asked. "Not that I'll ever retire," I said. "I'm too much like Granny, and we love this place too much to quit or leave it."

Colton cocked his head and leaned closer. "Really? There isn't anywhere you'd like to go on vacation?"

The question stumped me. I waited for something appealing to come to mind. New York or Chicago? LA or Hawaii? None of those places seemed like somewhere I belonged. "I'm not sure," I admitted. "I've never really been outside the state. We took lots of little trips when I was growing up, but we never had . . ." I searched for the right word. "Extra." Time or money. Farming was hardly a rich man's business, and it was absolutely a full-time job. I dropped the wet rag on the counter and made big, sloppy circles over the bar. "We camped, hiked, and fished, but mostly took day trips. It's probably part of the reason I'm such a local historian and a West Virginia enthusiast. There's not too many places around here that I haven't seen."

"You smile when you talk about it," he said. "Must be good memories."

"The best," I said. "Plus, there's just so much here to explore and such a rich history of diversity, tenacity, and innovation. Take these old Mail Pouch barns, for example. Advertising outdoors like this began in Wheeling. And the first women's publication was printed in Harper's Ferry, right up the road from here. And," I said slowly, proudly, feeling my inner feminist rise, "the first woman to win a Nobel Prize in Literature was from Hillsboro. The first African American woman to serve in any government body was from McDowell County, and she served in the House of Delegates. Also, we had the first brick road, the first pilot to break the sound barrier, and an Italian American baker who wanted to make something coal miners could pack for lunch without spoiling. He created pepperoni rolls."

Colton smiled. "I'm not sure why anyone lives anywhere else."

"Exactly." I folded my rag over the sink's edge and smiled back.

I watched him closely, gauging my timing. We'd had a good day, and I didn't want to ruin it, but I had something I wanted to say. "I know how you can capture Samuel Keller."

Colton's smile fell. His brows knitted, and his eyes narrowed. "Winnie."

"Hear me out," I said. "He's haunting me. He ruined Grampy's truck. There's a nasty bruise across my chest from the seat belt that aches and reminds me of him anytime I lift my arm. I'm under his finger, and I hate it. At least listen to my idea."

He stretched back, extending his arms and leaning away from me on the stool. "If it involves using you as bait, I don't want to hear it."

"Use me as bait," I said.

Colton let his head hang forward a moment before lifting it once more. "No."

I scowled and pressed my hands against my hips. "We need to flood this town with lawmen until Keller blows a gasket."

Colton groaned. The sound rumbled in his chest like a growl. "That'll spook him. The marshals are doing a good job right now. Slowly. Covertly."

"You mispronounced 'ineffectively,' " I

said, dragging the final word for emphasis.

He groaned again, coming forward on his stool. He locked me in an intense and unreadable gaze. "Keller told you personally that he'd kill you if he felt hunted. And your suggestion is to make him feel hunted."

"Exactly." I rushed around the bar and took the stool beside Colton, twisting the seat to face his so I could plead more effectively. "Keller's going to keep coming at me as long as he's free and you keep trying to find him. But you can't stop looking for him because it's your job. You have an obligation to protect our county and see that he carries out his sentence. I don't want to spend the unforeseeable future in fear. I want to end this, and what better way to flush him out than to put a lawman on every corner? Have them walk the streets with his photo in hand, asking loudly who has seen him?"

"He'll come for you," Colton said. "He'll be angry, and he'll strike to kill. I can't have that."

"Or," I said, "you can stay with me. Set him up to lash out, then arrest him. Again."

Colton's eyes lit, and a coy smile curled his lips. "Clever."

"Thank you."

He rubbed his chin and tapped the bar

with his thumbs, drumming out a plan. "I don't have access to that kind of manpower. There are only two marshals on the case because they only have two to spare for this."

"Do they have to be real lawmen?" I asked. "Because I know where to find about sixty trained actors who just finished pretending to be Civil War militia and Marines. I bet they'd pretend to be lawmen for a good cause." I wagged my brows. "And your brother knows them all personally now. He can ask some of them to stick around awhile and wear deputy uniforms. All they'd have to do is lurk and linger, flash Keller's photo, say his name a lot. Make him feel generally pressed and pursued. So he knows we aren't afraid and we aren't obeying him."

Colton watched me, processing, contemplating. Listening. "He'll know I'm with you when he doesn't see me with my fake men."

"He would," I said, "but have I ever told you how much Blake looks like you? Same build and stance. Same height and profile. At arm's length you're very different, but from afar, Keller would never know. Plus, Blake is a sheriff, he knows the job. He'd fill the role believably."

Colton scrubbed a hand over his lips, and I knew I'd won.

The barn doors opened, and a little crowd of women drifted inside, going immediately to the walls to take in the décor.

"I'll let you think about it," I whispered, then went to welcome my guests.

Colton spent the rest of my workday on the phone, making calls and sending texts. He walked away on occasion, especially when a guest or two ambled in, but he kept me in his sights until the world grew dark and it was time to go home.

He walked me to my door after work and paused there. "I'm running home for a shower, then I'll be back. Blake's on his way here now, so you'll only be alone a few minutes. We'll talk logistics and see about getting our hands on sixty believable federal agent's badges. Then the reenactors can just wear suits."

"So, you're going to do this?" I asked, rocking onto my toes with glee.

Colton shifted, looking both tremendously hopeful and painfully nervous. "We've got forty-eight hours before eighty percent of the reenactors go back to their real jobs. It's a Hail Mary at best, but we can try."

I set a palm on his chest and huddled in closer as the wind blew. "Don't look so distressed. We've got nothing to lose, and you'll be with me the whole time."

"How can you be so upbeat and confident when your life's at stake?" he asked, heartbreak in his tone.

"Because I trust you, and we make an excellent team."

His lips curved in a lazy half-smile, and he covered my hand with his. "How about when this is over, we take up a less-dangerous team sport? Like bungee jumping."

"Deal."

Pride swelled my chest even as fear worked to constrict it. Colton had listened to my idea, and he'd found value in it. It was more than I could have asked for, and for the first time in months, I had hope that Samuel Keller would be found.

Mr. Potter's killer could breathe easier for a day or two because this weekend would be all about capturing a fugitive.

CHAPTER TWENTY-FIVE

Blake and Colton stayed late at my place, then spent most of the next day at the cider shop, plotting to make our scheme believable. Blake left first to organize an informational meeting for the reenactors who had agreed to help. Colton walked me home at dinnertime, then left me with Hank, who was preoccupied with his own drama.

"I can't believe nothing I did made a difference," Hank said, hunched over his laptop at my kitchen table. "People were really receptive to registering for licenses. Heck, even all those church ladies showed up. So, why does this article say numbers are still on the decline?"

I went to stand behind him at the table and examine the article from over his shoulder. "Maybe all the new registrations haven't been recorded yet."

He made a noncommittal noise and slumped over the keys. "It just stinks that so many people did their part, and it wasn't enough to change the trend."

"Well, for what it's worth, I think what you did matters," I said, sliding around to look him in the eye. "You educated us. Most people around here have been buying a hunting license since high school, so you were kind of preaching to the choir on that, but not too many people knew those registration fees went to the DNR. And you can't forget that most of the folks you spoke to up at the fort were from out of town. They might still go home and register to hunt in their state, or make a donation to their local wildlife program. You made people think, and you made them care. That matters."

Hank's gaze slid back to his screen.

"And don't forget that Blossom Valley's total population is less than some big city apartment complexes, so even if every eligible person registered, it probably wouldn't have been enough to change the state's overall percentage of registered hunters."

Hank looked up at me, marginally less miserable. "I hate when you use facts and logic to improve my mood."

"Glad I could help."

He worked the cursor over his screen. "I told my boss I could run a campaign that would get people registering again and sway lawmakers from targeting oil companies to make up the lost revenue. I don't like having to go back and tell them I was wrong."

I rested my backside against the table and folded my arms to think. "How many people signed your commitment sheet?"

"Almost four hundred."

"Hank," I said flatly, "that's practically half the people in this whole town. And you got all those signatures in a week. That's impressive any way you look at it. You should be proud of those numbers. Why not suggest that your boss and the other oil companies take a lesson from what you accomplished here and run with it? They have the means to initiate a statewide campaign reminding folks that registering to hunt helps local parks and wildlife. The ads can encourage donations to make up for lost hunting registrations. There's so much your company can do, and you have proof that people will listen."

"Maybe," he said, unconvinced and clearly determined to be in a sour mood.

I poured another cup of coffee and took my time with it. I hated Hank's moods, and he had a lot of them. Funny how I hadn't noticed while we were together. Only in hindsight and now in real time.

He typed something on his keyboard, then looked up again. "Did I tell you that I talked to a couple of game wardens who were willing to check on the random cornfields I spotted near tree stands?" he asked. "They agreed the setup was likely meant for poaching."

"See," I said, "you're making a difference."

"Come here," he said, swiveling the laptop in my direction.

I carried my steaming mug back to his side and watched the grainy footage of deer eating corn in the forest. No hunter in sight. "You're a regular one-man sting operation," I said, giving him a playful nudge.

"If someone shoots one of these deer, and I get it on camera, the hunter will be in big trouble."

"Is this live?" I asked, imagining Hank indefinitely glued to his laptop, waiting for a deer to be shot.

"No. There's no internet available out there, so I have to go to the cameras and download the footage to my computer to watch it. I don't mind," he added. "At least I don't have to go through days of footage. The cameras are motion-sensitive, so they only record when there's activity in the area, and they stop recording when there hasn't been any motion for a set amount of time."

"Huh." I processed the information slowly, making a connection I hadn't made before.

A broad smile spread across my face. I grabbed my coat from the rack and threaded my arms into the sleeves. "Nate has trail cameras along the edge of his property where it meets the Potters'. He said bad things go on in the Potters' corn maze, and I blew it off. There's no way any cameras on his property could get a good look at who goes in and out of the maze, let alone what happens inside it. And I'm positive Mr. Potter would've noticed a camera hidden on his property. But a camera on Nate's property near the main road would have a good shot of where I parked the day Mr. Potter died. I was a long way from the pumpkin patch, but not so far from Nate's place." A thrill shot through me at the possibility that we'd had Mr. Potter's killer on camera all along. I snagged my keys and headed for the door. "If Colton and Blake come back before me, tell them I won't be long. I'm only going to drive by and see if there's a camera near where I parked that day. I won't stop or get out, and I'll call if I see a camera, then Colton can go get it and review the foot age."

"Hold up," Hank said, stretching onto his

feet and puffing his chest. "You're not running off on your own with some unhinged nutjob after you. That's how you always wind up nearly dead."

"Fine, come with me," I said, "but don't forget the last time I was nearly dead, I had the sheriff with me, and we were in one of Grampy's vehicles." I spun Sally's key ring on one finger. "Ready?"

Hank's cheeks paled, but to his credit, his expression didn't change. "After you."

Sally carried us toward Nate's place in a rush, eating up the dark, winding roads and bringing me closer to the camera I hoped existed.

Hank sent Colton a text to tell him what we were up to as the lights at the pumpkin patch came into view.

I slowed at the sight of Mrs. Potter and Wes talking outside the main barn. Wes was smiling, a good sign, and Mrs. Potter shook his hand. She headed for her house, and he turned for the field. "What do you think that's about?" I asked Hank.

"I don't know what you're talking about, but I think that's a camera." Hank's attention was fixed on a cropping of trees outside my windshield. "See it?" He pointed into dark limbs and branches.

I pulled Sally off the road, and Hank hopped out.

I joined him, and the porch light flashed on at Nate's house.

"Who's there?" Nate hollered. "What are you doing?"

"Winnie!" Wes called from the Potters' place.

I jerked my head in his direction.

He waved a hand overhead. "Thank you!"

Hank stepped close to my side and lowered his mouth to my ear. "I'll talk to Nate," he said. "My family's known him all his life, and I just spent an hour up at the fort telling him about my suspicions on local poachers. I can ask him for a look at his camera footage because I suspect someone's hunting on private property, and I want to see if they've made it out this far. Heck, I could even tell him I think Mr. Potter was picking off the deer that came for his corn maze." He straightened and looked me in the eye. "Trust me. I can get that footage. You can go talk to your friend." He nodded toward Wes, who'd gone back to work. "I won't be long. Besides, it's probably best you keep your distance from Nate if he is guilty and knows you're looking for proof."

The plan made sense, and while I didn't want to bother Wes while he was working, I also didn't want to wait alone in the car on a dark country road.

"Okay." It would be nice to know how he'd gotten his job back.

Had Mrs. Potter changed her mind about selling the farm? Did she decide to run the place with her boyfriend? I took a step in that direction. "Call me if you need me," I told Hank as I broke into a jog, eager to get beneath the bright lights of the pumpkin patch.

"That's supposed to be my line," he called after me.

"I said! Who's there?" Nate hollered again, his band of obnoxious hounds baying and wailing at his side now. "This here is private property!"

"Good luck with that," I muttered, thankful I didn't have to deal with the hounds again.

I crossed the well-lit parking area toward the gates to the pumpkin patch, then slipped inside, closing up behind myself. The place was bright, but felt a little eerie without people. Darkness loomed on the perimeter, untouched by the spotlights Mr. Potter had long ago erected overhead.

I stuck to the main path as I moved, keeping Wes in my sights and biding my time before calling out. I didn't want to startle

379

him or alert Mrs. Potter to my presence. As odd and grouchy as Nate was, Mrs. Potter's affair and underhanded play for the farm's money had me wondering if her husband lost his life because she'd wanted out and had no intention of settling for just half of their farm.

Wes straightened in the field up ahead and surveyed his work. He nodded, satisfied.

"Wes," I called in my regular speaking voice, willing him to hear me at that decibel.

He didn't. He dropped his hoe and shovel into a wheelbarrow and lifted its arms to push.

"Wes!" I called more loudly, picking up my pace to close the space between us before he went any farther.

He set the wheelbarrow arms down and turned. "Hey! Winnie! I thought that was you. My mama said you stopped by. She said you were with the sheriff. I hope everything's okay."

"Things are fine," I said.

He smiled, but a bit of crimson touched his cheeks. "Sorry if she wasn't herself."

"Don't worry about it," I said. "So, what's going on here?" I motioned to his tools and wheelbarrow. "You got your job back? Is the farm staying open?"

"Nah, I'm just helping close up properly

380

for the winter. It'll get me a few more paychecks at least, and that'll help us get by while I look for more work." He looked at his dirty hands, then the wheelbarrow. "Give me a minute to put this away and wash up?"

"Sure."

He pushed the wheelbarrow into a large red barn fifty yards away.

I moseyed toward the corn maze, drawn by stories of shenanigans and debauchery, but careful to keep my distance. A tingle of residual fear raised the hairs on my arms and along the back of my neck. I could practically see the larger-than-life trash-bag spiders from my childhood waiting inside for me as I approached.

I scanned the distant trees in search of hidden trail cameras while keeping an eye on the dark, yawning mouth of the maze.

Gentle thumps echoed through the walls of the barn, where Wes had gone to put the tools away. The faint but familiar melody of a Willie Nelson song slipped around the door frame as I passed.

I stopped at the maze entrance, curiosity pricking my skin. What had Nate and his wife really seen here? Something? Nothing?

The soft notes of the distant song ended, and several perimeter lights blinked out.

"I guess that's it," Wes said, his footfalls

echoing in the silent night.

I turned to smile at him, thankful again that he wasn't completely out of work just yet.

He looked over my shoulder and laughed. "Were you thinking of trying your luck in there?"

"Definitely not," I said with a laugh. "I haven't been inside since I was a kid, and once was enough for me."

"The maze was easier before," Wes said. "But Potter planted the stalks closer these last few years to cut down on cheaters, and he added about a thousand new plants. The maze is nearly twice as big as it was when I was a kid."

I gave the foreboding path another long look. "I didn't know that."

"Most people don't bother going in anymore. It's a tough maze, and it takes forever if you don't know your way. Thankfully, I do. I helped plant it. Are you sure you don't want to give it a try?"

"I'm positive. The maze isn't my idea of a good time," I said, smiling at the horrendous understatement. "Did you know, the neighbors seemed to think things went on in there that shouldn't? Do you have any idea what they could've seen?"

Wes crossed his arms and nodded with a

grin. "Yeah. Kids from the high school come up here to fool around or drink. I find empty beer cans and trash every once in a while. I know it's kids because I found a pair of student IDs once. Don't ask me how that happened." He chuckled. "Potter hated it. He worried someone would get hurt out here one night and he'd be sued even though they were trespassing after hours. He patrolled on weekends. Lost sleep for it and felt awful the next days, our busiest of the week, but he was dedicated. He loved this place."

"The neighbors probably saw all of that." The people going in and out. The alcohol. Even Mr. Potter with his flashlight checking on things, and assumed the worst, then blew that up in their minds to be some ludicrous on-goings. *Maybe things they felt that had to stop,* I thought.

I looked across the broad expanse of fields toward Nate's place, struck with sudden concern for Hank. The dogs had gone silent, and I had no idea what was going on over there. "I'd better go check on Hank," I said. "He went to ask Nate about the trail camera, but he's been in there awhile."

"What trail camera?" Wes asked.

"The one near the road. By overflow parking."

My phone buzzed, as if on cue. Hank's number centered my screen. "Speak of the devil."

I swiped the screen to check the message and found a small, grainy photo sent from Hank's phone. It was tough to make out the figures, but it looked a lot like Wes standing behind Mr. Potter at my truck's tailgate. A shovel poised over his shoulder like a baseball bat.

The text beneath the photo simply said: **Get out of there.**

I lifted my stunned gaze to Wes, who was no longer smiling.

He motioned me into the maze with the flick of his wrist, a handgun now in his grip.

CHAPTER TWENTY-SIX

The shocked and panicked expression on Wes's face likely matched my own. His hand shook, and the gun vibrated in his unsteady grip. "Move," he said, stepping forward as I stepped back, the corn maze entrance only a few feet behind me.

A familiar red truck arrived in the distance, and I considered screaming for help, but Wes's unsteady hand stopped me. The way he was shaking, he'd likely kill me completely by accident if I tried anything. The truck door slammed, and I peeked again in that direction, the interior light slowly fading away as Mrs. Potter buckled into the passenger seat.

"They're going out," Wes said without taking his eyes off of me. "We have the place to ourselves. Keep moving, please."

I took another step backward, and the stalks of towering corn obstructed my view of the world. There was nothing to do now but navigate it. I ground my heel into the earth at the first turn, then dragged it a bit to mark the direction we went from there. "What are you doing, Wes?" I asked. "I don't understand. I thought we were friends."

"Left," he said, his voice shaking nearly as much as his hand.

"Wes," I pleaded. "You don't have to do this. Whatever is going on, I can help you."

"No," he said, exhaling to steady himself. "I didn't know there was a camera. Now I have to deal with that *and* you *and* Hank, maybe Nate and his wife." His Adam's apple bobbed long and slow. "I don't want to do all this."

"Don't," I said. "Let me go. I won't say a word."

"We'll go to the center of the maze," he said, more softly, working out a plan. "I'll call for help until Hank comes to play hero. Then I'll take care of him too. The pumpkin patch is closed for the season, maybe forever. No one will look in here. You'll both be hidden until they raze the maze. Plus, winter's coming. So it's possible animals will take care of moving your bodies or they'll at least destroy the evidence of what really happened here."

"Animals," I squeaked, stumbling over my

386

feet and hidden rocks on the shadowy path. "Wes! You're going to shoot me and leave me for animals to eat?"

His distant gaze snapped back to mine, and remorse bled across his face. "I'm sorry."

Sorry? I thought, fighting the urge to grab the gun and kick him hard where it'd hurt the most. *Sorry? I brought his mama staples from my pantry! I worried about him, and now he is okay letting animals eat me or drag my body away?*

"You can't just apologize, then do the wrong thing anyway," I said, marking our next turn with a hard press of my heel. "That's not how this works."

"Yes, it is." The fear in his eyes turned hard, and his expression settled into something like disgust. "My dad beat my mama for years before he was arrested. When the sheriff finally did something about it, Mama filed for a divorce and a restraining order, but that only made Dad mad. He apologized through his court-appointed attorney, and the judge turned him loose a few days later. Dad came straight for her."

"I'm so sorry. I had no idea."

Wes made an ugly, choking sound. "Everyone's sorry. Dad was sorry. But he still came at Mama every way he could until that old, fat sheriff finally quit sending cruisers out to help when we called. The last time the sheriff showed up, he told my folks to find a better way to work out their differences. He thought Mama could arrange some marriage counseling and Dad could consider anger management. Dad put her in the hospital for a week that night, then he came home and beat me. I was eleven. When squirrel season opened a few days later, my dear old dad had a hunting accident." A malicious smile spread over his usually sweet face.

"You shot your dad?" I asked, shocked and stumbling over a dip in the earth and a scattering of loose twigs.

"I did what the sheriff wouldn't do. I protected my mama. She was supposed to be happy, thankful, even proud when I told her what I'd done for us, but instead she started drinking, and I don't think she's stopped."

My jaw dropped, and my heart sank. "Wes, I am really and truly sorry."

He hitched his chin high and squared his shoulders against my pity.

Then I finally understood. Wes had killed to protect his mama once, and he'd do it again. Killing me would keep him out of jail so he could provide for her, and that was all he wanted.

What I didn't understand was why he'd killed Mr. Potter. "What about Potter?" I asked. "You respected him. You said he was good to you." I dragged my heel once more.

Was that four? No, five turns. Was it left, left, right, right, left? Or left, left, left, right, left?

My thoughts scrambled as the rows of corn grew thick and deep around me. We had to be close to the center now, and I wasn't sure I could even see the marks I'd left on the ground in the darkness. The bright property lights were too far away to illuminate the base of the looming stalks.

"I needed this job," Wes said, scrubbing his trembling fingertips against the skin beneath his eyes. "Mama found the money I hid to refill the propane tank for heat this winter, and she took it. She bought booze and treated all those drunks at the bar to beer and pool and wings. Why would she do that?" he asked sincerely, desperately. "Now it's cold outside, and we're cold inside."

I bit my tongue against the urge to say I was sorry once more. The cards life had dealt Wes weren't fair, and I wasn't sure what I'd have done in his shoes if someone had beat up on Granny every day like that, if I'd grown up surrounded by anger and fear instead of love and protection. I didn't know, and it didn't matter. I couldn't let him kill again.

"Let's stop and talk," I said. "Please?"

He waved the gun and I hurried on.

"You're the one who took money from the register," I said, feeling the final pieces fall into place. "Mr. Potter assumed it was his wife, but you found a way to do it because your mom took the money you needed for heat. You probably planned to pay him back, but he caught you and he fired you. Then you couldn't pay him back or pay any of your other bills either."

"He caught me putting some of it back. I wasn't taking when he saw me, I was returning. Making a payment toward the whole, but he wouldn't listen," Wes said. "I begged him to let me explain, but he said he wasn't a fool, and he told me to go home. And not come back."

"You followed him to my truck, still trying to convince him to listen. When he wouldn't, and he turned his back on you, you hit him with a shovel."

Wes lowered the gun slightly, tears falling freely over his ruddy cheeks. "I didn't mean it. I was just so angry. When he didn't get back up, I hid him in your truck. There wasn't time to do anything else."

I felt the same way. We'd reached the center of the maze, and I had to do something or die without a fight. And that just wasn't in my blood. So, I took a chance on the only idea I had.

"Ah!" I yipped and pretended to twist my ankle in the dark. I faked crumpling to the ground and hoped Wes's distress would mask my poor acting skills. I kept my feet under me as I crouched, whimpering and holding one ankle. Not my finest moment, but I was out of time and options.

When Wes reached for me, I shoved upright with the full strength of my legs, ramming my head into his and creating a thunderous crack with our skulls.

He cussed and dropped his gun in favor of clutching his face.

My vision blurred, and my ears rang as I flung myself past him, back in the direction we'd come. The top of my forehead ached where it had connected with Wes's nose.

He screamed profanities behind me as I made hasty turns in every direction with no regard to the marks I'd carefully left to lead myself out.

I made the next turn while looking back over one shoulder, straining to locate Wes's position behind me. And I collided full-speed into a broad wall of muscle.

Colton clamped a giant hand over my mouth before I could find my voice and scream. He pressed one finger to his lips, then released me slowly. I formed my fingers into a gun and waved it around, warning him that Wes was armed.

Colton nodded. He tapped the sidearm in his holster, then moved into the narrow walkway as I slunk back into the dead end where I'd so gracelessly arrived.

A moment later, Colton's voice rose firm and clear into the night. "Jefferson County Sheriff. Drop your weapon."

The blessed thud that followed sounded a lot like the sound Wes's handgun had made when he'd dropped it in my presence only moments before.

I waited for the precious jangling of cuffs, then stepped onto the path and followed the sounds of Miranda rights being read by my hero. I could see the outline of him just opposite the next wall of corn, and I breathed easier, cradling my aching head in one palm. I'd surely have a goose egg tomorrow. But at least it was over, and headbutt aside, no one had been hurt this time.

"Ah, ah, ah," someone whispered.

A figure stepped into my path from the false turn a foot away and pointed a gun at my heart.

I stared, stunned and helpless, as Samuel Keller moved in close and curled a gloved hand around my throat, then positioned himself behind me. The barrel of his gun pressed against my spine. "I told you what would happen if you didn't leave me alone," he whispered, his hot, sticky breath clinging to the frozen skin of my neck and cheek.

"I listened," I whispered, and his fingers tightened against my throat in warning.

"I saw all those suits with your Sheriff Wise today. Federal agents, right? They're not in uniforms, so you didn't think I'd know who they were? You must truly think I'm stupid."

Kinda, I thought angrily, even as I forced my lips to say, "No."

My heart thundered painfully as I struggled with the new predicament. Colton and I had both killers in one corn maze, but he didn't know about the second one yet, and I had no way to tell him.

The massive maze suddenly felt stifling and small. Not nearly big enough for three men, three guns. And me.

Worse, what if Hank wandered in looking for me and was shot, or Colton did something stupid to save me and was shot? What if Wes became collateral damage?

What if I didn't make it out alive?

"Call to him," Keller whispered as Colton finished reading Wes his rights.

I pressed my lips together, refusing his request.

The gun moved away from my side until Keller's hand rested in its place, the barrel turned away. "Do it or I'll shoot him."

I didn't have to look to know he'd aimed the gun at an unsuspecting Colton through the cornstalks.

When I didn't comply, I heard the telltale click of the gun's hammer being cocked.

"Colton," I called hastily, the word warbling on my tongue. The fear in my tone was unmistakable.

Colton paused a moment. His head tipped slightly, as if listening to something, then the corner of his mouth curled gently, if only for the briefest of moments. "Winnie? I'm coming. Stay put."

Keller moved against my back, pushing us forward. The gun pressed firmly against my ribs once more.

Colton's blank expression didn't change as he led Wes to a halt before us. "Let her go, Keller."

My captor chuckled near my ear, sending a wave of icy chills down my spine. "Nope. Now, let your man go or I'll kill him. This is between you and me." He lifted the gun toward Wes's head, and Colton shoved Wes into the corn. "Go," Colton said.

Keller nearly buzzed with delight. "That's better. Now I can savor the moment. A beautiful night, a private place to play, and this lovely woman, whose life means so much to you." He nuzzled my cheek, and I fought to keep my dinner down.

Colton raised his palms to us, then rested one on the butt of his sidearm. "I have both hands free now. You should probably start running."

A hint of movement in the cornstalks drew my attention, and my muscles tensed impossibly further. Had Wes decided to stay and help? Had Hank arrived from next door?

I strained to see more clearly, losing track of the threats launched between Colton and Keller, focusing hard until I finally made out the figure in the shadows.

Blake was there. And he wasn't alone.

Suddenly, Colton launched at us, and the booming gunshot that followed momentarily silenced my world. Colton went down in a heap, and my ears rang anew.

I flung myself free of Keller's grip and crawled across the cold, rocky earth with thoughts of nothing but Colton's safety. "Colton!"

Around me, the world lit in a series of lights and activity.

"Samuel Keller," an unfamiliar voice called. "Drop your weapon. You are under arrest."

Blake stepped through the rows of corn alongside two marshals and the better part of our sheriff's department. They manifested from the shadows, like a cavalry of ghosts.

Emergency lights flashed red and white in the sky. Static from walkie-talkies and voices over radios joined the mix of footfalls and chaos.

"Colton," I cried, pressing my palms to his cheeks and willing his eyes to open. "Colton!"

He moaned, then pressed upward onto his knees. "I'm okay." He rocked upright and extended a hand to pull me up. "Nice work, Montgomery." He unzipped his jacket with a wince, then unfastened the bulletproof vest beneath. "I guess you were right. Keller didn't like seeing all those fake lawmen."

I touched the vest, in awe. "You planned this?"

"We improvised after I noticed Keller lurking outside the empty storefront where we organized all those reenactors in suits with bogus badges. As you suspected, Keller hated it. When I got the video text from Hank and another saying you were here with Wes, I made sure to announce that I was meeting you at the pumpkin patch. I was more covert while rallying my team."

"You used me as bait," I said, suddenly unsure how I felt about it.

"Not really. I was coming for you regardless after that text. I just took advantage of the marshals and available deputies in case it was a two-for-one night. We could've all shown up just to take Wes in."

I looked in the direction Wes had run.

"He's in custody," Colton said, pulling an earpiece from his right ear. "My men were waiting for him when he left the maze."

I leaned into Colton's embrace, careful not to press against his surely bruised chest. "You were shot."

"I suspected I would be, so I came prepared," he said. "Being shot tonight was a good thing. Keller just made it a lot more unlikely that he'll find leniency in the eyes of the court."

"You can't hold me," Keller seethed, his arms wrenched behind him and locked in cuffs. "I'll get off or out, and I'll come for you."

Colton raised the dented vest. "You're not going anywhere, Keller, and they'll be prepared for you this time, when you're being transferred to the maximum-security prison where you'll spend the rest of your life. You can be sure about that."

The marshals yanked Keller's arms, and he spun away with them to face whatever fate awaited him. Whatever it was, he'd earned it.

"You okay?" Colton asked, wiping the pad of his thumb across my tearstained cheek and tucking wild, windblown hair behind my ear.

"Thank you," I said, winding my arms around his waist. "You saved my life again."

"You were in danger again," he said, pressing me to his chest and tightening his protective arms around me.

"I'm sorry," I whispered. "I know you must be sick of this."

"I will always come for you," he whispered, lowering his cheek against the top of my head.

And I believed he would.

CHAPTER TWENTY-SEVEN

Granny outdid herself for Thanksgiving. The house was covered in holiday cheer, the table and counters lined in food. She'd decided to serve the meal all day this year and do it buffet-style, then she'd invited everyone she'd seen, spoken to, or passed on the street these last few days. She didn't even care whether they knew her. And the guests had arrived in droves. All day, stopping in before or after their own festivities, many with a dish to share. Some ate until they could burst. Others opted for coffee or dessert only, but all were welcome, and Granny made sure that every soul that passed through her door knew it.

Colton had come early and stayed all day, helping haul in and clean up extra tables and chairs from storage.

I sipped hot cider from my seat near the fire and enjoyed the tender moments of community and belonging all around me. I wished, stupidly, as I always did during the holidays that my long-lost mother would show her face and reveal that she was okay, but in keeping with her longest-running tradition, she did not.

Colton made his way in my direction, having helped Granny refill some empty serving bowls, and put on a new pot of coffee. "How are you doing?"

"I'm good," I said. "You?"

"Good." Colton smiled and tapped his mug to mine in cheers. "I'm feeling better than I have in a very long time. It's nice."

"Looks good on you too," I said.

He'd worn a simple black V-neck over a gray T-shirt with jeans, but he looked a lot like a man who was fast stealing my heart. The semi-permanent scowl he'd worn since we'd met was gone today, replaced with a reluctant but brilliant smile. That alone made me happy to see Samuel Keller behind bars. I'd had no idea how much capturing the fugitive had weighed on Colton until that weight was finally lifted.

"You think Keller will find a loophole and get off?" I asked. "Or escape again?"

"Not a chance." Colton said. "There's not a lawman around him who will let their guard down again. After killing my partner, then his transport guards, and taking that shot at me in the corn maze, he's pretty well sealed his fate."

I sipped my cider, content with that outcome, but concerned about another. "Were you able to see Wes?" I asked. "Any chance they'll go easy on him?"

"He was with the court-appointed attorney when I got there, but I'll do what I can for him," Colton said. "He had a lifetime of extenuating circumstances, but he killed a man. Two if you count his dad, and he had every intention of killing you."

"The old sheriff should have helped him," I said. "It's not right."

Colton nodded. "It's not substantiated either. It's hearsay from an emotionally wrecked kid, but it's being looked into. Meanwhile, I have some related, but better news. I found Wes's mom a place where she can get help. I know a guy at the detox and wellness center in Clarksburg who'll treat her and keep her pro bono. If she sticks it out, she can start over."

"Do you think she will?" I asked, a bubble of hope in my chest.

"The way I see it, she's got nothing to lose, but it'll be hard work, and it'll have to be her choice."

"Thank you," I said, reaching out to squeeze his hand. "Wes will be glad. I know

401

he wants to be a good man for her."

"A boy and his mother," Colton said.

"Do you try that hard to please yours?" I asked.

He smiled. "Not quite, but my mom has always given her unconditional love, so I've had plenty of room to be myself. She loves all of us right where we are. Good or bad. You know?"

I raised my eyes to Granny, refilling cups and plates inside the fullest kitchen in town and smiling with pure, selfless joy. "I do."

Colton watched the crowd, eyes busily surveying the scene. I supposed you couldn't take the cop out of him, whatever the occasion. He chuckled at the sight of another guest bringing a pumpkin roll.

"We love our pumpkin rolls," I said as Granny stacked it with three others on the dessert table. "Wait till next month. They'll all be ho-ho cakes, though I think I prefer pumpkin."

"Did I tell you I saw Mrs. Potter yesterday?" Colton asked. "She was at the post office. She had a moving truck and was going to stay with her family until the farm sells."

"Thank goodness for family." My phone buzzed, and I dug it free from my pocket to check the message. "I'm hoping this is Dot.

I have something I want to do in a bit, but I don't want to miss her when she gets here."

"Where is she?" he asked. "Working late?"

"She's at Doc Austin's. The truffle hog took a turn for the worse. I left another voice mail with the mushroom hunters' group today because they hadn't called me back after my last message. This time I gave a long, detailed explanation of what's been going on and Dot's number instead of mine. Hopefully she has good news. Either about the hog's progress or about finding his family."

I swiped the screen to read the message. My heart sank with each word.

"Was that her?" Colton asked. "Is she okay?"

"She's okay, but she's not coming." I put my phone away and counted silently to ten, reining in my temper before speaking. "She says it's been touch and go with the hog, and the mushroom hunters finally reached out to her. They told her to put him down. They'd assumed he was permanently lost or dead and weren't interested in accruing medical expenses for him."

Colton cringed. "Ouch."

I rolled heartbroken eyes up to meet his. "What's wrong with people?"

Colton squinted, thinking, it seemed.

"You want to get out of here? Maybe take Dot a plate? I've got my phone if anyone needs me and a deck of cards in the cruiser. We can keep her company so she's not alone and miserable on Thanksgiving."

"Yes." I smiled. "She'd like that." And so would I.

I sent a return text to Dot, who responded with a series of crying emoticons. "She's happy," I reported. "But first, we have something else to do."

Colton hiked a brow. "Yeah?"

I rose from my chair with a smile.

Hank's laughter turned my head, and I laughed along with it. "He's such a nut," I said. "And that laugh is obnoxious." Completely over the top. Carefree and contagious. "He's feeling like a champ right now because his company loved his suggestion to launch a Support the National Parks campaign."

Hank took notice of us staring and headed our way.

"I'm calling it a night," he said, shaking Colton's hand, then hugging me tight. "Dad's picking me up before dawn tomorrow for a little deer hunting with my uncles, so it's probably time I head home."

"You're going hunting?" I asked. "Your dad must be thrilled." Hank's family was full of hunters and outdoorsmen, but Hank had never quite fit that mold. It would mean the world to his dad to have him along.

"I'd rather sleep until sunup and then go for a run, but Dad doesn't do either of those things," Hank said. "I don't know how many more deer seasons I'll have with him, so I figured it's time I start making the memories I should've been working on years ago. I missed out on hunting with my grandpa. I don't want to have that same regret with Dad."

"Smart man," I said. It didn't matter how people passed the time spent with loved ones. It only mattered that they took the time to be there.

Hank kissed my cheek, then went to say good-bye to Granny.

"He's growing up so much," I told Colton. "Feel like going for a walk?"

Colton furrowed his brow. "Is it a walk to the thing you need to do before taking your best friend dinner?"

"It is." I took his hand casually and led him toward the door. I jumped back when it swung open and Harper bustled inside.

"I'm here," she said brightly. "I can only stay a moment, but I'm here. Happy Thanksgiving!"

I hugged her, then pointed her in Granny's

direction before slipping on my coat. "I love her," I told Colton as I fastened my scarf and zipped my coat.

"Where did you find her?" he asked, holding the door while I passed onto the porch.

I gave the yard a careful scan for signs of Waddles or Boo. They'd both been put up for the night, but neither was great at doing what was expected of them. "I found Harper at school, why?"

He looked away and stuffed his hands into his pockets. "Because I ran her prints after you found that pocketknife in your cider shop table. She's new and has access to your entire property, so I wanted to be sure she wasn't here for nefarious reasons."

I imagined Harper, the human equivalent of sunshine, as a harbinger of evil and laughed. "Harper is wonderful," I assured him. "And she has a clean record. I looked her up myself on the public database before I hired her."

"You're right. Harper Mason doesn't have a record," he said, "but that's not your orchard manager's real name."

I paused at the bottom of the porch steps. "What? Why not?" I looked back at the house, confused. "Why would she lie about her name?"

He lifted his shoulders, then let them

down slowly. "Hard to say without asking. My best guess is that she's hiding from something. Or someone."

I grabbed his sleeve and towed him away from the house. "Who is she really?" I asked.

"Amber Houston. She doesn't have a record either."

"I guess that's something."

Colton nodded. "You might want to talk to her about it sometime. See if she'll talk to you. Tell her I'm here to help, but go easy. Something tells me that if she finds out her cover's blown, she'll run."

I hooked my arm in the crook of his and contemplated the number of secrets kept by the people around me. How complicated we all were and how little most people ever knew about one another. "I hope she's okay," I said.

Colton covered my hand with his, curving warm fingers against mine on his arm. "With a friend like you, she will be."

We walked across the field between houses, then on past a number of outbuildings and rows of trees in sweet silence. Behind us, Granny's home glowed warm with light and laughter. Above us, the stars lit the way.

"Where are we going?" Colton asked.

"You'll see. It's not far now."

Several minutes later, we arrived at the top of a small hill over a winding creek a few dozen yards below. "It's no cliff, but it'll do," I said. Bending to reach a pair of preselected sticks at my feet, I handed one to Colton. "Now put a mudball on it."

He laughed. "Seriously?"

I released his arm and pushed a completed ball onto the tip of my spear. "Yep. It's more like damp dirt, but it's ballable," I said.

Colton crouched to pinch the ground and gather his medium. " 'Ballable?' "

"Ready? Watch closely, because I'm a professional." I pulled the stick back and whipped it forward, dislodging its spherical cargo. The ball vanished into the night, leaving an audible trail as it knocked into limbs and leaves and branches on its way to the water below. "Now you."

Colton mashed a too-large blob onto his stick and swung. The hunk landed about six feet in front of us.

"Too big," I said, then I flung another little sphere into the night.

Colton did better the second time, and we continued, catapulting dirt and laughing for a long while. Mudballs in the moonlight. A moment I wouldn't soon forget.

Eventually, he passed me a handkerchief, and I rubbed the dirt from my fingers.

"Thanks for this," he said. "You're right. It's fun."

"Told you." I slid my hand into his as we made our way back through the chilly night, to fix a plate for Dot and let her know she was loved.

"Can I make you dinner sometime?" Colton asked, twining his fingers with mine.

"Sure. Why?" I slowed for a better look at his face in the night. "What's up?"

He barked a sharp laugh, then went back to walking, tugging me along at his side. "Blake's right. I'm really bad at this." He glanced sideways at me, not losing step. "I'm asking you out. Officially. I'd like to make you dinner and serve it to you at my house. Anything you'd like, as long as it's available for carryout somewhere in town."

"Okay." I laughed, my heart full and my thoughts aflutter. "I'd like that."

Colton dipped his chin, a broad and genuine smile on his truly handsome face. "Well then, it's a date."

It certainly was.

ACKNOWLEDGMENTS

Thank you so much, dear reader, for joining Winnie and Granny on another Blossom Valley adventure. These books bring me so much joy to write, and I couldn't do that without you. You make my dreams possible, and for that, there simply aren't words. Additionally, I want to thank Norma, my blessed editor, who makes me feel like I can conquer the world, one story at a time; Kensington Books, for allowing me to be part of their amazing team; my literary agent and biggest cheerleader, Jill Marsal; and my critique partners, Danielle Haas and Jennifer Anderson. And thanks to my family, who tolerate a pajama-wearing, sleep-deprived, daydreaming, silly heart of a wife, mother, and friend, thank you for loving me exactly as I am.

ABOUT THE AUTHOR

Julie Anne Lindsey is a multi-genre author who writes the stories that keep her up at night. She's a self-proclaimed nerd with a penchant for words and a proclivity for fun. Her titles include *Prophecy* and *Goddess*.

Lindsey lives in rural Ohio with her husband and three small children. Visit her website at: Julieannelindsey.com, tweet her @JulieALindsey, and find her on Facebook.

The employees of Thorndike Press hope you have enjoyed this Large Print book. All our Thorndike, Wheeler, and Kennebec Large Print titles are designed for easy reading, and all our books are made to last. Other Thorndike Press Large Print books are available at your library, through selected bookstores, or directly from us.

For information about titles, please call:
   (800) 223-1244

or visit our website at:
   gale.com/thorndike

To share your comments, please write:
   Publisher
   Thorndike Press
   10 Water St., Suite 310
   Waterville, ME 04901